What people are saying about . . .

Pennsylvania Patchwork

"Love is in the air in Kate Lloyd's *Pennsylvania Patchwork* as the tale of three generations under one roof continues. Holly Fisher has been looking for love and suddenly finds herself pursued by multiple suitors. Her very Amish grandmother Anna disapproves of Holly's choice (a Mennonite vet) and takes pains to end the romance. Esther, Holly's mother, has a love story of her own brewing. Then an unexpected delivery forces Holly, Esther, and Anna to face issues long ignored and, surprisingly, brings healing and forgiveness. Lloyd's very enjoyable read has just enough twists, turns, and romance to delight the Amish fiction reader."

Suzanne Woods Fisher, bestselling author
of The Stoney Ridge Seasons series and
The Lancaster County Secrets series

Praise for ...

Leaving Lancaster

"A lovingly written tale of family, forgiveness, and redemption. Readers of Amish fiction will love every moment."

Hillary Manton Lodge, author of the
Carol Award Finalist *Plain Jayne*

"In *Leaving Lancaster*, Kate Lloyd gives us a fascinating glimpse into a tightly knit Amish community—and the terrible impact a daughter's thoughtless rebellion has had on three generations of women. This novel is well crafted and compelling!"

Serena B. Miller, author of *Love Finds You in Sugarcreek, Ohio*

"Kate Lloyd explores familial bonds in this warm and moving novel. She deftly captures the complicated relationships between mothers and daughters, exploring both expectations and disappointments. This talented and capable writer will leave you wanting more."

Suzanne Woods Fisher, author of the
bestselling Lancaster County Secrets series

"In *Leaving Lancaster*, Kate Lloyd has penned an inspirational novel about a long-kept secret that threatens to destroy an entire family. While the truth seems painful at first, Kate's beautiful story demonstrates how forgiveness can heal even the deepest of wounds."

Melanie Dobson, award-winning author of *Love Finds You in Amana, Iowa* and *The Silent Order*

Pennsylvania Patchwork

Pennsylvania Patchwork

~

A NOVEL

KATE LLOYD

David C Cook®

transforming lives together

PENNSYLVANIA PATCHWORK
Published by David C Cook
4050 Lee Vance View
Colorado Springs, CO 80918 U.S.A.

David C Cook Distribution Canada
55 Woodslee Avenue, Paris, Ontario, Canada N3L 3E5

David C Cook U.K., Kingsway Communications
Eastbourne, East Sussex BN23 6NT, England

The graphic circle C logo is a registered trademark of David C Cook.

The website addresses recommended throughout this book are offered as a
resource to you. These websites are not intended in any way to be or imply an
endorsement on the part of David C Cook, nor do we vouch for their content.

This story is a work of fiction. Characters and events are the product of the author's
imagination. Any resemblance to any person, living or dead, is coincidental.

Unless otherwise noted, all Scripture quotations are taken from the
King James Version of the Bible. (Public Domain.) Scripture quotations
marked NIV are taken from the Holy Bible, New International Version®,
NIV®. Copyright © 1973, 2011 by Biblica, Inc.™ Used by permission of
Zondervan. All rights reserved worldwide. www.zondervan.com.

LCCN 2013935960
ISBN 978-0-7814-0873-8
eISBN 978-0-7814-0961-2

The author is represented by MacGregor Literary, Inc. of Hillsboro, OR.

The Team: Don Pape, Jamie Chavez, Nick Lee, Renada Arens, Karen Athen
Cover Design: Amy Konyndyk
Cover Photos: Steve Gardner, Pixelworks Studios
and Bill Coleman, NoToCo, LLC, www.amishphoto.com

Printed in the United States of America
First Edition 2013

2 3 4 5 6 7 8 9 10

060513

To Corinne Lloyd, my fabulous mother-in-law

Note to Readers

Thank you for joining my fictional characters in Lancaster County, Pennsylvania, a unique and glorious location I hold dear to my heart. Any resemblance to real members of the Amish or Mennonite communities is unintended. I ask your forgiveness for any inaccuracies.

I am with you and will watch over you wherever you go,
and I will bring you back to this land. I will not leave
you until I have done what I have promised you.
—Genesis 28:15 NIV

PROLOGUE

Standing at the kitchen counter, Anna Gingerich noticed her granddaughter Holly's slim silhouette and wavy brown hair out of her peripheral vision. Anna wanted to meet her Maker with no regrets, but she blamed herself for inadvertently orchestrating Holly's ill-fated course. The young woman teetered on a precipice that could forever ruin her life.

Anna's arm ached as she lifted a plastic mixing bowl from the kitchen cupboard; her favorite ceramic bowl was too heavy. Weak as she was, she'd cling to life until she saw Holly follow in her mother's footsteps and become baptized Amish. Ach, how Anna loved Holly and wanted to see her for all eternity.

As she opened her cookbook, Anna found herself scheming to influence her lovely granddaughter before it was too late and she wed a Mennonite—a man with a despicable past, according to what Anna had recently learned. She vowed to do whatever it took to steer Holly on the right path.

Anna straightened her prayer cap to hide her balding scalp. She should concentrate on thanking the Lord her daughter Esther—Holly's mother—had returned to the fold as if she'd never taken off so many years ago, and was getting baptized—an occurrence Anna had scarcely dared hope for. But no use rehashing the past when it was the future that needed fixing.

CHAPTER ONE

For the first time in my life I, Holly Fisher, felt like a real woman! No Cinderella—not at my age. But my dreams were wonderfully, miraculously expanding into reality, like a three-dimensional fairy-tale ending.

I hummed the first stanza of "Here Comes the Bride" as I arranged five settings at my grandmother's kitchen table—six chairs and a bench around its perimeter. I figured Mom's fiancé, Nathaniel, would meander over from next door and claim the prestigious head of the table. I noticed Mom had tidied her skirt and blouse and patted her bun into place.

"Did I tell you I invited Zach to lunch?" I said to her and my grandma, who stood at the counter opening a cookbook. I was unable to contain my exhilaration; I hadn't seen him for days.

"Yes, we know," Mom said.

"He should arrive in twenty minutes." As I folded napkins, I envisioned myself promenading down the aisle in a satin gown with a flowing train, and perhaps wearing a veil edged in lace. Unless an ornate wedding dress was too fancy for Zach's church. Not to mention my dearest grandmother—I called her Mommy Anna—Old Order Amish to the core, with her ever-present white heart-shaped prayer cap and her black apron fastened together with straight pins. I might have to compromise, but what else was new? I'd learned life was akin to one of Mom's knit sweaters—a single tug of the thread and the whole garment could unravel. Yet those smoke-and-mirror days had delivered me here, so how could I complain?

I looked around the kitchen and saw peach-colored sunlight slanting through the window and dappling the linoleum floor. In late morning, no one would know we lived without electricity.

"Has there ever been a more glorious day?" I asked, and received a sluggish nod from my mother.

She removed two loaves of whole wheat bread from the oven and deposited them on a cooling rack on a counter, then slid a casserole into the oven. I sidled over to the counter with a serrated knife in hand and sliced into a spongy loaf. A burst of steam escaped; my nostrils inhaled the nutty aroma. I lathered the slab of bread with butter and strawberry preserves. As I swallowed a mouthful, my taste buds savored the scrumptious medley of flavors.

"I wonder what kind of cake we should serve," I said, and took another nibble. Mommy Anna and Mom glanced at each other a nano-second too long. "At my wedding," I said, when neither responded.

My mother produced a meager half smile.

"What gives?" I asked her. "I assumed you'd be ecstatic. You've wanted me to tie the knot and have kids since I graduated from college." And here I was in the second half of my thirties.

"Well, now, that's true, but—" My mother had mentioned that rumors about Zach were circulating around the county, but I'd chalked it up to Mom's being influenced by Mommy Anna, who suffered from memory problems.

"Ach." Mommy Anna opened a canister of flour with wobbly hands.

"Are you okay?" I set my unfinished bread aside on a plate. "Do you need help?"

"*Nee*, I'm fine, Holly. Just thinking." She measured a couple cups of flour and dumped it into the bowl; a cloud poufed out, dusting the counter. "God has been answering my prayers left and right, and I'm ever so grateful." She added baking powder and salt haphazardly. "Holly, are you sure you and Zach aren't getting ahead of yourselves?" She'd already talked me out of searching for an ornate engagement ring because Amish women don't wear them at all, and I'd caved because I did want to fit in. But eventually Zach and I would choose wedding bands. I could hardly wait.

"You sound like his mother," I said. "She's acted lukewarm toward me ever since Zach told her we were getting married." I'd hoped Beth would offer to help make my wedding gown, since Mom showed little interest, and I couldn't sew worth a hoot. And my funds were sparse; since I'd lost my job in Seattle, I was practically broke.

Mom moved closer. "Beth might have something—"

"What, you and Beth in agreement? Have you two finally resolved your feud?" A dispute to do with my father, a man I'd never met.

"Well, I wouldn't go that far. We took your grandma to the doctor's together because we needed Beth's minivan, but it was mighty tense. Beth did all the talking, like I wasn't even in the room." Mom spaced the plates equally, straightened the cutlery. "Did you and Zach pray about your impulsive decision?" She sounded preachy. Which irked me. But I was determined to keep my mind from returning to her past indiscretions. Her downright lies. How dare Mom criticize me!

"Yes, we have." I brought out coffee cups. "Have you and Nathaniel?"

She faced me straight on, her stare uncompromising. "Yah, and we've spoken to the bishop and gotten permission to marry early, after I get baptized, Nathaniel being a widower and all."

"Why does that matter? And why are you on my case?" The last thing I wanted was a hassle.

"Holly, you know their situation is different than yours." Mommy Anna leaned against the counter. "Esther and Nathaniel knew each other growing up. And Esther will be baptized and join the church. 'Tis God's will for the two of them, for sure."

"And change her last name. No longer Esther Fisher. That's fine because I'll change my last name too. Holly Fleming." I should start practicing my new signature.

Mommy Anna wiped her hands on her apron. "Yes, Esther will change her surname and truly become one of us."

"And I won't?" A few weeks ago, when I'd first returned from Seattle, my grandmother had acted like I could do no wrong. But I'd perceived a subtle shift in her attitude toward me. "I'm moving clear across country to live near you," I said. "I thought you'd be thrilled."

"I surely am." Mommy Anna extracted an egg from the refrigerator. "I've waited so long." She cracked the egg on the side of the bowl, splitting the shell unevenly, a jagged piece plunging into her concoction. "And I could wait even longer for you to find an Amish beau."

I reached over and plucked out the shard of eggshell. "Did I hear you right?" My words clotted in my throat, coming out raspy. "What's wrong with Zach?"

"I like him …" A befuddled expression warped her round face as she rechecked her cookbook for the corn muffin recipe.

"Good, because he'll be here soon." I reminded myself my grand-mother's mental clarity was clouded. I mean, she'd read the recipe at least ten times and hadn't added the cornmeal. And occasionally her balance tipped off kilter, although she'd refused to see the doctor again to discuss her latest lab results.

My grandmother had lived her entire life in this slow-motion world of horse and buggy; my sudden choice to marry Zach probably seemed like a runaway train. Old people tended to fret, part of their nature, and my mother wasn't exactly young herself. I should cut them some slack. Mommy Anna was the woman I'd waited a lifetime to meet.

As I found a container of cornmeal and put it on the counter next to the mixing bowl, I heard tires grating into the gravel on the lane at the side of the house. I dashed to the window and saw Zach's pickup idling while he spoke on his cell phone.

"There he is! He's early."

An unanticipated gush of apprehension washed through my chest like a rogue tidal wave. What if Mommy Anna was right about Zach and marrying him was a horrendous mistake? I'd been exhausted when my flight landed upon my return to Lancaster County a few weeks ago. Zach had fetched me at the airport—no big deal. But on the drive here, he'd pulled off to the side of the road and kissed me—a knock-your-socks-off kiss I'd never forget—then proposed marriage. And I'd accepted—a lifetime commitment on a whim.

But I'd hardly seen him since that glorious night. He'd attended a conference last weekend and before that had claimed he'd been buried with his work as a veterinarian.

Gazing through the windowpane, I admired his thick sandy-colored hair and his classic profile. I watched his mouth move as he spoke—the soft tender lips I relished—and was aroused with desire. He didn't seem to know how handsome he was, a fact that made him all the more appealing.

Striding to the back door, I heard his engine revving. I grabbed my teal-blue jacket off a peg and trotted through the unlit utility room and onto the stoop in time to see his pickup swerve onto the main road. His brake lights blinked red—had he seen me? His pickup slowed, then he gunned the gas and sped away without waving.

In a blink, the sun hid behind clouds, as if a curtain had been let down. The remaining fall leaves lost their luster, the side of the white barn turned drab, and the air nippy.

My previous joy evaporated. It wasn't as if I weren't used to disappointments; I'd endured plenty. I heard crows quarreling in the harvested cornfield on the other side of the barn, and a cow mooing in the distance. I reasoned: maybe a farmer had summoned Zach with an emergency, needing immediate assistance with birthing a calf. Or was this the wrong time of year for calving? As a veterinarian's wife, I'd need to learn these details, and a thousand more.

Chilly air surrounded me; I realized I was shivering. I started toward the kitchen but couldn't face my mother and grandma. I was flabbergasted with their attitude toward Zach. I refused to believe their innuendos about a skeleton in his closet. But I'd been wrong about a man in the past.

I poked my fists into the jacket sleeves, made a U-turn, and headed across the barnyard, which seemed eerily vacant. Before my uncle and his family moved to Montana two weeks ago, he'd sold most of his Holsteins, and all his draft horses and hogs to Nathaniel, next door. Nathaniel had recently hired his youngest brother to come over each morning to milk Mommy Anna's one remaining cow and tend to the two buggy horses and chores. In the past, I'd avoided the barn. I'd always felt the conviction of my uncle's hawkish ministerial stare.

Entering, I noticed all stalls were empty, save one. The barn's interior was neater than when my uncle and his family lived here. I guessed Uncle Isaac had his hands full as both farmer and minister, a man chosen by God according to Amish tradition.

The sweet fragrance of hay engulfed me. I saw Mommy Anna's aged mare, Cookie, in a stall munching on grain. I'd been told she was too frail to pull a buggy. I wondered how old the sway-backed, barrel-ribbed white horse was. Would she outlive my fragile grandmother? If only Zach were here, he could answer my questions.

I spun around and bumped into an Amishman wearing a straw hat. He reminded me of Nathaniel: same chocolate-brown eyes and shaggy haircut—like a barber had placed a bowl over his head and clipped—but no beard, meaning he wasn't married and never had been. His brawny chest and muscled arms filled a blue shirt nicely. Suspenders held up his dark work pants. He stood one or two inches shorter than Nathaniel, but his wide stance gave the impression of superior strength and stamina. This man must be thirty-five, maybe older, and what many women would call a hunk.

He gave me a quick looking over; I sensed he was judging my loose, shoulder-length hair and jeans, and liking what he saw.

"*Gude Mariye.*" His Pennsylvania Dutch—what my mother and Mommy Anna called *Deitsch*—greeting didn't sound foreign, yet his jovial sing-songy voice clashed with my tangled thoughts.

"My name's Armin King. I'm Nathaniel's younger *Bruder*." The corners of his mouth quirked down.

"Hi, I'm Holly Fisher, Esther's daughter. Why haven't we met before?"

"I just returned a couple days ago. I've been livin' in upstate New York, among other places—on and off for over eight years. I come back every now and then."

Mom had often advised me to count to ten before speaking, but I rarely did. "Why did you leave?" I asked, then realized I sounded like a busybody.

He paused for a moment. "I was undecided about joining the church," he finally said. "Nathaniel's been pressuring me to get down on my knees in front of the bishop and congregation for years." Armin removed his hat, revealing espresso-brown hair like Nathaniel's, and slapped it on his thigh. "No one to blame but myself for wavering."

It occurred to me he was like my mother, only she'd left for decades. I gazed up into Armin's handsome, suntanned face—he appeared to have broken his nose in the past, which added a rugged, manly quality—while Zach's features were finely chiseled.

"I'd best get back to my chores," Armin said. "Nathaniel will accuse me of slackin' off again." He repositioned his hat atop his head.

"Sorry to slow you down." Cold air traveled up my jacket's sleeves, and I zipped it to my neck.

"Nee, don't be. I'm glad for the company. It's too quiet around Nathaniel's."

I speculated how either he or Nathaniel could be lonely with Nathaniel's spritely and curvaceous housekeeper, Lizzie, flitting about, but managed to curb my tongue. "You live with him?" I asked.

"Yah, for now. Until I can afford a place of my own."

"I might stay in the barn and pay Cookie a call, if you don't mind." I hoped she didn't nip or kick.

"Cookie would be loving a visit, poor girl. Her limp is getting worse. I don't dare put her in the pasture with Anna's buggy horse and Holstein without Nathaniel's permission."

I wandered over to the mare and saw her white hair was yellowing to the color of oatmeal and missing in patches; her tail was short and scraggly. As I approached, she turned her head and gazed at me with soulful eyes.

"So Nathaniel calls all the shots around here?" I asked Armin over my shoulder. I wondered if bad blood ran between the two brothers.

His long legs easily caught up with me. "Yah, for the most part." He gave Cookie a pat on her bony rump, and she went back to eating. Armin's knuckles were hefty—assertive workingman's hands, able to tackle any job. "I suppose he was right when he told me not to leave. Ya see, I wanted to be a horse jockey."

"You're kidding. You're way too tall and heavy to be a jockey."

"Not that kind. 'Tis what we call men who buy and sell horses. I've got a *gut* eye for them, if I do say so myself. But to be a horse jockey, I needed to drive a truck to deliver horses twenty to fifty miles away. Sometimes farther. So I kept putting off being baptized, and then I met a woman up in New York State and stayed on."

"And?" I tilted my head. "What happened? Don't leave me dangling."

His mouth flattened into two lines.

"Are you still seeing her?" I persisted.

"Nee." He stroked his rectangular chin. "And you. Are ya single?"

"Not for long. Do you happen to know Zach Fleming?"

"The veterinarian?"

"The one and only." Standing taller, I felt myself growing in height—even if still only five foot three.

"Yah, our paths have crossed most of our lives." One eyebrow lifted. "I heard tell his long-lost love is back to reclaim him. And she brought a surprise no man could ignore."

"What are you talking about?" My heartbeat began to accelerate as if I were running up a sand dune; I couldn't catch my breath. "You must have the wrong Zach Fleming."

"Beth and Roger Fleming's son?" he said.

I nodded, a spasm searing from my abdomen to my throat, suffocating my words. My hands flew up to cover my ears as I rushed past him to flee from the barn, only to trip on the toe of his boot.

His hand swung out to catch me at my waist. "Something wrong?" he said, helping me regain my footing.

I stepped away from him, fluffed my hair, and tried to appear dignified as ziggy-zaggy notions squiggled through my brain like newly hatched tadpoles.

"No—" I said. "I mean, yes. Everything!"

CHAPTER TWO

Esther sequestered a damp rag and polished the lip of the sink. She was determined to settle her scuttling thoughts as she watched her mother flipping through the pages of the cookbook she must surely know by heart—or used to. Alas, Mamm's memory was vaporizing like frosty dew on a sunny autumn morning, but she had refused to see the endocrinologist again. Mamm's lab results were available, and the doctor was anxious to speak to her. Esther's mamm might have forgotten how much she'd liked Dr. Brewster.

Esther bet Mamm hadn't forgotten Holly's revelation that she and Zach were engaged, or that Zach's sterling reputation was tarnished. Since Holly's return, Esther and Mamm shared a common cause, to keep Holly and Zachary Fleming from getting married—but for different reasons altogether. And Esther feared their truce was temporary. Beth's charm might outweigh Esther's wishes because Mamm loved Beth more than she loved Esther—her own daughter—a wretched reality making Esther's whole stature shrink in on itself.

Her mind skittering through the past like a mouse in the barn, she recalled, at age fifteen, rigging up the open buggy without her parents' permission and sneaking out to meet her beloved Samuel, in part because she suspected Beth was determined to steal him away. A coyote or dog had spooked Dat's pony, and the animal reared, then hurtled off aimlessly, landing them both in a ditch—and Esther in a wagonload of trouble. Dat had watched her like a hawk after that night. But not well enough.

A lifetime ago, she thought. Her father and her former husband were in heaven, and Esther was a grown woman with a daughter to fret about. Imagine, Holly marrying the last fellow on earth Esther would have chosen for her. Unlike Mamm, Esther could live with the fact Zach was Mennonite, although about as liberal a Mennonite as you could find, judging from his and Beth's worldly attire and lifestyle. But Esther couldn't tolerate lying, if that was what Zach had been doing. Not after a deceitful cad in Seattle had already broken Holly's heart.

Esther needed to get honest; Zach's svelte, flaxen-haired mother still rankled her. When he and Holly wed, Beth would transform into her full-fledged relative, an integral part of Esther's life, the other grandma should Zach and Holly have children. Grandma Beth. The words resounded in Esther's ears, bringing on a headache.

She rinsed the rag and folded it in half. She'd sworn she would no longer dwell in the world of what-ifs as the bishop had suggested. Esther would reclaim the serenity she'd awoken with this morning. She'd concentrate on her Nathaniel ambling over for the noon meal. Envisioning his lanky frame, she felt like a teenager with a crush— her heart fluttering with a crescendo of emotions she had thought she'd never experience again.

She glanced out the window hoping to catch a glimpse of him, but saw only the barnyard, the main barn, the vacant gable-roofed cow barn, the outbuildings, windmill, silo, and cylindrical tin-roofed corncrib—and a loose chicken. Another hole in the coop needing mending? She'd ask Nathaniel's younger brother Armin to patch it, although Armin seemed to ignore her requests.

"Did you hear an automobile come and go a while back?" Mamm said, snagging Esther's attention.

Glad for the diversion, she set the cloth aside. "Yes, when Holly went outside. But no door opening and closing, just spinning tires."

"It sounded like Zach's pickup. But it took off in a flash."

"With Holly in it, do you think?"

"Nee." Using an elbow, Mamm supported herself against the counter. "Even our fast-footed Holly couldn't have caught up with it."

"Then, where is she?"

"Waiting, perchance on the back stoop." Mamm let out a prolonged sigh. "We've got to put a stop to her foolishness, don't you agree?"

"Yes, absolutely. But she seems determined."

Mamm shook her head. "Lovesick is what she is. Ach, she'll be heartsick when she learns the truth about Zach."

"We don't know it's true. I'm not going to say a word without proof."

Mamm flopped onto the rocker, coming down hard enough to make the hickory chair creak. "Oh dear me, I forgot to put the muffins in the oven."

"Stay where you are." Esther slipped her hands into potholders. "I'll place them next to my casserole." As she opened the oven door and set Mamm's muffins alongside her bubbling casserole she was enveloped with a splendid swoosh of hot air smelling of noodles, ham, and melted cheddar cheese. She hoped Nathaniel would relish her cooking. She'd be the best wife ever. Pleasing him and God would be her top priority.

"Would you go check the mail for me, Essie?" Mamm started the rocker in motion with the balls of her feet. "Remember how you used to love to wait for the mailman when you were little?"

"Yah, I remember." But Esther felt merely a shred of happiness when she recalled her childhood. She knew her mamm was longing to hear from her sons in Montana. Esther also could see from her mother's pale face, awash with tiny wrinkles, she was too fatigued to make it to the front porch, let alone down the steps without tripping.

"Mamm, you leave everything to me. I'll be right back." Esther left the potholders by the stove and set the timer, cranking it to twenty-five minutes. She walked through the sitting room, opened the front door, and moseyed onto the porch into the brisk fresh air. She glanced up the road to Beth and Roger Fleming's twentieth-century fieldstone home, with its sweeping lawn enclosed by a split-rail fence, and saw Zach's pickup sitting in their driveway.

Esther descended the steps and strode to the galvanized mailbox—not the homemade birdhouse-shaped wooden one of her youth. She opened it and recognized her brother Isaac's handwriting on the top envelope, addressed to Anna Gingerich. Esther doubted he'd included a note to her. Fair enough: Esther hadn't contacted him. She might gather her courage and write to him, or at least his wife, to see how they and their *Kinner*—children—were settling in. She might skip mentioning she was hiring a driver and taking their mother to the doctor's office the day after tomorrow.

Across the road stood giant maple trees, most of their leaves fermenting on the knee-high grass. In the distance stretched the most sublime farmland on earth. She didn't miss Seattle's hustle and bustle or the odor of automobile exhaust, but couldn't help wondering how the Amish Shoppe was faring in her friend and partner Dori's care. Esther considered visiting Seattle one more time before she started her baptism classes. She would ask Nathaniel's opinion when he arrived.

She longed for his embrace—when Mamm wasn't looking, of course. Public demonstrations of affection were not the Amish way.

Letters in hand, a few of them bills, she entered the kitchen and saw Mamm had fallen asleep, her head at an angle. A formal sounding rap-rap on the back door shattered the silence. The door slowly swung open.

Nathaniel stood in the doorway wearing his hat and work boots. "*Gude Mariye.*" His words seemed stilted.

Esther breezed over to greet the man she'd spend the rest of her life with. He grew better-looking every time she saw him, and soon they'd wake up in the morning together …

Warmth traveled up her neck and into her cheeks. She must be blushing something fierce. "Hello, Nathaniel. You don't need to knock. *Kumm rei.*" Come in.

He swiped his hand across his bearded chin. "I shouldn't." He took a step back, jammed his hands in his pockets. "I need to get home and speak to Lizzie."

"You'd choose spending time with your housekeeper over me?"

He stared at the floor. "Nee, you know that would never be so."

"Can't you speak to Lizzie after we eat?" Esther tried to sound playful, when in fact she felt her chest tighten and her throat close around her words as she envisioned the flirtatious young Amish woman. "We're almost ready. Except for Holly. Have you seen her?"

"No, but I heard voices in the barn. I'll go look."

He moved into the utility room. Esther followed him and took hold of his forearm. "I've been missing you, Nathaniel. Even though I just saw you last night." She surveyed his somber features. "What's wrong?" She took his hand and felt clammy skin. "I can tell something's the matter."

"Nothing for you to worry about." He worked his mouth, his lips so close she considered kissing him. But he withdrew his hand and reached for the doorknob. "Like I said, I need to get back home. And the bishop may stop by."

"Has he put the kibosh on our wedding?" she asked. Nathaniel seemed to be deep in thought. Or maybe he didn't understand. "Did you speak to the bishop again?" she said.

"Yah, but not about us." He turned away from her and opened the door. As he and Esther stepped into the cool air, Holly stalked out of the barn. On her heels sauntered Armin.

Nathaniel plodded down the steps and Esther followed him. "Hullo, Holly," Nathaniel said.

"Hi, Nathaniel, how's it going?" As Holly and Armin neared them Holly glanced toward the lane leading to the road.

"Hello, Armin," Esther said to Armin, who scuffed the cement with the toe of his work boot.

Esther was aware of a lack of eye contact between Nathaniel and Armin; maybe Nathaniel wanted time alone with his footloose brother, which made sense. He might wish to encourage Armin to marry and settle down. In fact, cute and sassy Lizzie would be a perfect fit.

Nathaniel had called his younger brother a rolling stone. The description made her think of the old Temptations song, which brought Samuel to mind—her former husband always shadowed the back of her brain. He'd been pronounced dead, missing in action during the evacuation of Saigon, when the popular tune reached its peak. And back then she'd wondered if her Samuel were indeed wandering somewhere, not ready to be found. A preposterous thought.

Esther said, "Want to join us for lunch, Armin?"

"Well, now, I don't know. I haven't finished with Cookie's ointment."

"Please come in, both of you," Esther said. She'd only greeted Armin briefly the last couple days. He'd made himself scarce every time he saw her. Did he not approve of her marriage to Nathaniel? "Our table seems too empty with my Bruder Isaac's family gone. We'd love to have you."

"Are we going to stand out here all day?" Holly asked.

Esther could tell her daughter was irritated, but doubted their conversation was the source of her agitation.

She glanced up to the brewing sky, clouds crowding in from the west, and asked the Lord who was the right man for her one and only Holly. Mamm was dreaming if she thought Holly would dive into the Amish church and be content driving a horse and buggy. Nor would Holly pitch her cell phone and laptop. Yet this Armin chap didn't look so bad, though Nathaniel said he wasn't even baptized.

CHAPTER THREE

The four of us stood in the barnyard waiting for someone else to make the first move.

My mother, all moony-eyed, gazed up at Nathaniel, but his attention was riveted on Armin, who turned his head to watch an undulating flock of starlings. Mom patted her hair; her hands paused at her nape, her fingers searching for loose strands at her bun. Her cheeks wore a flushed girlish hue. She bore little resemblance to the independent woman who owned and operated the Amish Shoppe and had stated she'd never marry again.

Against all logic, nausea snaked through my stomach as I envisioned Nathaniel King caressing her. My molars clamped together. Their courting, as the Amish called it, bothered me. I needed to change my immature attitude, but the child in me clung to my dream that Dad would return—talk about fairy tales. I should be thrilled Mom had found an upright and kind man who adored her. I'd have to get over it: Mom was infatuated with Nathaniel, like my father never existed. Until recently, she'd referred to my dad as the love of her life, a man no other could replace.

"You coming in to join us?" Mom asked Armin.

"Yah, I'll stay. *Ich bedank mich.*" Thank you.

"Unless Lizzie's waiting for you both," Mom said, which struck me as odd.

A smile fanned across Armin's face. "I'm not the man Lizzie's hopin' for, am I, Bruder?" Armin wore a goofy grin and Nathaniel scoffed.

"We'll both eat here, thank you," Nathaniel said.

"Gut." Mom rubbed her fingers against the palm of her other hand. "We've got plenty."

Hey, wait a minute, why hadn't Zach called to say he'd miss lunch? How rude. An insult to my mother, who'd prepared the meal, not to mention me.

Anger and frustration coiled through my mind.

Mom, Nathaniel, and Armin moved toward the back steps. I followed in their wake like a shriveled-up leaf on the creek behind the pasture. I didn't want Zach finding me standing alone out here looking desperate when and if he arrived. I increased my pace until I'd caught up with them. In the kitchen I stepped into my suede moccasins I'd brought from Seattle. Armin and Nathaniel left their boots in the utility room, washed their hands at the small sink just outside the kitchen, and entered sock-footed. They removed their hats and hung them on wooden pegs by the door.

"You should bring over a pair of slippers," Mommy Anna told Nathaniel, as he planted himself at the head of the table. "You own this house now."

"It's on loan to you, Anna." He scooted in his chair. "For as long as ya want."

"You're a generous man, Nathaniel," she said. "I'll find you a pair of slippers myself, the next time I'm out shopping."

I pulled out a chair for Mommy Anna at the middle of the table, and Armin sat across from her as if avoiding Nathaniel.

In a flurry of seamless motion, my mother set the casserole and muffins on the table, and brought three-bean salad, sliced tomatoes, broccoli salad, and chow-chow from the refrigerator. Then she glided onto the seat next to Nathaniel.

"Shall we thank the Lord?" Nathaniel made his usual guttural sound, and we all bowed our heads as he led us in a silent prayer. Was I praising God? Not really; my thoughts scattered like dried dandelions in the autumn wind.

When Nathaniel cleared his throat and the prayer ended with "Amen," my mother spoke. "Mamm?" Mom brightened her voice; I recognized the shimmering quality of her sugarcoated incentives. "How about we go shopping for Nathaniel's slippers after your doctor's appointment the day after tomorrow?" she said.

"What appointment?" The corners of Mommy Anna's mouth veered down. "Ya made an appointment without asking me?"

"I was going to tell you as soon as we prayed and served the food." Mom unfolded a napkin, stretched it across her lap.

"Is Beth taking us?" Mommy Anna asked.

"No, Beth doesn't know a thing about it. I'm your daughter, and I'll hire a driver."

"Why didn't you tell me sooner?" My grandma had become surly the last couple weeks.

"I only found out yesterday afternoon. Dr. Brewster had a cancellation, and I wanted to set up a ride before I told you."

"That's wonderful." I felt a smack of contrition for not placing Mommy Anna's health issues ahead of everything else in the world.

"Ach, I still haven't located a driver," Mom said. "I got distracted."

"Maybe Zach could take us," I said. "Or would we all fit in his pickup?"

"I doubt it." Mom wrung her hands. "He's such a busy man."

In a flash, my mind catapulted back to our Seattle home, to the evening she unveiled her well-kept secrets. She'd claimed—my whole life—she had no living relatives, even though she knew I'd longed for a humongous family. I thought I'd forgiven, but I didn't completely trust her or understand her motivation.

"Mom, do you know something I don't?"

She passed the butter. "Not exactly."

I'd endured a lifetime of my mother's sidestepping the truth, so I pressed her for details. "Please, if there's something I should know."

"I saw Zach's truck in Beth's driveway a little while ago."

"It must have been someone else's." I selected a muffin, then passed the cloth-lined basket to Armin.

"I recognized his pickup." Mom ladled casserole onto Nathaniel's plate. He seemed awfully quiet. I reminded myself he wasn't a chatterbox type to begin with, and he'd no doubt been up since dawn milking his cows.

"There must be a hundred pickups like his." I slathered a muffin with butter, watched it soften and melt.

"No, there aren't," Nathaniel said. "I can recognize almost every pickup in the county."

"Remember, I've ridden in it." Mom served my grandmother a scoop of casserole and placed her fork on the edge of her plate like Mommy Anna was a child.

"Why would Zach drive to his mother's, when he knows we're expecting him?" I persisted.

"Unless she summoned him," Mom said.

"I surely hope Beth's okay." Mommy Anna had yet to taste her meal.

"I'm sure she's fine." My mother speared a slice of blood-red tomato with her fork. "Maybe she ran out of sugar."

"Zach's a mamma's boy?" Armin said, and smirked. He glanced my way as he served himself chow-chow.

"How dare you?" I placed my elbows on the table.

"What?" Armin shrugged one shoulder. "Isn't mamma's boy an *Englisch* expression?"

Mom covered her grin with her napkin.

"You're bad-talking my fiancé," I said, "and I don't appreciate it."

"Is it really true you're marrying Zach Fleming?" He scratched his head in what appeared to be an exaggerated manner. "I guess I have my facts mixed up."

"Armin, have you heard what I've heard?" Mommy Anna said.

All eyes pivoted my direction.

"Best not to spread *en Gebrummel*—a rumor," Nathaniel said.

I filled my mouth with muffin so I wouldn't have to partake of the conversation, but it tasted of baking powder and was too salty. Mommy Anna had forgotten sugar and not added enough cornmeal.

My mouth puckered. I gulped a mouthful of water and struggled to swallow.

"Zachary Fleming is a respected veterinarian now," Nathaniel told Armin. "He brought that ointment for Cookie's leg."

"Yah, I know him, not a bad fellow." Armin dished himself a plateful of casserole. "And you're planning to marry him, Holly?"

"Yes, I am." I considered marching over to Beth's house to see if Zach were really there.

Nathaniel swallowed a mouthful. "Armin, it isn't polite to pry, and you know that. You've been living an Englisch life too long."

Armin patted around his mouth with his napkin. "Sorry, Holly, no offense meant."

"I accept your apology." Armin had a charming personality, not to mention his looks. I bet many women found him irresistible—like hummingbirds hovering around a feeder full of sugar water.

I recalled being drawn to Nathaniel when I'd first met him weeks ago. How dumb was that? But Armin possessed all Nathaniel's good attributes plus a feistiness I found appealing. Or would have, if I were not in love with another man. The moment Zach appeared, Armin's appeal would fade away. Like this nasty-tasting muffin, looks could be deceiving. I set the rest of my muffin aside and hoped Mommy Anna didn't notice.

"You've come home for good, Armin?" Mommy Anna said.

"For a while, anyways."

My appetite diminishing, I forced myself to consume a few bites of Mom's noodle casserole; I realized she'd been cooking Amish my whole life, but how would I have known?

"Are you planning to join the Amish church?" I asked Armin, and Nathaniel stopped chewing for a moment, as if to better hear his reply.

"I haven't decided." Armin sneaked a glance at Nathaniel.

"And what's keeping ya?" Nathaniel's terse question came out in staccato.

"I've only been home a few days, and already you're on my back." Armin set his napkin on the table. "Is this why you invited me in?"

"No, don't leave, please," my mother said. "Let's all get to know one another."

"Yah, Armin, I wantcha ta stay," Mommy Anna said. "No bickering at the table, and no more questions." Her brows—mere wisps—met over graying sage-green eyes. "We're going to be family soon."

As if standing afar, I examined my life in fast-forward. I listened to a car putter by, and a horse's clopping and buggy's steel-rimmed wheels on the road out front of the house. But of course Zach wouldn't be driving a buggy. When it came down to it, every man I'd ever loved had cheated and left me. Not that Dad cheated, but he left me when he hadn't needed to. Mom said he was a nonresistant conscientious objector and could have avoided military service during the Vietnam War by applying for a farm deferment. I couldn't fathom why he and my mother didn't return to the safety of the Amish community, where he could have worked for his father or another local Amish farmer.

A truck pulled beside the house and shut off its engine. "Zach." I folded my napkin, set it next to my plate.

"Nee, 'tis a delivery truck dropping off a package," Nathaniel said.

"But it could be—" I shot to my feet. "I'll go check."

CHAPTER FOUR

While she waited for Holly's return, Esther topped off Nathaniel's, Mamm's, and Armin's coffee. Then she heard the truck's engine gunning. Holly would no doubt come back inside moments later with a dejected expression on her face. How Esther wished she could spare her daughter sadness.

Esther sat again, and passed the sugar bowl to Nathaniel. As she watched him add a tablespoon and swirl the white crystals into his coffee, she recalled conversing with Mamm at sunrise today while preparing breakfast. *Subterfuge* is what Holly would call Esther and Mamm's scheming to derail Holly and Zach's wedding. She knew Holly would be furious. But on the other hand, finally, Esther and Mamm were on the same page, in agreement. A new experience for two old women, Esther thought, and chuckled to herself. Well, apparently she wasn't too old to fall head over heels in love with Nathaniel. Nor too old to bend at the knees and join the Old Order Amish church, which she should have done decades ago. The picture of herself confessing her sins—all of them—in front of the congregation and her family and before God, made her insides shudder as if she'd swallowed an ice cube. At least Beth would not be in attendance, since she was not a member.

But as Esther watched her mother nibble her meal, then set her fork aside, she worried Mamm's allegiance to Beth could be an impediment. Surely, Mamm understood that Zach was Beth Fleming's son, unless Mamm's mind had gone *verhoodled*.

Esther listened to the truck jerk away. Moments later, Holly slogged into the kitchen carrying a package. "FedEx," she said, and handed Esther a carton big enough to hold a shoe box. Esther recognized the return address: The Amish Shoppe. She had to admit to herself she missed the store—her dream child. But not half as much as she'd miss Nathaniel, her mother, or Holly should Esther return to Seattle.

Holly plopped down on her chair. "I wonder what Dori sent you, Mom."

Esther set the package at her feet. "Maybe she found more yarn."

"Then why not give it to me when I flew here?"

"She might have just discovered it." Esther nudged the package out of sight with the side of her foot. "I'll open it later."

A dog woofed outside. "That's my Rascal," Armin said. "He must have broken loose when he heard the truck."

"I love dogs." Holly's soprano voice sounded invigorated. "Let him in."

"Nathaniel won't allow Rascal in the house and won't let me bring him over here while I work."

Nathaniel tapped the table with his knife handle. "Did he or did he not kill my favorite Rhode Island hen a couple days ago? And he steals eggs." He was acting uncharacteristically grumpy, but Esther could understand he'd grow weary of the dog's shenanigans.

"He won't do it again," Armin said, between bites.

"Dogs that kill farm stock don't belong on a farm." Nathaniel forked into his meal.

"Rascal won't misbehave now that I told him not to," Armin said. "He was brought up in a town, ya know. At least I think he was. If you'd let him in the house he wouldn't go looking for trouble."

Nathaniel gulped a mouthful of coffee. "Dogs don't belong inside and that's that."

"Since when?" Holly demanded. Esther thought she sounded impertinent.

"Our *Mudder* never did," Nathaniel said. "And she was right."

"What kind of dog is Rascal?" Holly asked Armin.

"Mostly collie. The prettiest dog you'll ever see." Armin emptied his coffee cup. "Come on, I'll introduce you."

"You haven't eaten dessert," Mamm said.

"No matter, I'd better get my chores done." Armin pushed his chair away from the table. "Looks like it may rain later."

Nathaniel narrowed his eyes at Armin. "Take that mutt back with you, before he catches one of Anna's chickens, if he hasn't already. You hear?"

"Yah, yah, I heard ya." He stood. "Come with me, Holly. But you're not wearin' those moccasins outside again, are you?"

She giggled as she got to her feet. "Oops, I forgot. No wonder the FedEx driver gave me a double look."

"He did that because—" His cheeks brightening, Armin glanced down at the floor.

"Because she's prettier than any *Maedel* in the county," Mamm said.

Now Holly's cheeks were as pink as Armin's.

Armin nabbed his hat off a peg, and Holly her jacket.

"Wait, we haven't prayed again," Nathaniel said.

"All right, can ya do it now?" Armin bowed his head.

Nathaniel's eyelids compressed and his brows furrowed, he lowered his head for a few moments. The second he lifted his chin, Armin helped Holly wriggle into her jacket and the two were out the door. Their voices wove together as they trailed through the utility room.

"Nathaniel," Mamm said, "do you think Armin will stick around this time and get baptized?"

"No way of telling. I've never been able to figure Armin out. I don't think he knows what he wants, himself. Too many choices out in the Englisch world. A man should stay in the community."

"And find a good wife." Mamm winked at Esther. "He'd make a right fine match for Holly, don't ya think?"

"Not unless Holly got baptized." Nathaniel's hand moved to the back of his neck and he gave it a squeeze. "Sorry, Anna, but I can't see it happening. The both of them? And her with another man courting her?"

"You're probably right. Well, of course you are. Unless your brother—" Mamm sent him a coy grin.

"I wouldn't count on it," Nathaniel said.

"Armin's the type of man Holly likes," Esther said. Not just his handsome face and stature—almost as good-looking as her Nathaniel—but he was a tad prideful and full of himself, personality traits Holly seemed to be attracted to for no reason that made any sense to Esther. Not like Zach, who was polite and gentlemanly, and equally as handsome if not more. Esther found it extraordinary some

Englisch woman hadn't already snapped him up. Maybe Mamm was right: Zach's distraction—why he was always too busy for Holly— was another woman.

But no matter; Holly was here with her. Three generations of women dwelling in the same household. For now, anyway. She and Nathaniel had still not agreed where the two of them would live when they wed. Probably here, since the *Daadi Haus* was already erected for Mamm—unless Nathaniel built one attached to his home.

Esther removed Nathaniel's plate, every scrap of food eaten, a sign he'd enjoyed her cooking. Gut. "Can I serve you some lemon chiffon pie or peanut butter cookies?" she asked him. "Freshly baked this morning."

"Sorry, I don't have time." He gazed up into her eyes and she felt alive with giddiness. Who would have predicted this at her age? Thank the good Lord Esther had not remarried and settled for second best the way many women did. If she'd saddled herself with someone else, her whole life would be topsy-turvy. Yet she could feel, deep in her belly, the grip of guilt for not clinging to her Samuel. Esther had watched a movie, *The Odyssey*: the ancient Greek hero's wife waited years and years for her husband's return in spite of many suitors. She should ask the bishop if she truly was free in God's eyes to marry Nathaniel. She and Nathaniel both should; they floated in the same boat, now that she thought of it.

"Not even a cookie or more *Kaffi*?" Esther said.

"Nee, I must be on my way." He shot to his feet, strode to the back door, and grabbed his hat. Esther listened to his footsteps on the stoop.

"Do you think something's wrong, Mamm?" Esther asked. "Seemed like Nathaniel couldn't wait to get out of here."

"He's got an afternoon of labor ahead of him," Mamm said. "You don't expect Nathaniel to sit around and yak with the womenfolk all afternoon, do ya?" Mamm straightened her wire-rimmed spectacles, which had slipped down on her nose. "Esther," Mamm said, "you have a faraway look in your eyes."

"Just thinking about Holly and Armin." Esther glanced around the spacious kitchen, not an electrical appliance in sight, although the gas-generated refrigerator looked like one. And she didn't miss them. Well, maybe the blender. "You don't really think there's a possibility, do you?"

"I prayed every day you'd come home, and here you are." Her eyes glistened with moisture. "So yes, I think anything is possible."

"But they'd have to wait so long for children." They'd have to attend baptism classes before they could wed, and Esther knew full well how long that took. "If she marries Zach, they could start trying for a family right away." Esther felt awkward speaking of such personal matters with her mother, or anyone. Old customs from her childhood clung to her like moss on the shady side of a pine tree.

"There are no easy answers in life. If only your brother Isaac were here. He'd know what to do, being a preacher and all." Using her hands, Esther's mamm pushed herself halfway up. She tried again, without success.

Esther rushed around the table and supported her mother at the waist. "Let me help you."

"I've been a little dizzy for the last couple days. Nothing serious."

"*Was fehlt dir denn?* Why didn't you say something?" Esther could feel her mother's ribs. "Have you lost weight?"

"What does it matter?" Mamm sank back onto the chair. "Ya say I'm going to the doctor's soon. Yah? Maybe she'll have the answer. Or maybe my time has come. Although I don't want to meet our Maker until I see both you and Holly baptized and married—to Amishmen."

Esther didn't want to disappoint her mamm, so it was best to agree, at least in part. "I'd hoped Holly would be married by now, while she's still young enough to bear children," Esther said.

"She is young enough. Why, I was her age or even older when I had your brother Isaac." A look of confusion crossed Mamm's face. "And I had another child after him, didn't I?"

"Not that I know about."

"I guess I don't remember much of anything anymore." Mamm knocked a spoon off the table with her elbow. "Ach, I'm clumsy as a chicken up a tree." She leaned down to retrieve it and her gaze landed on the FedEx carton. "Are ya going to open the box, Essie? Aren't ya curious?"

Esther envisioned her mother's letters inside; Mamm had sent numerous entreaties over the decades pleading for Esther to return. Rehashing old grievances would most likely make her faithful mamm melancholy.

"I'll open it later," Esther said, and hoped Mamm would forget she'd ever seen it. With her toe, Esther prodded the carton farther under the table.

CHAPTER FIVE

My fingertips luxuriated through Rascal's silky fur as the dog sniffed my pant legs, then licked my hand. He did look to be mostly collie, but darker and with a black muzzle. Maybe some Labrador retriever mixed in.

"Have you had him since he was a puppy?" I asked Armin as we stood at the bottom of the back steps.

"No, he was a stray, sort of like me." Armin hooked his thumbs in his suspenders. "I was inspecting a pair of mules, and Rascal latched on to me, started following. No one knew where he came from, but he was sure hungry enough. And he was fine around the horses."

"Are you a good boy?" I said, all the time my mind volleying back to Zach.

Rascal wagged his plumed tail and bowed, stretching his forelegs out in front of him like I was royalty.

"He likes you," Armin said, fluffing Rascal's coat. "I can't say that about everyone."

"You mean like your brother Nathaniel? Maybe Rascal prefers women over men."

One corner of his mouth lifted. "Some more than others."

My curiosity piqued, I said, "What's the story? Did you and your lady friend in New York break up for good?"

"Yah, a few months ago. It's all over."

"Is that why you left?" I tilted my head. "And why you're here now?"

His features stiffened. "You surely ask a lot of questions."

Guess my interrogation was over. "Sorry, Armin, I don't mean to put you on the spot." But growing up, I hadn't asked enough.

I listened to cars motoring out on the road, a horse and buggy clip-clopping, but no pickup. No Zach.

"Come on, I'll show you the shortcut to Nathaniel's," Armin said. "He told me to bring shingles over to mend the roof on Anna's shed."

"Give me a minute, okay?" I dug into my pocket for my cell phone. It had enough juice for several more calls. I punched in Zach's number and got his answering system, informing me to try his veterinary office. Then I tried Beth. I really did need to borrow her electrical outlet. And I missed her.

"Hello?" Beth's voice sounded reticent.

"Hi. It's me, Holly." I figured she'd seen my number on her caller ID. "How are you?" I wanted to ask if Zach was standing in the very room with her. Then it occurred to me Zach had stopped by to talk about the joyful news—our upcoming wedding.

"What can I do for you?" Beth sounded too formal, like a recorded department store operator, her voice devoid of tenderness or affection. Something was wrong.

"I'm trying to track Zach down." I did my best to sound upbeat, while uncertainties and reservations rioted through my brain.

"Uh— just a moment," she said.

I heard muffled voices—one, another woman's. Beth must have her hand covering the mouthpiece to keep me from hearing her. Maybe a family dispute that had nothing to do with me, I told myself. Zach might be miles away, or at his office performing surgery. My mother had promised she wouldn't fabricate, as she had in the past, but I wondered if she'd made up the story about seeing Zach's pickup, or if she'd mistaken it for another. I suspected Mom needed glasses for distance, not just cheaters for reading.

"You still there, Holly?" Beth eventually said.

"Yes." With my free hand I stroked Rascal's neck, and he leaned into me.

Beth paused. In my mind's eye I saw her trying to hand Zach the phone, but his refusing to take it. Finally she said, "He'll have to get back to you." Meaning he was there?

"While I have you, Beth, may I bring my phone and laptop over to get them recharged?"

"No—this isn't a good day." I heard a click; she'd hung up without saying good-bye. My lungs seemed to collapse, emptying themselves of air. I felt sadness enclosing me.

I reminded myself Beth had a husband who often traveled for work. Maybe I'd caught her while he was leaving, amid an altercation. And she had a daughter. I didn't know the situation and was letting my imagination take hold of me.

The sun unmasked itself, revealing azure sky and filling the air with the aroma of warming soil on this coolish mid-November day. Growing up in Seattle, I'd rarely enjoyed a white Christmas, but had heard Pennsylvania winters could be frigid. I looked forward to snuggling by the fire with my honey-bunch while feathery snowflakes drifted to the ground, cloaking Lancaster County. But I wondered if Zach would be stoking the hearth or if I'd spend my days confined to the house alone. Would I be happier living here with Mommy Anna?

"Armin, I'll take that walk with you," I said, ignoring my heavy legs and sudden weariness.

With Rascal leading, I followed him and Armin out of the barn-yard. We crossed the dirt-and-gravel lane and approached a fenced field, which used to be Nathaniel's boundary before he bought my grandmother's property.

Armin unhitched a gate, then closed and secured it behind us. We trod across a harvested cornfield, then stepped through another gate and into a grassy pasture, cushioned with moist soil.

Ahead Nathaniel's black and white Holstein herd grazed. A couple of cows eyed us, but paid little attention. Birds trilled in the background.

"Ya better watch where you step," Armin said, glancing over his shoulder at me. "Aren't ya glad you wore those rubber boots?"

"Yes." As I circumvented a pile of manure, I caught sight of Galahad, Nathaniel's dappled gray thoroughbred gelding—a retired racehorse, according to Nathaniel. I felt my skin turn itchy as the rambunctious horse raised his head, ears pricked.

I'd once groomed this majestic animal, but Galahad had worn a halter and was tethered in a stall. Even then, I'd been anxious.

As if reading my mind, Galahad shook his head and trotted toward us, his tail flagging. Could he smell my fear? I slipped my hand in the crook of Armin's elbow.

"Don't be *naerfich*—nervous," Armin said, and strode toward Galahad. I hoped Rascal would bark and scare the horse away, but he dodged behind Armin and me, a sure sign trouble was approaching.

Galahad picked up speed, now loping directly at us. I clutched Armin's elbow, ducked my head.

Armin raised both his hands and yelled, "Whoa!"

Galahad stopped short, then pawed the ground. I thought he'd rear up and trample us, but he lowered his head submissively. Armin strolled over to the horse, grabbed hold of his mane, and in one smooth maneuver, swung his leg over Galahad's back.

Armin patted the horse's arched neck. "Gut boy." He reached his other hand toward me. "Ya want a ride?" he asked. "We'll make quick time if we do."

I shrank back. "Without reins or a saddle?" I tried to sound brave while my heart flung itself against my ribs. "Uh—no thanks." I'd never ridden a horse, other than the ponies at Woodland Park Zoo as a child.

Armin chuckled, then slid off Galahad's back and landed gracefully. As if nothing out of the ordinary had occurred, the horse began nibbling the grass among the herd again.

"How did you do that?" I said, impressed with Armin's attitude and ability. "I thought he was going to run over us."

"Nee, he would never hurt me. I told you I know horses, and they can sense it. I've always been like that, even when a youngster going to the auctions in New Holland with our dat. When I helped Nathaniel choose Galahad at an auction several years ago I warned him the horse might be too boisterous. He's a gelding but acts like a stallion half the time."

"You helped Nathaniel buy Galahad?"

"Yah, Nathaniel had asked me to keep my eyes open for a horse that could pass any buggy on the road. I teased him that racing his buggy was prideful. Ya know, just to give him a bad time, because I feel the same way. I selected Galahad here, and told my brother I'd take him off his hands if Nathaniel couldn't handle him. But it's worked out fine."

"I thought you said you lived in upper New York State."

"Yah, that's where I finally settled. Every couple years I'd pass by this way, but never stayed. I'd feel like a caged tiger after a few weeks. Strangled, really. I hated to break my mamm's heart over and over, I truly did. But she's gone now and so is our dat, a month after she passed. Nathaniel sent word. I drove home for the funeral, and I considered staying, since my parents wanted me to have the farm, my being the youngest son and all."

As we crossed the pasture, I inhaled the multilayered farmland aromas and felt my pulse return to its natural rhythm. Almost. I was still out of my element. I'd need to get used to these animals, I told myself. As the wife of a veterinarian …

I realized I didn't even know where Zach lived. In an apartment or a small house, with a roommate? What kind of a goofball was I? I'd agreed to marry a man I hardly knew.

"Why didn't you return earlier?" I asked Armin, to keep my spinning thoughts from tangling into a knot.

"I was tidying up, you might say. Packing and selling my truck and trailer." He kicked a pebble. "It wasn't easy giving up my keys."

"Or girlfriend?"

"I had no choice there."

"What's her name?"

"Lynnea."

"A beautiful name."

"Well, she's a beautiful woman." He gazed at an oak tree, its elegant branches reaching for the sky.

"Tall and slender?" I said.

"Yah, she is."

The fact he loved a willowy young woman made me feel short and homely.

"Amish?" I said, and he nodded. "How come it didn't work out?"

"She's still living with her family, and her father told me to ske-daddle until I went home, repented to my bishop, and got baptized."

"Aha." In other words Armin wanted to marry Lynnea. "But couldn't you just get baptized in New York State?"

"It's more complicated than that. There's another fella—" He pulled his earlobe. "How about you?"

"You know I'm engaged."

"I don't see an Englisch engagement ring."

"I decided I don't want one—too fancy for these parts." Zach had been called to a medical emergency each time we'd set aside to select wedding bands.

"When's the wedding?" he asked.

"We have yet to confirm a date."

"Ya don't seem very excited about it." His hand swiped across his mouth. "Never mind, Holly. 'Tis none of my business."

We ambled over to one of Nathaniel's small outbuildings, next to his statuesque barn, silos, and windmill. Armin yanked the out-building's door open, and a musty smell laced with the aroma of milled cedar filled my nostrils. Inside stood stacks of plywood, two-by-fours, and bundles of roofing shingles.

Armin took off to hitch a buggy horse to an open cart, but Rascal stayed with me, supplying the company I desperately needed. As I surveyed the back of Nathaniel's white clapboard house, I noticed the kitchen window was cracked open several inches, allowing the scents of melting butter, vanilla, and cinnamon to escape. I saw movement in the kitchen and made out Lizzie, his housekeeper. And Nathaniel, who must have jogged alongside the road to beat us here.

Through the glass windowpane, I admired Lizzie's plain attire: her lilac-colored dress and dark apron, her pressed white cap, its dainty strings dangling behind her. I recalled the enjoyment I'd experienced dressing Amish for a few days. I'd felt connected to my heritage, like a taproot to past generations. Except I'd never parted my hair down the middle and worn a cap like Lizzie. I might ask my grandma if I could try on one of hers. Yes, I would.

Nathaniel and Lizzie's voices raised in volume. They were speaking Pennsylvania Dutch much too rapidly for me to make out their words. Curiosity spurred me to move closer.

Then Nathaniel switched to English. "How dare you?" he said. "Ya had no right!"

CHAPTER SIX

Esther breathed in a lungful of contentment. With Nathaniel next door tackling his afternoon chores and Mamm resting under a patchwork quilt on the sitting room couch, she settled into an armchair. After Mamm fell asleep, she would *redd* up the kitchen without worrying about her mother trying to help and putting items away in the oddest places. It seemed Mamm had forgotten that all clean cutlery was compartmentalized, the forks collected together, facing up, not dispersed amongst the knives and spoons.

Mamm's lids drooped closed. Esther reached down for her knitting bag and brought out the skein of nubbly indigo blue wool yarn Holly had delivered to her, selected by her friend Dori. Esther's eager fingers wound strands into a ball; it was a lovely feeling to be beginning a new knitting project.

One of Mamm's eyes cracked open a sliver, then both widened. "What are you up to, Essie?"

"I'm making a sweater." Esther had performed this task so many times, her hands moved as if they had minds of their own.

"For yourself?"

"No, for a man." Esther felt her cheeks blush.

"Ya don't mean an Amishman, do ya?"

"Well, yes, I was hoping—"

"That he'll turn Englisch? Did you ever see your dat wearing a knit sweater?"

"No, I guess not." Her fingers slowed their tempo.

"You're the one who needs to do the changing, daughter of mine. If you wish to join the church."

Esther's mind spun back to her childhood. Decades had passed with so many changes. Why, children pushed themselves on two-wheeled rubber-tired scooters and wore Rollerblades these days, and farmers drove tractors in the barnyards, even though not in the fields. "Men can't wear sweaters?" Esther said.

"Not in this district, that I know of. Maybe, if it were black yarn. Better ask the bishop if you want to know for sure. I suppose you could knit a lap quilt or shawl for yourself." Mamm fluffed a pillow to support her back. "Knitting seems such a private endeavor, not like quilting, where everyone tells stories and laughs. Ya know what I mean? Only one person can knit at a time."

"Not really. My friend Dori holds a knitting class and the women chat up a storm." And after a busy day at work in the Amish Shoppe, Esther had always relished the quiet solitude as she knitted.

Paralyzed by Mamm's disparaging stare, Esther's hands came to rest on her lap. She'd envisioned herself and Nathaniel sitting in front of the hearth on winter nights after they were wed. In the picture, he was wearing a blue cable-knit sweater, but she imagined Mamm could be right. Esther needed to explore and learn the rules of the Ordnung, the unwritten code of conduct for her district, to become baptized.

"When will you start dressing plain?" Mamm said. "Don't think the People and the bishop, preachers, and deacon aren't keeping an eye on you."

"Soon." Esther knew her mother was correct. "I was planning on sewing myself a dress. Maybe on the way home from the doctor's the day after tomorrow I can buy the fabric."

"How about Holly?" Mamm asked. "Can she sew?"

Feeling deflated, Esther dropped the half-balled skein back into her knitting bag. She'd like to be fashioning pink or blue infant clothes, or a baby blanket, but knew she needed to accept the fact she might never have grandchildren.

"That's another matter I've neglected. She can't even hem a skirt." Esther had failed her daughter in a multitude of areas.

"She can certainly learn." Mamm pointed to a hamper of clothing. "The darning's been stacking up now that your brother's Greta is gone. You can start Holly on mending some of those garments. My fingers hurt too much."

"I'm sorry, Mamm. So very sorry." If only Esther had returned years ago, but no use crying over spilled milk, as she'd said to Holly many times—words her own parents had taught her as a child.

"Never mind, I've grown used to the discomfort, but my fingers and arms are too stiff to be of much use." Mamm massaged her shoulder. "Now that you and Holly are here, 'tis easier to ignore."

Esther glanced out the window and saw a red coupe whisk by, then veer into Beth's driveway without slowing down. "Looks like Beth is having company. I wonder who it is." A surge of animosity clenched Esther's stomach, but she admonished herself. Bearing malice against one's neighbor was a sin. She'd better face the fact she and Beth would be neighbors, if nothing more. And without a car, Esther might depend on Beth in a moment of crisis, as a last resort.

"We need to get Holly back into a proper dress and apron," Mamm said, her voice growing in animation. "Remember how pleased she was dressing Amish? I can tell Holly loves the Amish life."

"I can't disagree. Holly got the biggest kick wearing Nathaniel's daughter's old dress and apron, straight pins and all."

Mamm cocked her head, as if listening for Holly's voice. "I wonder where your *Dochder* is. I'll bet ya anything, she's with Armin." Mamm grinned, the creases in her cheeks deepening. "I saw a twinkle in Armin's eyes when he spoke to Holly. Something's going on there. He's a fine young man, he really is, once he straightens his ways and joins the church."

"The chance of those two getting together is slim to none. Although Holly dressed plain for a couple days, I doubt she'd give up her modern conveniences."

"With God, anything's possible. I heard tell of a woman down in Paradise ... or was it Bart?" Mamm glanced up to the ceiling for a moment, then her shoulders lifted. "Anyway, don't you see the beauty of it? The Lord brought Holly and Armin together so they can both be saved and start a family. I'm sure of it. Your daughter paired up with your future husband's little brother? 'Tis more than a coincidence."

"My daughter isn't as fickle as that." Esther sat with her knees together, her big toes touching. "If she says she's marrying Zach, then I believe her."

"Maybe not, after what the grapevine's been saying about him."

"She'll come unglued if it's true." Esther wondered if Mamm had her facts straight or if she'd dreamed up the whole tale. "How did you first hear of it?" Esther asked.

"A couple days ago. Lizzie stopped by with a gift from her mother." Mamm straightened her cap. "Strawberry preserves and apple butter."

Esther recalled the tasty preserves, but had assumed her sister-in-law had made them. "When was this? I didn't see her."

"You were in the chicken coop."

"Well, at this point all this talk about Zach is hearsay."

"You never can tell what the Lord Almighty has up his sleeve. Some day Armin may own part of Nathaniel's farm. Maybe that's why Nathaniel bought this place. For Armin."

Esther allowed herself to imagine Holly mistress of this acreage, the barn, the outbuildings, the plentiful fields—she recalled her brother Isaac had said he owned eighty acres.

"Don't forget, once you marry Nathaniel, he could be nominated for your brother Isaac's vacant position as minister. Nathaniel is well respected, that's for sure."

"Ach, I hope not. An unpaid, full-time job on top of running his farm? I'd never see him."

"Every Amishman must promise to be available to be chosen by lot when he's baptized."

"Yah, and I've seen a few men cry, even when selected to be bishop."

"By God, remember. 'Tis his choosing."

"I assume the man's family and children must be in good standing with the church. Holly isn't Amish nor is Nathaniel's brother baptized."

"Not yet." Mamm let out a yawn, then her head slumped to the side and her breathing slowed. Her mamm had complained her sleep was paper-thin. Esther knew she missed her sons and grandchildren. Mamm probably prayed into the night for their well-being and safety setting up and equipping their farms in Montana. And the hullaballoo of having Holly here, wanting to use this very house for her non-Amish wedding reception, would be enough to keep anyone from sleeping soundly. Esther hadn't slept well last night herself.

With Mamm snoozing, Esther moseyed into the kitchen. She'd get twice the cleaning accomplished in half the time by herself. Soon Holly would return to help her. Esther wondered if that girl of hers was trouncing around with Armin. The old saying about switching horses midstream wrangled in Esther's mind. She recalled how Holly's old beau—they'd dated for years—had unceremoniously dropped her and married someone Holly called a *bimbo*.

As Esther pushed the chairs against the table she noticed the box Dori had sent her. "Why on earth?"

Esther recollected putting the shoe box full of Mamm's letters pleading with Esther to return home on the top shelf in the back of her closet in Seattle. Holly might have taken them out, dug through the envelopes again, and asked Dori to send them. Esther wondered what Mamm would think if she saw them. Maybe it would warm her heart to know Esther hadn't thrown them away. But now was not the time.

Yet, she found her fingers removing the scotch tape and lifting one edge enough to reveal a box covered with brown paper inside, not the Keds shoe box she'd expected to find. A note from Dori was affixed to the top of the box saying: *Esther, when this arrived I started opening it, then realized it must be personal. Sorry!*

The box inside was addressed to Mrs. Samuel Fisher—her name used only in correspondence with the army years ago. After Samuel died, Esther had given up being Mrs. anything and went by her first name.

Esther lifted the carton's other flap and saw the return address on the label: Chap McLaughlin from Clearwater, Florida. She didn't recognize the name or location. Most likely a disgruntled customer, a complete stranger. No, not a client. Who would call her by her former husband's name? Few of her customers knew she'd ever been married.

Esther shook the box—about the weight of the letters—and felt a solid mass sliding inside.

A shroud of dread and uncertainty descended upon her. Her hands shook. For no reason, she assured herself. But the kitchen table was the worst place to open the package, what with Mamm, Holly, and possibly Armin scrutinizing her at any moment. She should disclose its contents with Nathaniel present. She would, of course, when they were alone together.

Esther cradled the carton, left the kitchen, and stealthed past her mother toward the stairs to her bedroom.

CHAPTER SEVEN

I saw Lizzie glance out the window of Nathaniel's kitchen and spot me staring up at them. Oops, she'd caught me eavesdropping. "Look, that Englisch girl is spying on us," I heard her say through the cracked window.

"Don't try to change the subject." Nathaniel's voice blasted out gruffly; I'd never seen him angry before. "You were the storyteller at the quilting frolic, weren't you?" he said. "Ya know what the Bible says about a wagging tongue? Proverbs 20:19: 'He that goeth about as a talebearer revealeth secrets: therefore meddle not with him that flattereth with his lips.' In other words, Lizzie, you betrayed my confidence. I'm to avoid those who talk too much."

"I was repeating what I heard, not making up lies." She lapsed into rapid-fire Pennsylvania Dutch, no doubt so I couldn't understand. Lizzie strutted over to the window and shut it.

With Rascal at my side, I turned on my heels and headed back to the shed just as Armin led the horse and cart toward me.

"I think I'd better go home." I gave Rascal a fluff.

"Wait a minute and I'll take you." Using swift movements, Armin's muscled arms tossed several bundles of roofing material onto the cart.

As I lingered beside the shed, I brought out my cell phone to make sure it was really on. I was going to have to get to a source of electricity. Maybe Armin knew someone.

Armin closed the shed. "There, that didn't take long. We can drive back on the road." He put out his hand to help me board the cart. His large hand was rough and calloused and warm. It seemed he held on to mine too long.

I settled onto the bench. In the back of my mind, questions churned about Zach, but the air was alive with delicious layers of farmland smells and the songs of birds chirping elaborate melodies. For several minutes, my spirits soared. Who knew, we might find Zach in Mommy Anna's kitchen enjoying a cookie and waiting for me. Or would I, as a veterinarian's wife, always be waiting for Zach? His patients would come first. I couldn't fault him for his dedication—I admired his work ethic. Still, he should have called.

Armin steered the cart along the road to Mommy Anna's lane. I craned my neck. No pickup, meaning no Zach. Then I stood, my hand on Armin's shoulder for support, and spied the pickup at Beth's house and what appeared to be the roof of a red car. I told myself it didn't bother me, but felt anger brewing in my chest. I recalled the stunning blonde I'd met on the plane a few weeks ago, and the business card she'd so seductively handed Zach in the airport baggage claim. Hold everything! I should be more concerned with an old girlfriend reappearing to claim him.

Once in the barnyard, I sat on the cart's bench as Armin unloaded the bundled shingles. "Need help getting down?" he asked me.

"No thanks." I shut off my phone. Zach knew where to find me. I jumped and landed on both feet: one small victory.

"How well do you know Zach Fleming?" I asked.

Armin tied the horse to a post. "I've known him my whole life, although we attended different schools and we were never friends. And then he left for college. He treats Nathaniel's cows suffering from mastitis."

I nodded my head, when in truth I had no idea what he was talking about. Some sort of bovine illness.

"I could drop you over at his mother's if you like."

"No, thank you." Beth had clearly not wanted me there. I wished my feelings weren't so easily bruised by what seemed like a brush-off. I felt like the only girl in my third-grade class not invited to a birthday party.

"We could drive by," he said. "People drop in on each other around here." He chuckled. "It's written all over your face you want to see him. Maybe his mother would be second best."

"What I need is someone with electricity so I can charge my phone and laptop. Is there anyone other than Beth on the road who has it?"

"Something wrong with Beth?"

I tried to sound nonchalant. "No, but I'd rather find someone else."

"Sure, okay. Let me work on the roof for a couple hours and I'll take you there."

"Thanks, that would be great." By then Zach would have shown up. And I had a hankering to know what FedEx had delivered to Mom.

CHAPTER EIGHT

Carrying the parcel, Esther slunk past Mamm, who still reclined on the sitting room sofa.

"What ya got there, Essie?" Mamm raised herself on her elbows.

No more duplicity, Esther told herself as she prepared to answer her mother's question. Esther could think of no reason not to be honest with Mamm, yet she was riveted with fear, a prickly feeling reminding her of walking through nettles as a child.

Silently, she asked God for fortitude. After decades of secrecy, she wondered when her first reaction would be total honesty.

"Dori, my friend and partner, the woman who's running the Amish Shoppe, sent me this," Esther said, and held it out.

Her mamm could always tell when Esther was fudging the truth, Esther recalled from her youth. "I thought they were the letters you sent me, but it turns out they aren't."

"Ya saved my letters?"

"Yes, of course."

Mamm's speckled hand moved to her breast. "I didn't know if you'd ripped them into shreds, or what. You answered so rarely."

"I did answer them. Every one. But Mamm, I'm sorry. I have no excuse. It just seemed the deeper I wandered into the mud the more I got stuck in it. Like a hog sinking into the pigsty."

"Satan got his grip on you, Esther. But you're forgiven. You heard the bishop. And I promise I've forgiven you." She patted her chest. "An empty hole sat right in here for the longest time, but it's full again."

"Thank you, Mamm. I don't deserve it."

"None of us does, but you heard Bishop Troyer. God is all-merciful when we repent." She scooted around to a sitting position. "Now, open the box. I'd like to look through those letters, like a history book, since my memory's fading."

"I don't know what's inside, as it turns out. There's a container from a stranger I've never heard of. And it's from Florida, where I've never been, nor do I know anyone there."

"We have relatives who retired to Florida."

"But how would they know about my store? Unless you told them."

Mamm's forehead creased. "I don't think so. And it's highly unlikely your brothers told anyone. They didn't know the store's name or address. Ach—you call it the Amish Shoppe?"

"Yah." Esther was grateful Mamm didn't rant about the name; Mamm had every right to complain. Esther was pretty sure it went against the Ordnung to use the word *Amish* to prosper financially. She'd have to ask the bishop. Then what? Change the store's name or sell her share to Dori, making Dori the Amish Shoppe's sole proprietor?

Esther scanned the label. "The sender's last name is McLaughlin, which I assume is of Scottish origin."

"That wonders me." Mamm pressed her palms together. "Enough of this chitchat. Let's open it up and find out."

"I was going to wait until Nathaniel was here."

"You two aren't married yet. Don't you think he's busy enough? It might be a fine-gut surprise."

"I'd rather we read my brother Isaac's most recent letter."

"Never mind about your brother and my grandchildren. Open the package and take my mind off of them for a short while, won't ya? Unless there's somethin' you're keeping from me."

"No, Mamm, I don't have a clue. Honest, I don't."

The kitchen door swung open. "I'm home," Holly said. Esther heard pounding—a hammer on nails—and figured Armin was working on the storage shed's roof.

As Holly entered the room, Mamm stood and snatched the carton from Esther.

"Give that back!" Esther grabbed the box. Mamm lost her footing and thudded down onto the couch.

"Ow, my sacroiliac." Mamm's hand moved to the base of her spine.

"What's going on?" Holly galumphed into the room. "Can't I leave you two alone for a minute?"

"It's not what you think." Esther hugged the carton to her breast.

"Yah, your mother and I are getting along like two peas in a pod."

"Having a tug-of-war? Mommy Anna, you could get hurt."

"We weren't arguing," Mamm said, and nodded at Esther, who feigned a smile. "Not really." Mamm checked her prayer cap. No doubt about it, she was going bald, in the front at least.

Esther recalled Mommy Anna's visit to Dr. Brewster's several weeks ago. The endocrinologist had asked about Mommy Anna's temperament: was she becoming crotchety? Esther had admitted she didn't know Mamm well enough to discern if her occasional cantankerous outbursts were a recent development.

"How was your time with Armin?" Mamm asked, as if the previous scene had never occurred.

"Fine, he's a likeable guy." Holly's cheeks were glistening and her brown eyes alive. Esther wondered if Armin had snagged her attention. Then Holly's features turned serious. "I don't suppose Zach stopped by."

"No sign of him," Mamm said. "Didn't you say he was coming for the noon meal?"

"Yes, but he might have misunderstood and thought I meant tomorrow."

"He may be at Beth's," Esther said. "Like I told you, I saw his pickup in her driveway."

"Are you trying to start trouble?" Holly's words lacked conviction. She didn't even peer out the window toward Beth's house.

"No, I'm being honest, like you asked." Esther wished she could dispose of the carton unnoticed.

"Hey, what were you two arguing over?" Holly said.

"We weren't arguing." Mamm smoothed her apron. "Just jabbering. Ya see, a package came for your mother and I admit I was being overly persistent trying to get her to open it."

"The missing letters from my Grandpa Jeremiah?" Holly said, catching Esther off guard. "In which case, whatever's in that box also belongs to me."

"Why would you suggest such an illogical thing?" Ach, Esther had hoped Holly had forgotten about Jeremiah's claim he'd sent letters.

"The carton's the size of a shoe box," Holly said, "but I can't imagine you'd hide Mommy Anna's letters twice."

Esther felt as if she were juggling hot coals. "It's addressed to me, Mrs. Samuel Fisher." Her words burbled together.

"That makes sense if they're from Jeremiah," Holly said. "How else would he and Grandma Beatrice reach me?" She marched over to Esther. "Have you hidden his letters for years and years?"

"No, I swear, I never saw them. And Dori forwarded this from Seattle." Esther swung around to face her mother. "Mamm, do you have them?"

"What letters are you two talkin' about? Jeremiah never sent me letters."

"He told me last month that he wrote us letters and asked my Grandma Beatrice to give them to you," Holly said. "You were supposed to forward them to Mom and me."

Mamm gnawed her lower lip. "I don't recall letters, but my brain's so addled these days I could have forgotten."

"You haven't forgotten your sons and all their wives' names, have you?" Esther said. "Or that they live in Montana now."

"No, I recall that just fine. But there are some things …"

"In any case, I want to see what's in the carton," Holly said. "Please open it, Mom."

Esther tried to stall. "They were sent by a gentleman in Florida—"

Holly's hand reached out and filched the box from Esther. "I'm sorry, Mom, but we might as well get this over with." She removed the carton from the box and gave it a shake, much as Esther had done.

"Chap McLaughlin?" Holly lowered her eyebrows in Esther's direction. "Please, Mom, don't tell me you have a boyfriend lurking in your past."

"Absolutely not."

Holly coughed out a sputter of mock laughter. "Let's not get indignant, after all the baloney you've fed me over the years."

"You're right, Holly. I've given you little reason to trust me in the past. But I affirm before God that your father is the only man I ever loved—until Nathaniel. And I'll bet even he still misses his first wife, like I miss your father." That sad fact flooded Esther's chest with unforeseen grief. Did Nathaniel pine for his first wife?

Holly turned the carton over and ripped off the brown paper covering. She set the mailing label on the table. She opened the box and out fell an envelope, closed but not sealed. On the cover the words *To Mrs. Samuel Fisher* were printed in a strong masculine hand.

Esther reached out for it. "I know I've earned your distrust, but the letter's meant for me."

With Holly still clasping the box, Esther opened the envelope and read:

"Dear Mrs. Fisher, if I've finally found Sam's wife, then I'm carrying out his final wish. At least, his request the last time I saw him during the evacuation. Maybe he made it back to the States and he's fine and dandy. I've been looking for you for ages. As you might have heard, much of the archives in Saint Louis burned, and searching the Internet got me nowhere. Through a fluke last week, I ran into an old war buddy who thought a Samuel Fisher's widow lived in Seattle and owned an Amish

store. *(I think Sam said he was Amish.) Is that you? I figure Sam never made it out alive. Or did he? Please get back to me and let me know. Tell Sam he owes Chap ten bucks.*"

Holly, a tear escaping from the corner of her eye, held on to the carton like it was the only life jacket on the sinking *Titanic*.

Mamm said, "What's in the box? Someone's gone to a lot of trouble to find you, Essie. Aren't you curious?"

Holly gave the carton to Mamm, who removed the lid to expose crinkled tissue paper. Mamm flipped the box on its side without ceremony, like it was any old sack of cauliflower headed for a vat of soup.

Out slid an object a foot in length, wrapped with fuchsia silk cloth, like an Egyptian mummy. Mamm set the box aside and tugged at the end of the fabric, unrolling a doll—an exotic grown woman. It flopped onto her lap.

"An Englisch Barbie doll?" Mamm said with disdain, as if someone had offered to pour arsenic into her coffee.

Esther moved closer and scooped up the doll. The figurine was the opposite of soft, flexible Amish dolls—alien to anything Esther had ever seen. It was hard to the touch, with a ceramic face, its eyes rimmed with makeup and its mouth rhubarb-red. The doll wore a long and shiny tight yellow silk dress with a mandarin collar and turquoise-colored high heels. Her black hair, piled high on top of her head, was also fashioned into two long braids, affixed with bows that matched her shoes.

"That's no Barbie doll," Holly said.

"My Samuel bought this?" The hairs stood up on the back of Esther's neck.

"It must have been a gift for you." Mamm lowered her brows in Esther's direction.

"I never dressed this fancy," Esther said.

"Maybe it was for me." Holly took the doll and rocked it. "A gift from Vietnam for the little girl yet to be born. She's proof my father wanted a daughter." Her voice rose an octave. "He prayed for me before I was born."

"But how would he know Esther was carrying a girl?" Mamm said. "We didn't have those newfangled ultrasound machines back then."

"If we did, I didn't use one," Esther said. "I had no idea you were a girl until the moment you were born."

Cradling the doll to her breast, Holly seemed deep in thought. "What shall I name you?" she asked it.

CHAPTER NINE

I was stunned, reeling in a fragile state of mystification and grate-fulness. Was Dad trying to reach me from beyond the grave? I didn't believe in telepathic hocus-pocus—séances and psychics who claimed they could conjure up ghosts—but this doll was tangible evidence my father lived and was planning to come home to Mom and me.

I hoped.

"Could this be a prank?" I asked my mother and grandmother, the three of us in the sitting room.

"I can't imagine it's a joke. Who would do such a lousy thing?" Mom examined the fuchsia fabric—about three yards of the most exquisite silk I'd ever seen—its surface glinting from a ray of sunlight entering through the window, revealing metallic green threads. But Mom was going Amish; I couldn't imagine she'd be allowed to use it.

Mommy Anna polished her glasses on her apron, reset them on her nose, and peered at the fabric, then the doll. "They look new. Never used, anyway."

I sniffed the doll's dress; a mustiness pervaded my nasal cavity, bringing on a sneeze. "It smells decades old."

Mom stroked the silk, I assumed marveling at its weightless splendor. "A better question would be: Would a stranger hold on to a doll for all these years and never take it out for his own child?"

Mommy Anna harrumphed. "No God-fearing Amishman would give it to his *Kinner*, that's for sure. I won't have such rubbish in my house."

"Maybe Chap doesn't have children." My mind floundered for an explanation. "Or not a daughter, anyway."

"The letter says he's been looking for me for ages," Mom said. "Is that possible?"

"Anything's possible with the Internet," I said. "How long did you search for Dad after he was declared missing in action, hoping he was in a hospital with amnesia?" Also my pitiful fantasy—that he'd miraculously appear. I felt the familiar aching in my chest. Maybe the void left by Dad's absence would never be filled. I thought Zach would take away the emptiness, but I'd been wrong.

"I wonder what I should do with the doll," Mom said.

"Are you joking?" I hugged the doll, but she was unyielding and attached to a platform to keep her standing. "I want it. Not that a memento will bring my father back."

"Samuel might have intended it as a gift for someone else." Mommy Anna arched a brow. "I've heard men do strange and *greislich*—horrible—things during times of war."

"Please, Mamm," Mom said. "Don't make me feel worse than I already do."

"How a young Amishman ended up in Vietnam in the first place is beyond me," Mommy Anna said, as if trying to antagonize my mother. "Samuel's parents said the army would have released him as a nonresistant conscientious objector if he'd come home to work on an Amish farm."

"Eve tempted him, just like in the Bible." Mom gulped, then swallowed. "It was all my fault."

"But Adam should have taken control, been the head of the household," I said in Mom's defense. I'd never understand why Dad had acted so compliantly, just like Adam, now that I thought about it. "Adam should have tossed the apple out of the ballpark."

"That's kind of you, Holly." Mom draped the fabric over her arm. "Your father and I were so young and naive, and times were turbulent in San Francisco—frenzied. Radical protestors, marches, and mayhem everywhere. Your father got drafted, then falsely arrested during an antiwar rally, when he hadn't done a thing wrong. He landed in jail and was threatened with prison time. The prosecuting attorney and judge suggested plea bargaining: if your father enlisted, the court would drop all charges."

"Why didn't you hire a lawyer? Doesn't the court appoint one for free?"

"It's not our way to use them."

"But you were living like *Englischers*, as you call us." Her convoluted story still didn't ring true.

Mom's fingertips caressed the fabric. "I should have written his father for help. He and Dat might have come to our aid."

"It must have been God's will," Mommy Anna said.

Her rationalization was of little comfort. A monstrous hand seemed to squash my heart, like I was made of putty. I thought of the book of Job, all that innocent man suffered. It wasn't the first time I'd pondered why God allowed bad things to happen to good people.

I held out the doll and studied her face—definitely Asian. Her features were meticulously hand painted. I had no idea if it was from Vietnam. China exported so much these days, practically everything. Later, I'd check for a Made in China stamped on her somewhere out of sight, but I couldn't locate one now. Carrying home the silk as a gift made sense; it was nonbreakable, light, and easy to pack—the opposite of an exotic doll.

"What kind of a first name is Chap?" I tried to imagine a man persistent enough to track down my father. Most likely the two men had been tossed together at random like driftwood washed ashore.

"Sounds like a nickname," Mom said. "Short for something."

"Maybe he got his war buddies mixed up. And holding on to the doll for decades doesn't seem normal." I stood the doll on the mantel over the hearth. "I want to write this Chap McLaughlin guy."

"After I do." My mother held fast to the address label and letter.

"Yah, Holly, you let your mother handle this. I'm not convinced it isn't some mean-spirited hoax. Who ever saw a doll like that?"

"I want to run it past Nathaniel before I do anything," my mother said.

I decided to keep the argument I'd overheard between Nathaniel and Lizzie to myself. Why bombard Mom with more uncertainties?

———

Armin poked his head into the sitting room. "*Es dutt mir leid*—I'm sorry," he said. "I let myself in." He'd removed his work boots and hat. In spite of his mussed hair, I couldn't help but notice he was striking enough to pose in an Eddie Bauer catalog.

"Ya don't need to knock." Mommy Anna beckoned him to enter the sitting room. "You're always welcome, Armin. Are ya almost done out there?"

"Yes, but I ran out of nails and need to buy more." Armin's voice turned smooth as he directed his words to me. "Holly, I could take your phone and get it charged, if you like. Or you could come with me. It isn't far, but you'll be riding in the open cart." He really was a sweetheart.

"I figured that," I said, "unless you have a motorcycle stashed somewhere."

But if I left, I might miss Zach. "I'd better stick around here." As I spoke an idea sprouted. "I could take Rascal for a stroll while you're gone. Get us both exercise and keep him out of mischief."

"He'd sure love a walk," Armin said. "When I leave him alone in the cart he barks and the horse doesn't like it."

"Do you have him on a leash?" I asked.

He held out his arms to demonstrate. "A rope about six feet long. And he's got a collar."

"That would work."

He eyed the doll on the mantel, about his shoulder-height. "Whose figurine?"

"Remember the package delivered during the noon meal?" I relived the disappointment when I spotted the FedEx truck instead of Zach's pickup.

Armin drew closer. "A couple years back, I saw one almost identical to this in an antique shop in Philadelphia. The owner said it was from Southeast Asia."

"What were you doing in an antique shop?" my mother asked him.

"A better question would be what was Armin doing in Philadelphia?" Mommy Anna waggled a finger at Armin.

"Buying a present for someone."

"I hope you didn't purchase anything like this doll." Mommy Anna's words sounded like a reprimand.

"Nee." Armin skimmed his fingertips along his jawline. "As a matter of fact, I bought a teacup."

I wondered if the cup was for Lynnea, but would wait and ask later.

"Where did this doll come from?" he asked.

"According to a letter that arrived with it, my dad gave it and some fabric to a war buddy during the evacuation of Saigon." I pointed to the silk. "Apparently Dad asked the man to make sure Mom got these. The guy finally tracked her down. We think."

"He could have located the wrong Samuel Fisher," my mother said.

"Yah, there are many Samuel Fishers in this county alone," Armin said.

My shoulders slumped.

"No matter, I don't want that fancy doll in the house," Mommy Anna protested. "'Tis a bad influence on my grandchildren."

"They live clear across the country." Mom folded the fabric.

Mommy Anna pointed a gnarled finger. "That shiny material either, Esther."

"Since these items were sent to me, I should determine their fate," my mother said solemnly. It occurred to me she might be missing Dad as much as I did.

My mother picked up the letter with her free hand as Mommy Anna reached for it. "So, you're determined to write this fella," my grandmother said.

"Yah, I must." Mom's pale face appeared haggard. A nest of fine lines gathered at the outer corners of her eyes. "I can't ignore his gesture of kindness."

"If that's what it is," Mommy Anna said. "Don't it seem odd your Samuel would send you a doll wearing gaudy makeup and high heels?"

"Yah, that is a mystery," Mom said.

Mommy Anna's voice grew harsh. "That material was meant for a woman of the streets, if you catch my gist. And, like Armin said, there are many Samuel Fishers in these parts."

"But he sent the doll to Seattle, not here," I said.

"Don't get your hopes up, darling girl," Mommy Anna said to me.

I noticed Armin receding from the room. "Wait a second," I said. "I'll come with you." I funneled my words to my mother. "I want to look at the doll more closely when I get back."

"Okay, I'll put it in my bedroom."

"Thanks." For the first time I was grateful my grandmother had difficulty climbing the stairs.

I trailed Armin into the kitchen, grabbed my jacket, and followed him through the utility room and out to the back stoop. Rascal was tied at the bottom to the post railing. He yawned loudly, then yapped.

The sky was as blue and wide as an ocean, but a current of cool air tickled my cheeks. I was glad I'd remembered a jacket. Yet Armin didn't seem to need one.

"Want to go for a walk with me?" I asked Rascal, and untied the rope.

"Where ya headed?" Armin asked.

"I haven't decided. I might go to my other grandparents' farm. The Fishers."

"Jeremiah and Beatrice? Please don't take Rascal over there without me, what with their aggressive dog."

"Oh, yeah, you're right. They don't call him Wolfie for nothing." I recalled my encounter with their mongrel, one of the biggest, meanest looking canines I'd ever seen.

"And it's a long way on foot," Armin said. "I'll take you over there another time."

"In that case, we'll stick closer to home."

Minutes later, I watched Armin depart in Nathaniel's cart. Rascal barked and tried to follow him, but I gripped the rope with both hands and held my ground. When Armin was out of sight, I told the dog, "You be a good boy," then ushered him out of the barnyard and onto the side of the road. "We're going to have fun."

I might just scope out whoever was driving that red car.

CHAPTER TEN

Esther glanced out the sitting room window and saw Rascal tugging on his rope, pulling Holly north toward Beth's house. "I surely hope Holly's not chasing after Zach," she said to Mamm. "I can see his pickup and the red car are still at Beth's."

"'Tis difficult to watch your child traipse into a swamp of disappointment," Mamm said, from the couch. "I know all too well, having you live an Englisch life as a spinster all those many years."

"My life wasn't so bad—"

"Ach, I don't believe it for a minute. If that were true, what are ya doin' here?"

"Trying to make up for lost time."

"Have you considered Samuel bought that fabric for someone else?" Mamm got to her feet. "Why, for all you know, he could have been carrying on with a woman over there and calling her Mrs. Samuel Fisher."

"Why would you suggest such a ridiculous thing? He never would have."

"I've heard stories. Men do all sorts of irrational things in times of war. He could have decided he was doing her a favor. Why, she could have been pregnant with his child."

Esther wanted to plug her ears. Again, she recalled the doctor asking about Mamm's personality, and wondered if her mean-spiritedness was a symptom of a disease. Or was her mother losing her marbles?

"Mamm, I refuse to even listen to your preposterous ideas. Samuel didn't marry another woman. He wasn't that kind of man. He wrote me letters telling me how much he missed me."

"Now that Holly is gone, tell me the truth." Mamm eyed the fabric as if it were made of woven poison ivy. "Would your Samuel have bought that shiny silk? The color's almost blinding it's so bright, only the devil's mistress would wear it. And that *schlecht*—evil—doll?"

Esther stepped back, recoiling from her mother's verbal onslaught that rang all too true. Those last few months, his letters had become far and few between, and his sentences disjointed. She'd wondered if he was doing drugs, working with the wounded as he was, where pain medication would have been easy to access.

"I suppose I can't imagine he'd get this particular doll for me, either," Esther said, envisioning the faceless dolls of her youth. What had Samuel been thinking? "Maybe that's all there was for sale over in Vietnam."

Esther noticed talking about her former husband's death didn't quake her world as violently as in the past—his image at age eighteen used to visit her randomly throughout the day. She was glad she'd left his photo in Seattle.

"During a war they had such expensive things for enlisted men to buy?" Mamm said.

"He could have saved up and wanted to bring me a present."
Although he'd never mentioned it in correspondence and she'd
never requested a doll, only his safe return.

"You said in a letter once he was hoping for a son, didn't you?"

"He'd hinted he wanted a little Samuel junior, but added he'd
be just as pleased with a daughter who looked like me."

Mamm shook her head. "I ain't tellin' ya this to hurt you,
Esther, really I'm not."

"You could have fooled me." She felt like her mother had
driven a jackhammer into her abdomen. She silently asked God
for guidance. "I'll write the man who sent these to verify he has
the right Samuel."

"I'll bet ya anything he's got the wrong woman altogether,"
Mamm said. "Not that I would ever bet, for betting is a sin."

"Holly would be sorely disappointed, but it might be for the
best."

"In the meantime, give them to me to put in the Daadi Haus
in case someone stops by."

"No, I promised Holly I'd look after them." Her resolve to
show them to Nathaniel was dwindling.

Mamm bustled to the hearth, pushed herself up onto her
tiptoes, and swiped the doll off the mantel. She pivoted to face
Esther. "Now, give me the silk, too."

"Please, Mamm, let's not fight over this. I thought we'd come
to a permanent truce, you and I."

"Yah, we have, but I'm still your Mudder!" Mamm's voice
turned acerbic, but Esther was determined not to retaliate, no
matter what. Esther thought of old western movies she'd watched

on TV. A showdown is what they were having, but Esther wouldn't overreact or be insolent to her mother. Yet she couldn't let Mamm have her way.

"I'm going to keep this with me." Esther clutched the silk to her chest and raised her chin.

"Essie, you're disrespecting me!" Mamm lunged out, took hold of the fabric, and yanked hard. But her fingers turned rubbery and slipped. Esther's mouth gaped open as she watched her mother's torso twist and fall, her arms flailing. Mamm's forehead struck the coffee table, toppling it over. Esther reached out, but too late to keep her from hitting the wooden floor.

"Mamm!" Esther stooped down. "Are you all right?"

"Yah, yah, fine as I'll ever be."

"No, you're not. Your head's bleeding."

Mamm wiped her forehead, then observed her bloodied hand. "'Tis nothing that a damp rag won't fix."

"I should take you to the doctor. I think you need stitches." The sight of blood usually didn't bother Esther, but queasiness rippled through her stomach; she thought she might gag. She was tempted to use the silk to swab Mamm's gash, but figured Mamm would be offended.

"Nee, I'm fine, I tell ya."

A rap-rap-rap-rap on the door startled Esther.

"Who could that be?" Mamm said. "Hardly anyone comes to the front door."

"A salesman?" How would Esther explain the tableau: her mother sprawled out on the floor, the table on its side, the doll lying facedown. "I'll ignore it."

Mamm tried to sit up, but couldn't. "Ach, whoever it is heard us speaking and knows we're home. Go see who's there."

"All right." Esther hoped it wasn't the bishop. No, he'd come 'round back. But she could use help getting Mamm to her feet and assessing her injury.

Another knock, knock.

A sense of urgency slithered through Esther. She tried to help Mamm, but her mother shushed her off. "Get the door."

CHAPTER ELEVEN

Pretending I had no destination in mind, I glanced to the right, toward Nathaniel's farm, and to the left and caught sight of Beth's home, Zach's pickup, and a splash of red, which I assumed was another automobile. I wished I didn't care she'd not invited me over, or that she might be covering up for Zach, but I did.

His tail flagging, Rascal turned frisky as we ambled along the dirt-and-gravel path at the side of the paved road. The mellow scenery of rolling hills, farms, and pastureland unfolded ahead of us.

"Where shall we go?" I said to Rascal, as if I were wandering aimlessly. He tugged to the left toward a squirrel scuttling up a tree on the other side of the road. "Are you a rambler, like your owner?" I asked him, but the pooch's vision was locked on the squirrel, its furry tail twitching as it balanced on a limb.

Careful of an oncoming buggy, I allowed Rascal to drag me across the road. He heaved on the rope as another squirrel appeared, then scampered out of sight. Farther up the road, a dog barked, and Rascal quickened his gait. Unless we turned around in a few minutes, we'd parade right in front of Beth's house. Showing up at Beth's would be one of the most immature stunts I'd ever pulled. So I wouldn't. When Rascal and I got to her driveway, I'd cross the road.

As we neared Beth's, Rascal stopped to watch another squirrel zigzag up a tree, then the dog lifted his leg to mark the territory.

In my imagination, Zach's pickup motored down the driveway, then he stopped, jumped out, and gave me the hug and kiss I longed for. But no such luck.

Within moments Rascal and I were at Beth's driveway. I readied myself to cross the road, but a car was coming toward us. As I waited for it to pass I heard a child's voice, then a woman's calling. Rascal's ears pricked up and he looked toward Beth's house. I figured she had one of her grandkids visiting—she was preoccupied.

The woman's voice—not Beth's—grew shrill. "Justin, get back here!"

A little boy about three years old wearing shorts and a polo shirt came barreling down the drive. I heard a truck's muffler headed our way. A horrific scene detonated in my mind—a vehicle running over the youngster! I ran to successfully corral him before he reached the road.

Rascal yipped, and the little boy stopped short. "Doggie!" he said as the truck roared by.

The woman, wearing slacks and a cerise turtleneck, showing off a curvy figure, clasped the child's hand. "Don't ever do that again, Justin," she said to the boy, then noticed me. "He's never run away like that before."

Her eyes were swollen and ringed with mascara as if she'd been crying. But her frosted pink lipstick matching her sweater wasn't smudged. She was what people in Seattle might call classy; her short, coiffed golden hair had been highlighted, and a diamond stud adorned each earlobe.

I figured she was Zach's sister, making cutie-pie Justin his nephew.

"Hi, I'm Holly Fisher," I said.

She gave me a cursory looking over, but said nothing.

I heard tromping footsteps and saw Zach sprinting down the drive toward us. He seemed to glance at me, then his gaze honed in on the woman. "Thank the Lord you got him before he reached the road," he said to her. His face was blotched red and his breathing ragged.

"It's not easy being a single parent," she snapped. Her arm encircled the boy protectively. She was about my age, but Mom's height—several inches taller than I was.

"That's no excuse for negligence," he said, his nostrils flared.

"How dare you? Don't speak that way in front of your son." She picked up the boy, but he wriggled to get down.

I felt like I'd been sucker-punched; I almost doubled over.

"You've got your nerve coming here with pie-in-the-sky accusations," Zach said to the woman.

As if I'd suddenly materialized, he acknowledged me. "Hello, Holly. Sorry you had to see this."

Rascal growled at him. I was tempted to let the dog nip at Zach's pant legs. "Are you going to introduce us?" I said.

"Holly, this is Victoria."

"And Justin, Zach's son." Victoria lifted her chin.

I felt bile rising in my throat. I realized compared to this woman I was a plain Jane. Today, I'd combed my shoulder-length hair and applied a small amount of makeup, but I felt like a ragweed compared to this orchid. Then the jigsaw pieces fit into place: everyone else in the county knew the truth. Zach was involved with another woman! There was no way I could compete with her—his child's mother.

Victoria inclined her head toward me and said, "Is this the woman you're fooling around with when you're ignoring your own child?"

The little boy sobbed into her shoulder and sucked his thumb.

"You want your daddy, don't you?" Victoria said.

Her words were like knives, piercing me. I stood frozen, unable to move. Please, God, I thought, wake me up. Let this be a bad dream.

"I'll bet he does want his real father," Zach said.

Victoria stomped her foot. "How can you be so cruel?"

Zach turned to me. "This is not my child, Holly." As he stepped toward me, Rascal let out a throaty growl.

"You obviously don't need me around." My words tasted acrid. "I'd better leave."

"It's not what you think, Holly." Zach kept a couple yards away, thanks to Rascal's growling. "Victoria and I used to date, but she broke it off and got married."

"To a man with black hair," she said, ramping up her volume. I looked from Zach to the child. The boy's hair was lighter than Zach's sandy-colored hair, but I knew a child's hair could darken with age, as mine had. I tried to detect facial resemblances, but as far as I could tell the boy had inherited his mother's pert nose and rosebud mouth.

I heard Beth's voice calling from the house. "Justin, the cupcakes are out of the oven. Time to make icing."

Justin's face lit up, his blue eyes sparkling.

Victoria set him down. "Go to Grandma Beth," she said, and gave him a light swat on his rear.

His pint-sized legs hustled up the drive. I could make out Beth's tall and slim figure. She didn't wave. I almost jogged up the driveway to demand that Beth tell me the truth.

"Don't call my mother Grandma Beth." Zach pounded his fist against his thigh. "Victoria, why are you doing this?"

"Because I owe Justin the truth. And you, too."

I felt crushed, like a steamroller had mowed me over.

"I was just about to come and see you," Zach said to me, but his words were darts in my ears.

"And what? Tell me about her?"

"I was pregnant with Zach's son when I got married," Victoria said to me, as if she could hear my unspoken questions.

"I don't buy your story for a minute." Zach's voice seethed with bitterness. "I'm betting your husband tossed you out. Did you cheat on him like you two-timed me? You think dumb old Zach will come to your rescue?"

Rascal barked and ratcheted the rope out of my grasp. I turned and saw Armin steering the cart toward us. He brought the horse to a stop, and Rascal leaped up onto the bench next to him.

"I could hear y'all from a half-mile away," Armin said. "Am I interrupting something?"

"Yes, and your timing couldn't be better." I clambered aboard the wagon, and Rascal jumped in the back. "I've never been so glad to see someone in my life," I told Armin.

I recalled feeling the same way about Zach just this morning, but now knew why I hardly ever saw him.

Zach dashed over to me. "Holly, don't believe a word she said."

He seemed so earnest, I felt myself being drawn to him—an oblivious moth to a tantalizing flame. But I couldn't poke my head in the nearest groundhog hole and ignore the hellacious train wreck I'd just witnessed.

CHAPTER TWELVE

Esther raced to the kitchen for paper towels to blot the blood dripping from Mamm's forehead.

The knocking on the front door persisted.

"*Himmel*!" Mamm said. "Answer the door. Where are your manners?"

Esther placed several towels over the bloody gash and guided Mamm's hand to hold them in place. "Press on this," Esther said. Then she ran to open the door to find an Englischer clad in a button-down shirt, a tie, and khakis. She could tell from his short haircut and preppy attire he was not from around here.

"Yah?" She looked past him to see a sedan parked out front. "Are ya lost?"

"No, I think I have the right place. I'm Larry Haarberg, here to see Holly Fisher."

Esther recalled his name, a man Holly had met at church.

"She might have mentioned me," he said, his voice eager. He was a nice-looking fella, she guessed around forty years old. He seemed trustworthy—not a serial killer or burglar. And Esther needed help. It was times like this she wished Mamm owned a telephone. But whom would she call? Not Nathaniel, who also was without a phone.

"Holly's not home. Come in, would ya? I've got big trouble."

"Anything I can do to help?" He crossed the threshold. "Are you Holly's mother?"

"Yah, but—"

"She's talked about you, Mrs. Fisher. I'm from Seattle."

No time to ask what he was doing here. "Please—please come this way." Esther's hand motioned him to enter the sitting room. "My mother just fell."

"How serious?" Larry assumed a take-charge voice. "Is she unconscious? I learned CPR, but it's been a few years."

"She's awake, but I can't get her up off the floor. And she cut her forehead."

"Yow." Larry hurried over to Mamm and knelt down. "You must have taken quite a spill."

"It happened so quickly." Mamm winced. "Ach, my arm hurts something awful. And I bent my glasses."

Esther dabbed Mamm's bloodied forehead with fresh paper towels. "I hope you didn't fracture a hip," she said.

"My hip's perfectly fine," Mamm said brusquely. "Why do people always assume a woman my age has fractured her hip?"

Larry leaned in close to Mamm. "Looks like your forehead needs stitches," he said. "I'll take you to the nearest hospital."

"No need, I have a doctor's appointment coming up," Mamm said, and a smile spread across Larry's face. Not a bad chap, thought Esther.

"This can't wait," she told Mamm.

"I agree." Larry got to his feet. "Without stitches you'll have an unsightly scar across your forehead."

"I don't care. I'll cover it with a *Kapp*. And I have an extra pair of glasses—somewhere."

"That may be so," Esther said, "but I think a doctor should have a look at you."

"I'm happy to drive." Larry helped Mamm to her feet, but kept hold of her. "I'll see Holly when we return. She is staying here, isn't she?"

"Yah, she is and should be home soon." Esther dove into a coat, and located her purse and a coat for Mamm.

Larry propped up Mamm as she tottered to his car. "Please," Esther said to him from the backseat where she sat with Mamm, "could we make one quick stop?"

Adhering to Esther's directions, Larry drove onto the road, then swerved around the side of Nathaniel's house, and waited while Esther streaked into the barn to explain the status quo to Nathaniel, who stood gripping a pitchfork.

"I could come with you if you like." He leaned the pitchfork against a wall, then dug into the pocket of his black work coat and brought out a knife.

She would have loved his company but said, "You must have chores—"

"Yah, right now I'm pretty busy." He bent over, knife in hand, and slashed the twine encircling a bale of hay.

When Nathaniel didn't attempt to dissuade her, she spun on her heels and leaped back into Larry's car. Strange, she thought, that Nathaniel didn't wander out to wave at Mamm. But maybe he knew he'd only be slowing down their departure. Yet his stiff posture and grim expression bothered her. He couldn't be afraid of the sight of blood, Esther told herself. She doubted he was afraid of anything.

As Esther got back into the car she had noticed Larry entering the Lancaster General Hospital's address into the GPS system.
When her seat belt clicked, his foot shoved down on the gas
pedal and Esther felt the seatback propelling them. She inspected
Mamm's forehead. "Gut, the bleeding has stopped," she said.

A woman's robotic voice spouted directions from the GPS as
Larry whisked them back onto the road. He narrowly missed several horse-drawn carriages and a tractor.

"That didn't take long." Larry pulled up to the hospital's
emergency entrance's curb fifteen minutes later, and jammed on
the brakes. He jumped out, demanded a wheelchair, and pushed
Mamm inside the patient entrance, ignoring her protests that she
wanted to go home.

With Esther trailing, they passed a mishmash of people,
including an Amish family she didn't recognize huddled together.
When Esther checked in, the attendant at the front desk asked
about Mamm's insurance. The woman didn't seem alarmed when
Esther said her mother had none. The staff must be used to the
Amish, Esther thought. Old Order Amish in their district were
forbidden by the Ordnung from purchasing any type of insurance.

"I'll wait here," Larry said, and found an empty chair. Like
magic, a phone appeared in his hand and his thumbs moved rapidly across its face. Texting, Esther thought.

Finally, in a cramped exam room reeking of disinfectant, a
nurse carrying a clipboard came in. "Oh, my, what have we here?"

Esther was grateful Mamm said, "I don't quite remember how
it happened. I stumbled, not lookin' where I was going." Esther
wondered if Mamm really had forgotten or if she was covering

up for Esther, who once again felt like the worst daughter in the world. Just when she and Mamm were doing so well.

The nurse and Esther helped Mamm onto the exam table. After asking about medications—Mamm wasn't on any—and measuring Mamm's blood pressure, the nurse worked her fingers into latex gloves. "I'll need to remove your prayer cap, Mrs. Gingerich."

Mamm's good hand moved up to hold the blood-caked Kapp in place. "Nee, don't take it off."

"I'm sorry, the doctor will insist," the nurse said. "Then you can have it right back."

Under the glaring overhead lighting, Esther watched the nurse gently peel it from her balding scalp. "Once you see how it looks, I doubt you'll want to put the Kapp back on," Esther said.

"Then you should have thought to bring an extra." Mamm's mood seemed to be escalating from bad to worse, but Esther reminded herself Mamm was in pain and probably embarrassed by the whole ordeal. If only Esther had let Mamm have the doll, they'd be at home nice and comfy.

Ten minutes later, Mamm sat stoically, refusing pain medication, while a doctor stitched up her forehead.

"I notice your mother's lost a patch of hair in front." He directed his words at Esther. "When did that start?"

"I don't know. I haven't been living here." Esther turned to Mamm, whose eyes glanced upward for a moment.

"I can't recall. If I had my Kapp I could cover it up."

"I'm sure you could, Mrs. Gingerich—"

"Enough doctoring," she said. "I want to go home."

But he sent her for X-rays, which came back normal. When the three left the hospital, Mamm's wrist was wrapped in an ace bandage and in a sling.

"Nothing's broken," Mamm said. "See, I told ya."

"I'm glad," Larry said, and situated her in the back of his rental car. "There you go," he said, "all set." Next to her lay the coat Esther had brought, then forgotten about. Esther reached in from the other side and draped it over Mamm's shoulders.

Mamm sank low in the seat. "Ach, I'm glad the bishop can't see me without a Kapp."

"I'm sure he'd understand," Esther said, and opted to sit in front next to Larry.

"The Bible admonishes women to cover their heads when they pray," Mamm said. "I might want to pray on the ride home."

Larry climbed in behind the steering wheel. "I know that verse," he said. "First Corinthians 11:5." Proving to Esther he'd memorized scripture, he grew in her esteem.

"If you wish to pray," she said, "perhaps you could pull your coat up over your head. The Lord will forgive you under the circumstance."

"I'm not going back to the hospital, ever," Mamm said. "I should be home fixing supper."

"You can't cook with that arm of yours," Esther said. "Holly and I can take care of everything. The doctor recommended you don't lift anything over five pounds for a week."

When the doctor realized how confused Mamm was, he'd suggested she spend the night, but she'd flat-out refused.

"I can't wait to see Holly." Larry pressed his foot on the accelerator. "I tried her cell phone, but she must have it turned off."

Esther considered asking Larry to stop at an optician to get Mamm's glasses fixed, but decided against it. She'd already bothered him enough and he looked bushed. Esther opened her purse to make sure the glasses were there and noticed the letter from Chap McLaughlin. She couldn't pretend she hadn't received it.

One hand gripping the steering wheel, Larry checked his wrist-watch. "I'll need to find a hotel."

"We have plenty of room at our house," Mamm said.

Esther stiffened. "Maybe we should ask Holly first." Larry had yet to explain his sudden appearance.

"Nee," Mamm said. "After all he's done for us I wouldn't hear of his staying elsewhere."

"Thank you very much, Mrs. Gingerich." Larry tailgated a buggy until it pulled to the side of the road, then sped past it.

Esther cowered when she considered how she would explain Mamm's accident to Holly—when it wasn't an accident. Ach, the way Mamm's disposition fluctuated, there was no telling what she'd say.

CHAPTER THIRTEEN

Riding back to Mommy Anna's, I listened to the horse's rhythmic clip-clop on the paved road. The cart swayed as if trying to lull me. To the right and left, harvested farmland stretched placidly, cows and horses grazed, and birds chirped. I heard the flapping of mourning doves' wings—a unique sound I'd always enjoyed.

For a moment, I couldn't recall how I happened to be sitting next to Armin. My mind struggled to reconstruct the last twenty minutes. At first I drew a blank, then the tumultuous scene congealed behind my eyes. I saw haughty Victoria laying claim to Zach. Their son, Justin. Beth must believe Victoria or she wouldn't be baking cupcakes and calling him into her house. If Zach was the boy's father, I should step aside. I wanted what was best for the child, the darling youngster who'd followed Grandma Beth's voice.

I'd been dealt a bad hand, as they say. I'd been in the wrong place at the wrong time. No, quite the opposite; I was thankful the truth had surfaced before I'd married Zach.

"What was that all about?" Armin gave me a sideways glance.

Like a bird that had flown into a windowpane, I was in shock and agony—numb, unable to converse. All I could do was shake my

head in response. I knew if I spoke I'd cry, and the waterfall of tears
building up behind my eyes might never stop.

Hard as I tried to steady myself, I felt moisture seeping from the
corners of my eyes. I reached into a pocket, but found no Kleenex.

Armin steered the buggy off to the side of the road onto a wide
patch of dirt and offered me a clean, pressed cloth handkerchief. "Ya
want to talk about it?" he asked.

"There's nothing to say other than I'm a gullible fool," I sputtered between sobs. I guessed I didn't need to worry about the sexy
blonde from the plane anymore. Zach already had another dazzling
femme fatale throwing herself at him. And a son!

Armin didn't urge me to continue; he patiently allowed me to sit
beside him and blubber.

"You, Mom, and Mommy Anna were right. Zach's been lying to
me." I sniffed and wiped my nose. "He has a child. According to a
woman named Victoria—"

"Yah, I knew he dated her. I met her once several years ago on
one of my visits home. But Nathaniel said she up and left Zach, and
right off the bat married another man." He fingered the reins. "I can't
imagine Zach would abandon his own child."

"Maybe he didn't know he had one. Until today."

"Could be a lie. Word buzzes 'round this county like swarming
bees."

"Who'd make up a story like that?"

"You're not the only person suffering from gossip, Holly. Just
recently someone reported seeing Nathaniel's wife in Ohio, of all
things."

"I thought he was a widower."

"We all did. The coroner said she most likely drowned years ago, and our bishop agreed with the verdict. But now Bishop Troyer thinks Nathaniel should go to Ohio and put an end to speculation."

"Unless Nathaniel's wife hit her head and lost her memory," I said, and immediately regretted my words.

"His two daughters don't believe for a minute their mother would be living somewhere and not contact them." He took the handkerchief from me and wiped under my eyes. "Sometimes we have to come to peace with what we cannot see," he said. "That's called faith."

"You're right." I blinked. "Like my own father's disappearance in Vietnam." No matter how many times I'd tried to come to peace with it, the image of him on the helipad continued to saturate the back of my mind. I'd never get over missing him and wondering what happened. "Mom's never mentioned anything about Nathaniel's wife. How did you find out?"

"Lizzie was there when the bishop came, and she overheard their conversation."

"Eavesdropping?" What I'd been doing myself. "In other words, more gossip."

"I confirmed it with Nathaniel. The bishop wants him to go as soon as possible, and I told Nathaniel I'd look after his farm. Nathaniel hires a young Amishman who will continue to work alongside me."

"Does my mother even know about this?"

"I don't know." He searched my eyes. "Ya look *drauerich*—sad in your face. You want to go back and talk to Zach?"

"No, if he wants to speak, let him come to me."

Did I no longer love Zach because he had a child? Would I not help raise the little boy? I knew I would. I recalled Justin's adorable face, his excitement at the word *cupcake*. But I grew up without a dad. If Victoria was telling the truth, I'd be keeping Justin from his father. I couldn't do such a thing.

Armin jiggled the reins and the horse conveyed us to Mommy Anna's barnyard. He helped me descend; my legs felt like they might give out on me. "Thanks," I said, grateful for a friend. I dreaded facing my mother and grandmother. They'd been right about Zach; he was not the right man for me.

My head as heavy as a boulder, I trod up the back steps and into the kitchen, but I found it empty. "Anyone home?" I called. No one answered.

I discarded my jacket, stepped into my moccasins, and entered the sitting room.

An eerie feeling surrounded me when I saw the low table lying tipped on its side, and the doll sprawled on the floor facedown. Why would Mom leave the doll there? I recalled my grandmother disapproving of it but couldn't fathom Mommy Anna or my mother tossing and leaving it on the floor.

Then I noticed the fabric strewn across the couch, and spotted Mom's knitting bag by the chair. I didn't see Mom's purse and wondered if someone had broken in. Mom's handbag could be upstairs. But if someone had burgled the house the intruder might be there.

I hurried through the kitchen to the back door and called for Armin. "Can you help me?"

He came bounding up the back steps. "What's wrong?"

"I don't know. Someone might have broken into the house."

"It's unlikely. Why would you think such a thing?"

"Come look in the living room."

He led the way. "Where's your mother and Anna?"

"Could they have gone to Nathaniel's?" I said.

"And left the house in such disarray? I doubt it. I better have a look around." Armin scaled the staircase to the second floor, then returned. "No one there," he said and then jogged into the Daadi Haus to find it also empty.

I heard Nathaniel's voice, and moments later he entered the room.

"Have you seen my mom and grandmother?" I asked him.

"Yah. Some Englischer drove them to the hospital a while back. Anna took a fall. Nothing too serious. Apparently she could hobble to the car so I don't think she broke anything. But her forehead was bleeding."

As Armin righted the table, Nathaniel turned his attention to him. "Why aren't you working on Anna's roof?" Nathaniel said, his mouth severe. "And you've got that mutt over here again."

Nathaniel was one of the most gentle and even-tempered men I'd ever met; I couldn't understand what seemed like hostility toward his brother.

"I took Rascal for a walk," I said. "Armin gave me a lift and was just about to bring Rascal back to your place when I asked him to come in here."

Nathaniel stepped closer to me, took in my face. "Your eyes are swollen. Have ya been crying, Holly? Something *rilpsich*—foolish— my Bruder said or did?"

"No, quite the contrary. Armin saved me from an awkward situation and I'm very grateful." My vexation transferred to Nathaniel. "Does Mom know you're going to Ohio?" I asked him.

"I was planning to tell her today." He glared at Armin, who'd obviously spilled the beans. "I hate to worry her, since I went through the same routine several years back. Senseless titter-tatter is all it was." He raked his fingers through his hair. "But now, this time, I don't know—"

My poor mother, was all I could think.

CHAPTER FOURTEEN

"Mamm and I owe you a debt of gratitude," Esther said to Larry as they cruised up to the front of the house. My, how quickly he drove, but Esther certainly wouldn't complain.

She glanced over the seatback to see Mamm was yawning, rubbing her eyes, and apparently waking up—Esther hoped not in a grizzly-bear mood.

"Glad to help." He hopped out, came around the hood, and opened Esther's door, then helped Mamm exit the sedan. Quite a gentleman. But Esther recalled Holly's labeling Larry a Romeo, love-'em-and-leave-'em type. According to Holly, the two of them were just friends.

With Mamm supported by Larry, Esther walked ahead of them. As she turned the knob, Nathaniel opened the door. "Gut, you're back," he said, his gaze not meeting hers. He spoke to Mamm. "Anna, are ya okay?" He wore a dour expression, his brows drawn down.

"Yah, fine as ever." Mamm's hand tentatively patted her forehead. "Pay no heed to the bandage. It looks worse than it is."

"But your wrist," Holly said. "Why the ace bandage?" She and Armin stood nearby. "Mom, what happened?"

Esther noticed the table had been righted and the doll stood on the mantel, the figurine a conspicuous contrast to its surroundings.

"A small accident—a few stitches and possibly a sprained wrist," Esther said.

"Larry?" Holly's jaw dropped. "What are you doing here?"

He rushed over to hug her. "I told you I might drop by."

She gave him a one-armed, unenthusiastic hug. "You said you had an uncle in Philadelphia—"

"And that I'd always wanted to see Amish country!"

Holly's hands rose to cover her cheeks. "I can't believe you're here." Esther had never seen her look so perplexed. "How did you know where to find me?" Holly said.

"Remember, I asked for your address?"

"I thought you might send a postcard or letter, not show up."

He wiggled his brows. "I have a surprise I decided to bring in person."

"Larry kindly drove your grandmother and me to the hospital," Esther said. "Would you please introduce him?" She could understand Holly's feeling bamboozled.

"Uh—sure." Holly's eyes were veined pink and her lids swollen. "Larry Haarberg, I'd like to introduce you to Nathaniel and Armin King." Then she excused herself to use the bathroom.

Larry put out his hand to shake Nathaniel's. "Hi, there," Larry said.

"Gut ta meet ya." Nathaniel's gaze took in Larry's attire.

"Likewise." Then Larry shook Armin's hand, long and hard.

"Hullo." Armin's stare bore into Larry's eyes.

When the two men finally parted, both seemed to puff out their chests like a couple of roosters. Esther chuckled under her breath. Men were such funny creatures, she thought. Not that her Nathaniel would lower himself to such prideful behavior. Maybe he was keeping his distance from her because a stranger was in the house. Their engagement had yet to be published; it wouldn't be official until the bishop or a minister announced it to the community at church.

"I'll get supper on the table," Mamm said. She swiveled toward the sitting room; her toe caught on a rag rug.

Esther raced to the end of the rug, holding it in place, and took Mamm's good arm. "No, you don't, Mamm. We'll make up a tray for you and bring it in to the Daadi Haus."

"Yah, Anna, your arm looks like it needs resting." Nathaniel stepped to Mamm's other side and the two shepherded her into the Daadi Haus. Esther could always count on Nathaniel. Ach, how had she survived so long without him?

Holly came out of the bathroom with a freshly scrubbed face, all traces of smudged makeup removed. "I'll get the food out," she said. Esther could hear Holly explain to Larry that supper would be leftovers—plenty of cold cuts, cheese, and homemade bread.

"Sounds good to me," Larry said. "I'm hungry enough to eat a horse."

"Think I'll stay, too, if you'll have me, Holly," Armin said. "A meal other than horseflesh does sound good."

"Not literally eat a horse," Larry said. "Holly and I go way back, did she tell you that, Marvin?"

"It's Armin. Armin King."

Their voices muted as Esther and Nathaniel escorted Mamm to her bedroom on the first floor of the Daadi Haus, its door opening into the front hall. They guided Mamm onto her bed and covered her legs with a quilt. Nathaniel lit a fire in the heat stove. "We'll get

ya warmed up and comfy," he said. "If you want the kerosene heater
going too, let me know."

"*Ich bedank mich*, Nathaniel. My daughter's gettin' herself a fine
husband."

"*Gem gschehne*—you're welcome." He looked uncomfortable
with the flattery, but Esther reminded herself he'd been taught since
childhood to be humble.

Minutes later, standing alone with Nathaniel in the sitting
room, Esther heard Holly, Armin, and Larry chatting in the kitchen.
As Esther moved to the window she reiterated the hectic afternoon.
She thanked the Lord Mamm's injuries were minimal and that the
catastrophe was behind them.

Evening was descending earlier each day as autumn dwindled.
The lowering sun cast a coral-colored glow across the oak trees and
fields on the other side of the road, and on the resplendent barns and
silos in the distance. Serenity seemed to fill the valley as if a giant
locomotive had just rolled by, leaving in its wake quiet harmony. Yet,
she couldn't shake a feeling of unease.

"I need to tell ya something, Esther," Nathaniel said, and took
her hand—his skin was clammy. She thought he was going to pull her
toward him and steal a kiss, which she very much desired. Instead, he
said, "I've got bad news."

He released her hand.

"*Was is letz*?—What's wrong?" Her vocal cords tightened around
her words; her throat felt parched as if she were in the Sahara Desert.
"You know you can tell me anything."

"There's *en Gebrummel*—a rumor—going around in Ohio."

"I don't have a clue what you're talking about." Esther tilted her head, trying to evoke a smile, but his expression remained stony, his lips pressed together.

"According to my cousin, people claim my former wife is still alive," he said. "*Sie is schunn lang ab im Kopp*—she's been crazy for a long time—living in a shack by herself like a hermit."

"But it's a falsehood, isn't it? Surely after so many years she would have been found."

"I wish I could tell you with certainty. My daughters have probably been praying for years she'd come back ..." He stared at the floor. "Bishop Troyer says I should go check."

"Yah, I guess you'd have to make sure, once and for all."

His eyes glazed over with a veneer of moisture. "I can't believe I have to relive this nightmare, just when I've met you again, Esther." He finally glanced her way; his pupils were dilated. "I never loved her the way I love you."

Hearing his affirmation of devotion made Esther feel twenty years younger, but she said, "You shouldn't speak like that, Nathaniel. Of course you loved her." She tried to banish the image of Nathaniel and his wife becoming united at a Sunday service, surrounded by a couple hundred relatives, neighbors, and friends, then the two sitting at the corner table—the Eck—as they celebrated afterward over a bounteous meal at the bride's parents' home. They had two children together when she'd disappeared and had surely wanted more.

Nathaniel had never mentioned his former wife's parents. Esther wondered if they were still alive and served as grandparents to his daughters' children, whom Esther had only met briefly.

This myriad of thoughts tightened her chest; her breathing was so shallow she thought she might faint. Esther had asked God to show her his will for her life. She might have to accept that the Lord wished her to remain single, an atonement for her sins. She recalled one winter, as a child, a girl had crashed through the frozen pond and was imprisoned beneath the ice. That's how Esther felt at this moment, as if she were drowning.

"When will you leave?" She lay a hand on his shoulder, but he back-stepped as if she carried leprosy.

"As soon as I get my ride set up." He slipped his hands in his pockets. "I'll take the bus or train or hire a driver."

The kitchen door swung open and Holly shambled into the room. She reminded Esther of a wilted hydrangea—what Esther felt like. "You told Larry he could stay here, Mom?"

"Yes. He was such a help to us, and offered to take Mamm to Dr. Brewster's, unless her arm hurts too much."

"I should rent a car," Holly said. "Or buy one, my original plan—I'd have to take out a loan. But after today, I don't know what to do. Maybe I should pack my bags. No, I won't leave Mommy Anna just because a man's been lying to me."

"You mean Zach?" The hairs on the nape of Esther's neck raised. "Do you want to tell us about it?"

Holly's face contorted. "He fathered a child and is refusing to own up."

"Zach's not one of us, but he's an upstanding man," Nathaniel said. "Are you sure it's the truth?"

"I met the woman—Victoria—and saw the boy with my own eyes." Holly rubbed the heel of her palm against her chest. "And I heard the woman talking about Grandma Beth."

"I'm sorry, dear girl." Since Holly was born, Esther had tried to

protect her, but a never-ending stream of disappointments continued to assault her daughter.

"Mom, it's too painful to talk about in detail right now. Okay?"
She bit at the corner of her thumbnail. "Would you show me what
to put on Mommy Anna's plate, and then I'll take a tray in to her."

"Sure, darling. In fact, I'll bring her the tray. And a pair of
her old glasses—better than nothing." Esther could tell from her
daughter's bent spine her heart was breaking. Neither Mamm or
Esther had wanted Holly marrying Zach, and they'd been right all
along. Yet it was torturous to watch Holly suffer.

Out of the corner of her eye, Esther saw the doll on the mantel.
Ach, her whole world was spinning out of control.

CHAPTER FIFTEEN

I returned to the kitchen with Nathaniel and Mom on my heels, and found Larry, humming as he set the table.

"Armin took off, I guess to milk the cows." Larry did a drumroll on the counter with two spoons. "Bet you didn't know I was handy in the kitchen, Holly."

"You're full of surprises," I said.

He flashed me a smile of even white teeth, pretty enough for a Crest ad. Not that I should hold that or his stylish haircut against him. He worked at a downtown bank and was expected to dress smartly. "There's more to come," he said.

Nathaniel cleared his throat. "I'd better get back to my place too." He strode to the back door and lifted his hat off a peg. "I hope Armin's taking care of everything right."

"He's a lot more capable than you think he is." I recalled Armin's finesse in handling Galahad, and his sweet attention to me after my devastating meeting with Zach and Victoria at Beth's.

Nathaniel positioned his hat on his head, pushing his bangs over his bushy eyebrows. "Time will tell."

"As with all things." I thought he should give his younger brother the encouragement he needed to be successful.

"Will we see you after milking, Nathaniel?" My mother sounded like she was pleading with him. He must have told her about the rumors regarding his former wife because her face was ashen and her chin seemed to be trembling. I considered suggesting he hire a private detective. Or did he believe the story that his wife might be alive? If he married Mom he'd be a bigamist, and if he got a divorce I assumed he'd be booted out of the Amish church.

"Yah, probably. If I can."

"I hope so," Mom said to Nathaniel as she prepared a plate of sliced ham, cheddar cheese, dill pickles, and whole wheat bread for Mommy Anna's meal.

"Nice meeting you," Larry said to Nathaniel, and pumped Nathaniel's arm.

Not very often was I left speechless, but on this day of all days, Larry was the last person I wanted to see. But he'd obviously been a godsend to my grandmother earlier. I needed to extend her invitation to him. We had plenty of room in this large old house.

"Have you been visiting your uncle?" I asked.

"Nope, I came here to spend time with you, Holly. This trip is the most spontaneous off-the-wall stunt I've ever pulled. I figured if you permanently moved I might never see you again. I'd miss my chance to win you as my bride."

My mother quickly assembled a sandwich, set it and a cup of tea on a tray, and hastened from the kitchen.

"Did I hear you right?" I said, sputtering. "You and I came to an agreement to be friends and nothing more. Didn't we split the bill at dinner a few weeks ago?"

"Well, yes. But good friends are hard to come by, and I started missing you."

"Larry, we haven't spoken since I left. The fact is, I'm engaged."

His head jerked. "Since when?"

"Since right after I came here." Too excruciating to tell him my engagement was also the most impromptu action I'd ever taken, and was already collapsing.

"To one of those Amish fellows?" Larry said. "Please tell me it isn't Armin."

"What's wrong with him?"

"I can't picture you being happy with a know-it-all hick who wears suspenders."

"Armin's smart and capable, more than anyone gives him credit for." My voice went flat, monotone. "But he's not the man I'm engaged to—or may be engaged to, anyway."

"You might break it off? Super." He rubbed his palms together. "Come home with me to Seattle. You don't want to live on a farm in the middle of nowhere for the rest of your life, do you?"

"I happen to think this is the most gorgeous place in the world."

"Compared to Washington State—the Cascade Mountains and Puget Sound? Not to mention the Olympic Mountain Range." He had me there; Washington was hard to beat.

"But—uh—my grandmother lives here."

"With no electricity or telephones?"

Aha, my opportunity to change the subject. "I do need to get my cell phone recharged. And my laptop. Although I miss it less and less now that I'm not working. No need to send out résumés." I sighed as I remembered my last day at the brokerage and how inferior I'd felt being laid off.

"I'll take care of all that for you," Larry said. "And I'd fly you out here to visit your Grandma Anna once a month if that's what you wanted. Anything at all."

"No, I can't leave."

"You say you got engaged recently? Sounds like a whirlwind romance. In that case, why don't you give us a chance?"

"Larry, we've known each other for years, as friends. We don't have a romance."

He inched closer. "But I can really talk to you and you can talk to me. Am I right?"

"Yes, but—"

"I should have proposed to you years ago, Holly. I don't know what held me back."

"Other fascinating women with longer legs?"

"Yeah, okay, I've dated a lot of cuties, but none can compare to you."

He got down on one knee—like in the movies—and grasped my hand.

"Come on, Larry, stand up." But he shook his head. "I know several attractive women from church who'd make excellent spouses." I tugged on his arm, but he didn't budge.

"I guess I think too much, that's my problem. Each of those women has some flaw."

"And I don't? I'm a zillion miles from perfect, and you know it."

He was reminding me of myself—why I was still single. But if I'd married, Mom might have never confessed, and I'd never have met my grandmother. Being here with her was more important to me than anything.

"We'll have the spiffiest, most opulent wedding Seattle's ever seen," he said. "Nothing's too good for my future wife."

"Get married in Seattle, without my grandmother in attendance? I'd never do that. Anyway, Larry, we don't love each other."

A zany notion hit me like a hailstone on a summer's day: maybe Armin was the answer.

I heard a knock-knock on the back door and Larry scrabbled to his feet, looking suddenly awkward.

"I'll be right back," I told him, and strode through the utility room and opened the door to find my darling Zach.

No, he wasn't darling, nor was he mine.

"Holly, I'm sorry I didn't get over here earlier. Victoria wouldn't leave, and she was sucking my mother in at the expense of that poor little boy."

I hurried to close the door to the kitchen so Larry wouldn't hear us, then turned back to Zach, who'd shut the outside door and was heading into the utility room. I met him halfway, barring his entrance to the house. I reached up and lit the gas lantern with a match, illuminating his face. He looked wiped out, half circles under his eyes.

"Justin has your blue eyes," I said, reducing my volume.

"You'd believe that lying hussy over me?" Cynicism seemed to govern his voice.

"If you care for me so much, why haven't you called or come over?"

"I was here early for lunch and about to get out of my truck when I got a frantic call from my mother. I wish I'd ignored it."

"Zach, don't tell me I didn't meet Victoria, and that you don't have a son you've neglected to mention. Have you known about Victoria and Justin the whole time I've been back? When were you going to tell me?"

"I would have, tonight. And to get the record straight, Justin is not my son." He moved closer.

I felt a battle waging between my brain and vulnerable heart. My mind warned me to be wary, while warmth and tenderness filled my chest. I did adore him. But I'd been misled in the past. Three years ago, I'd gotten engaged to a wizard of a liar, a criminal defense attorney who could hoodwink any jury. I was fortunate I'd found out about his alcoholic binges before we tied the knot. Not to mention the tawdry women he'd picked up in bars.

"Can you prove that statement?" The air in the utility room was dank and chilly; goose bumps erupted on my arms, but I didn't want him meeting up with Larry. Another conflict was more than I could handle. "Are you doing a paternity test?" I asked, the logical side of my brain sparring for control.

"Victoria says she won't allow it."

"You could insist." I felt myself turning inward, withdrawing from Zach.

"Unless she asked for financial support, I don't believe I have legal grounds to demand one. I'll have to check with my attorney."

The lantern hissed. "Why would Victoria suddenly appear?" I said.

"She's been calling my mother. According to Mom, her husband ran off with a woman at work. Victoria signed a prenuptial agreement when she got married and was left penniless. Hard to believe a man would desert both his wife and child."

"Yes, and it's curious that Victoria would choose to reach out to your mother, of all people. And that Beth would have invited them in and baked cupcakes."

"Truth is, Mom had a fit when Victoria and I split up. My guess is Mom hopes Justin is her grandson. But he isn't." Zach looked bewildered, defeated—his cheeks sucked in. "I called my parents and told them the good news about our engagement the night you came back, weeks ago. They'd seemed delighted."

"Both parents?"

He took a lethargic breath. "Well, mostly my dad. I suggested we all get together to celebrate, but my father was about to hit the road again and Mom suggested we wait."

"It appears your mother doesn't like me after all." My throat constricted around my vocal cords. "I thought Beth and I were friends."

"She's not the one who wants to marry you." Zach's voice gained momentum.

I felt my resolve melting, then heard Larry cracking the door open and saying, "Holly, where are you? Let's eat!"

"Who's that?" A frown darkened Zach's face. I raised my hands to stop him from entering the kitchen to no avail. He brushed by me.

"Welcome, come on in," Larry said, like he owned the house. "I'm Larry Haarberg." He shook Zach's hand with gusto. "Are you Holly's new boyfriend, who hasn't bothered to call her and neglected to show up for lunch, according to her mother and grandmother?" Larry laid his hand on Zach's shoulder; Zach shrugged it off. "I'll be straight with you, buddy," Larry said. "I might marry Holly myself."

The corners of Zach's mouth pulled back.

"Cut that out," I told Larry. I steered Zach into the utility room, and closed the door behind us.

Zach's words turned bitter. "Holly, why would you accept my proposal if you already have a fiancé?"

"He's not my fiancé," I said. "We're just friends. I had no idea Larry would show up. He came without an invitation."

"Is our engagement one big game to you?" Zach's words bulleted into me.

"No, it isn't." I was overwhelmed by his accusation and felt myself breaking down from the inside out.

A gargantuan fact struck me: Zach wasn't telling me he loved me. I ached to have him sweep me in his arms, to have him assure me he adored me, and that everything was going to be all right. But he didn't.

"I'm out of here," he said, and I murmured a measly "Good-bye."

CHAPTER SIXTEEN

Esther perched in the Daadi Haus on the straight-back chair next to Mamm, who sat in bed with the food tray. Mamm still wore a sling on one arm but had already warned Esther she would discard it tomorrow. A fresh Kapp hid most of her bandaged forehead, but a purplish bruise radiated down to her eyebrows. Esther was glad Mamm didn't keep a mirror nearby.

Mamm picked up the ham and cheese sandwich with her good hand and bit into it. A slice of pickle plummeted out, landing on the plate.

"Are you sure you don't need help eating?" Esther unfolded a napkin and tucked it under Mamm's chin.

"Don't treat me like a child. I can take care of myself just fine." Mamm swallowed a mouthful. "It's you I worry about, Essie."

Now what? Esther waited for a lecture on forcing Mamm to go to the ER, on her mediocre parenting of Holly, or on the doll and silk, or her knitting. Esther recalled Mamm never seemed satisfied with any project she'd tackled as a girl.

"I know all about Nathaniel's wife resurfacing," Mamm said.

"Ach, you do?" Esther's cheeks stung as if she'd been slapped on the face. "What did he tell you?"

"Nathaniel hasn't said anything to me." Mamm sipped her tea and dribbled on the napkin. "Your cousin Martha in Ohio sent me a letter about it a few days ago. And Lizzie mentioned it when she was here."

"Why didn't you tell me sooner? I can't believe you'd keep it from me. Am I the last person on the planet to find out Nathaniel's wife might be alive?"

"Nee, don't be silly. I figure it's not true." Mamm brought the sandwich to her mouth. "You know how folks love to blather." She gnawed into it. A slice of cheese slipped out but she didn't notice.

"We're talking about my future husband." Esther reached out and put the cheese on the plate. "Why didn't you tell me? I deserved to know." She pressed her lips together to keep spiteful words from spewing forth like pesticide. She knew she shouldn't be angry with Mamm, but she was.

"I didn't want you fussing over nothing," Mamm said.

A taste like a rusty nail flooded Esther's mouth. "What if his wife is still alive?"

"I certainly never wished the woman dead, and I don't now," Mamm said. "That would be a sin. But in this case, her passing would make life less complicated for you." She chewed another mouthful.

Esther decided she had nothing to hide from her mother, who obviously knew more about the situation than she did. "Nathaniel just told me," Esther said. "I was so shocked I almost fell over. He'll search for her, once he checks the bus and train schedules, or hires a driver."

"Or maybe Zach will take him."

"How can Zach leave his clinic, let alone Holly?" Esther reassembled Mamm's sandwich. "Not that he hasn't made himself scarce for weeks. Why, if he doesn't shape up, someone like Larry will steal her away."

"Larry's not such a bad man. But too fancy. I doubt he's ever milked a cow, or used a hammer and nail."

"Not many cows in Seattle," Esther said. "I believe Holly and Larry met at the church's singles group. That carries weight with me."

"Unless he only attends church to meet women. I've heard of men like that." Mamm picked a bread crumb off her quilt and set it on the tray. "I'm still placing odds on Armin. Not that I believe betting is all right. But I believe Armin's the perfect spouse for Holly once she comes 'round. I see God's orchestration at work." She let her head fall back against the pillows. "Ach, 'tis been quite a day, with that doll arriving, and then that *unsinnich*—senseless—trip to the emergency room."

"Mamm, ya needed eight stitches." Esther noticed new creases around Mamm's eyes, as if she'd been squinting into the sun; her face looked weathered.

"We could have used homemade bandages right here. Or that silk scarf, then tossed it in the trash bin where it belongs."

Esther felt her shoulders tighten. "I'm ready to rewrap the doll and send it back to that Chap McLaughlin."

"A fine-gut idea. But I don't think your daughter will give up the doll without a fight. I heard her talkin' to the doll, asking it what she should name it."

"Meaning she's grown attached to it." In a way, Esther had too, but she knew its presence would build a barrier between her and Nathaniel.

CHAPTER SEVENTEEN

Out the kitchen window, I watched Zach sulk back to his pickup. The sun had sunk behind a bank of clouds; the sky grew dark, draining the color from the barn and outbuildings.

If I wasn't mistaken, Larry muttered, "Good riddance," under his breath. Half of me experienced the same sentiment. I mean, Zach had no right to be jealous of Larry. But on the other hand—

"I'll be right back," I said to Larry. "Please, go ahead and eat." Then I barged through the utility room and out the door. Zach was nearing his pickup.

"Wait, Zach." I tore down the steps and trotted over to him. "Can we talk?"

He paused, turned my way. "Looks like you've already found my replacement." His stare cut right into me. I figured hurt feelings were ruling his words. All day he'd been pummeled by adversity. But I couldn't shake the image of Justin's cherublike face.

"Zach," I said, "it's been a long day for both of us." I was afraid to ask him to stop by for lunch again. I couldn't stand another disappointment.

He took my hands. His fingers felt cool, lacking strength, as if he'd given away every ounce of energy and desperately needed rest and solitude. The temperature was dipping, and chilly air permeated my clothing, making me shiver.

"It may take months to detangle Victoria's cobweb of lies," he said. "Do you have the patience to wait?"

"I honestly don't know."

His fingers tightened around mine. "I'd better go," he said, and loosened his grasp.

My arms flopped to my sides. "Okay, see ya." I didn't ask when; I'd demeaned myself enough for one day.

He got in his pickup and drove away. As I returned to the house, I couldn't get Justin out of my mind. A multitude of questions and doubts threaded through my thoughts. If my father were alive, I'd want him to be proud of me, even if it meant sacrificing my own wishes. The young boy needed a father. Long ago, I'd concluded fathers were the most important person in a child's life.

Not fair. Mom raised me and made many sacrifices for my well-being, yet she'd neglected her own mother. I recalled my shock as Mom opened the Keds shoe box crammed with Mommy Anna's letters back in Seattle. Guess I'd never understand Mom's motivation for concealing the truth and wondered if even she knew. I hoped forgiving her meant I'd eventually be able to let go.

I scuffled back to the kitchen and saw Larry sitting at the table gobbling down a sandwich. He'd shed his tie and opened his shirt at the collar. He dabbed his mouth and hands with a napkin, rose to his feet, reached into his pocket, and held out a small blue box with a white bow. "I brought you something."

I recognized the signature blue. From Tiffany's! I stood for a moment frozen in indecision. My mouth shaped into an O.

"Take a peek," Larry said.

"A ring?"

"Yep. An incomparable one-carat solitaire diamond. Here, open the box."

"Larry, you and I agreed we're friends, nothing more." I held my hands behind my back.

"But, like I said, once you left Seattle I started to miss you big time."

"Please don't get me wrong. You're a terrific guy."

"That's what my mother says." He stood taller, but was still several inches shorter than Zach, not that his height should matter in the least. "Wait until you see the ring. The salesman at Tiffany's told me no woman could resist it."

"That's what I'm afraid of." I felt like I was being swept out to sea on a riptide of curiosity. "I've already made enough hasty decisions for one month."

I heard Mom coming through the sitting room, in our direction, and decided not to allow temptation to dominate my actions. She entered the kitchen carrying Mommy Anna's tray. Her eyes widened when she caught sight of the box. "I'm interrupting. Sorry."

"No, Mom, please stay." I budged away from Larry. "We were discussing a matter that we've decided to put on the back burner."

"We have?" Larry's demeanor fell, the corners of his mouth dragging down. "May I still spend the night here?"

"Of course." Mom set the tray on the counter by the sink. "I haven't properly thanked you for your help today. I'm ever so grateful you happened by when you did."

"I didn't just happen by. I'm a man on a mission. And I'm not giving up." He spoke to Mom as he rolled up his shirtsleeves. "I want to marry your daughter, and I'm officially asking your permission."

Such chivalry, I thought. I had to admire him. But, alas, I didn't love Larry, and he didn't love me. I'd never felt the spark of attraction between us.

"I have little doubt you'll find a better bride in the blink of an eye," I told him. "You're the most eligible bachelor at church." He was never without a woman fawning over him at our singles' functions.

"And you're the most eligible bachelorette," he said. "We'd be the perfect couple."

"I think I'd better leave and let you two sort this out," Mom said, back-stepping.

"No, Mom, please—"

A single rap on the back door silenced us. The knob turned slowly, and Nathaniel entered the kitchen and hung his hat on a peg. His hair was flattened on top, but he didn't rake a hand through it as he usually did when in proximity to Mom.

"Any luck finding a driver?" my mother asked in a lackluster voice.

"Nee, it looks like I'll have to use the bus. Armin can take me to the station."

As Mom and Nathaniel spoke to each other in hushed voices, I took Larry off to the side and quickly explained why Nathaniel was going to Ohio. "If his wife's still alive, Mom and Nathaniel's wedding is history," I said.

"Couldn't he get a divorce?" Larry said in my ear.

"No, it's against the Ordnung, the code of conduct the Amish must obey. If she's alive, Nathaniel may never marry another."

"Even if they don't live together?"

"Yup."

"Weird." Larry screwed up his features. "These Amish sure have a lot of rules and regulations."

"Yes, they do." I turned and saw my mother holding the seatback of one of the kitchen chairs like she couldn't keep herself erect.

Larry spoke to Nathaniel. "I'll drive you," he said, his words filling the room. "I've got a GPS system in my rental, not to mention my trusty iPhone. Just give me the address and I'll get you there."

"I couldn't trouble you." Nathaniel looked the shell of the robust man I'd met last month. "I'm thinking it's a six-hour drive to my cousin's in Holmes County."

"That's a long trip," Larry said, "but I'm on a two-week vacation and have nothing else to do. I'm not ready to return to Seattle yet, and I've never been to Ohio."

"Are you certain?"

"Yeah, it'll give Holly time to open the box and accept my proposal."

"'Tis too much to ask." Nathaniel shook his head; his beard swayed.

"You're in a jam and I'm up for an adventure," Larry said. "My phone will direct us from Starbucks to Starbucks. No offense to your coffee, Esther, but I'm craving a tall triple nonfat latte." He bounced on his toes. "I might be of some help. I'm savvy in the business world, so I figure I can communicate with the police and check their records more easily than Nathaniel, as well as use the Internet. And I'll call back here and keep you updated."

"Larry, that's the kindest offer ever," Mom said. "You truly are a gut man."

"Thanks, Mrs. Fisher."

"Please call me Esther. And we have a phone shanty not far away, so I can use that phone."

Larry scratched his temple. "But not own one? I don't get the logic." He glanced my way. "Want to come with us, Holly? Couldn't hurt to have an extra pair of eyes and ears."

"You'd be welcome to," Nathaniel said. He spoke to Mom. "I'd look after Holly like she's my own daughter. And of course she'd have her own bedroom at my cousin's house."

"Or we could stay at a hotel, my treat," Larry said.

The last couple of hours, Larry had shown a side of himself I'd never before seen. I wondered if men also had biological clocks that chimed at a certain age, telling them to settle down and get married. In any case, I appreciated his generosity. And he'd bought a ring! I thought even Mom was curious about the box's contents as Larry tucked it in a jacket pocket.

I was tempted to say yes to Larry's offer. To run away from this confusion with Zach, to run away from my grandma's doctor's appointment that might spell bad news.

"I can write this whole trip off as a business expense," Larry said, lifting on his toes.

Aha. His statement reminded me that in the past money and possessions seemed to be the center of his universe. And he was a show-off. If I married him I'd serve as his arm candy.

"I'd better stick around here in case I'm needed," I said. "If I hadn't gone for that absurd walk with Armin's dog, my grandmother might not have fallen and hit her head." And I would still be in the dark about Zach, which I might prefer. Justin's sweet face kept crystallizing in my mind's eye.

"How will your farm stay afloat while you're gone?" Larry asked Nathaniel.

"I hire a young man six days a week to help with milking, and several neighbors have offered to stop by." He rubbed the back of his neck. "And I have Armin, if he doesn't run out on me."

"He wouldn't do such a thing," I said.

"You have more faith in my little brother than you should," Nathaniel said, using a no-nonsense tone.

I felt like informing Nathaniel he had more confidence in my mother than he should. She was, after all, the woman who still owned a house in Seattle and 51 percent of her beloved Amish Shoppe. And she'd proven herself to be capable of lying to me.

"Larry," I said, "if I don't go with you and Nathaniel, will you fly home instead of driving him?"

"Not a chance. Granted, I'd rather you come with us." His hand reached into his pocket, I assumed to feel the box. "Maybe you'll change your mind by tomorrow morning. In any case, I'll drive Nathaniel." He turned to Mom. "Thanks for letting me stay here, Esther."

"We owe you a great debt of gratitude for all you've done and plan to," she said. "I can't thank you enough."

Armin breezed through the back door. He winked at me as he passed, then came to a halt in front of Nathaniel and made a mock salute. "Anything else you want me to do?"

"Yeah." Larry swaggered over to him. "You can keep away from Holly while I'm gone."

CHAPTER EIGHTEEN

With Nathaniel at her side in the kitchen, Esther heard Larry and Holly chatting in the sitting room, then Holly's footsteps climbing the staircase and Larry entering the *Kammer*, the bedroom on the first floor.

"Could ya step outside with me for a minute?" Nathaniel said.

Mamm was sleeping, and Esther had waited for hours to be alone with Nathaniel, but she hesitated. Under the circumstances, what would people—particularly the bishop, one of the ministers, or the deacon—think if they saw her and Nathaniel alone together? Yet this might be her last opportunity to clasp Nathaniel in her arms and savor his tender kisses. Every moment with him was precious.

She recalled her farewell embrace with her former spouse, Samuel—how wretchedly naive she'd been back on that San Francisco day he'd been inducted into the army. She'd been sure she would see her newlywed husband again. History was rerolling upon itself; Nathaniel was being taken from her.

She glanced up into Nathaniel's face and tried to decipher his faraway expression. He could be thinking about his wife and hoping she was still alive, for his daughters' sake if nothing more. Esther imagined their reunion, should there be one, and felt her scalp tighten.

"*Kumm, Lieb*—come, love." He spoke the words without emotion, as flat as a countertop. He handed her a jacket and she pushed her fists into the sleeves, then he guided her outside and down the back steps. At the bottom, Esther spun around to face him.

"What will happen if she comes back?" she blurted out. She'd meant to skirt the subject, not dive into it headfirst. Why, she couldn't even swim.

"If she is, I must accept it as God's will," Nathaniel said, his lips barely moving.

"Are you sure you have to leave? Can't the authorities handle it?"

"Not after the bishop instructed me to go, there's no way 'round it. You wouldn't marry a man who won't stand up to his obligations, would you?"

"But you're committed to me." Her tongue seemed to have a life of its own. "I'm sorry, I'm acting selfishly. But I'll miss you so." Her fears lay deeper than she could express.

"And I'll miss you, Esther." He stared toward the west, as if he'd already succumbed to the fate awaiting him in Ohio. "My other choice would be to leave the church," he said, shocking Esther. That he'd consider so great a sacrifice for her was a compliment, but the act would prove every complaint ever describing Esther—a she-devil, indeed.

"No. No, I wouldn't let you." Her words stumbled over each other. "You'd be shunned, excommunicated from church. You wouldn't be invited to dine with your daughters and grandchildren. They're more important than I am."

He took her hand, pressed it to his lips. They wandered into the barn. He flicked a lighter, raised a kerosene lantern's glass chimney; a small flame journeyed up its wick.

Esther had only ventured out here a few times since returning. The way her feet sank into the soft flooring, and the familiar bouquet of dust, hay, and *Mischt*—manure—hurled her back to her youth. She listened to the two horses shifting their weight, Cookie's irregular breathing, and Mamm's one remaining cow, Pearly, rustling.

He released Esther's hand. "If we can't be wed, would ya still join the church? You wouldn't have to." His words grew strangled.

"Without you, I don't know." Was God trying to tell her something? Please, Lord, help me out of this quagmire, she prayed silently. She recalled from the book of Job: Though he slay me, yet will I trust in him.

A sob threatened to escape from deep inside her belly. "I feel like I'm in the way."

He took hold of her upper arms. "Please promise me you won't disappear before I get back."

"No—I mean, yes, I promise. I couldn't run out on Mamm again no matter what happens between you and me. Oh, Nathaniel, ya must be torn up inside. If anyone can empathize, I can."

"I don't know what to think. Rumors about my *Fraa* have buzzed around before and it's never amounted to anything. But my cousin—" Nathaniel tugged his beard. "Well, he's not a man to be taken in by hearsay."

"The cousin you're staying with?"

"Yah, I figure I'd best step right into the eye of the hurricane." He gasped a chestful of air. "Neighbors claim she's living in a shack near the Tuscarawas River. That she's hard to recognize, wearing rags and her hair all *schtruwwlich*—disheveled. Whoever the woman is, she's said to be half-crazy. *Narrisch.* I'm sorry for her, whoever she is. I'm praying God's will be done."

"Yah, me, too." Esther would have to let the truth unravel itself like a ball of yarn. She'd never felt so helpless. Not true, she'd felt forsaken many a time, and always God had provided— although not as she'd expected or even wanted.

"Tell me what you think of Larry's driving me to Ohio," Nathaniel said, interrupting her reflections. "Should I take him up on his offer?"

"Yah, why not?" Her pupils were becoming accustomed to the barn's shadowy interior and she could make out the shapes of stalls, bales of hay. "I'm guessing his motive is to impress Holly, but I doubt his tactic will work. I don't know what my daughter will do next. After all these years of my praying she'd find a hus- band, I don't approve of any of her three possible suitors—making me a hypocrite."

"You want what's best for her, like any mother would. Which rules out my brother. He'll sneak out of town before long, I'm almost positive, so you don't have to worry about him."

"But if she marries Larry, they'd live in Seattle. I'd never see my grandchildren." She rubbed her temples as a headache encom- passed her skull.

"Everything's been spinning out of control like a helicopter landed in the cornfield since Holly came home."

He stepped closer and held her against his chest, but didn't kiss her. She contemplated telling Nathaniel about the carton and the letter with it, which had thrown Esther into a tailspin, but she didn't want to add to his burden of worries.

Tomorrow, she'd write this Chap person a letter.

CHAPTER NINETEEN

"I owe you an apology, Larry," I said as I carried a platter of scrambled eggs to the kitchen table the next morning.

We were the only two in the room. I'd brought Mommy Anna a tray so she could eat in bed, although she'd pooh-poohed it, insisting she felt gut, capable of coming to the kitchen while Mom wandered over to Nathaniel's to say good-bye to him.

I laid the eggs next to the bacon on the table and sat across from Larry. "I've been leading you on," I said.

"No way." He scooped eggs onto his plate. "You won't even let me kiss you."

"I went out to dinner with you in Seattle, and accepted lattes and scones." I watched him through the rising steam from the eggs. For the first time since we'd met, he was without a tie or pressed collared shirt. Today he wore a T-shirt, jeans, and a zippered hoodie.

"You've made it clear you only wish to be friends." He downed a mouthful. "That's one quality I find so fetching about you, Holly. Besides your cute and trim little self, you're smart, independent, and don't want anything from me but friendship."

I scooted the plate of toast nearer to him. "Then why did you come all this way?"

"I like a challenge." He slathered butter on a piece of toast, munched into it.

"You bought a diamond ring and came to Pennsylvania on a personal wager?"

He swallowed another mouthful down with coffee. "No, I'm not that shallow. Here's the deal: I realized there's only one Holly Fisher and I might never see her again when she moved here. I tried to think of one other woman I'd rather take out next weekend, and not a single face came to mind—other than yours. That's when I made tracks down to Tiffany's, to put my money where my mouth is."

"I feel rotten about it. I wish you'd called first."

"And have you turn me down over the phone? No sirree." He spooned strawberry jam on his buttered toast and smoothed it with a knife. "Sure you don't want to see the ring right now?"

"I'm tempted, but I'd better not. Because that would be leading you on too. Larry, I'm trying to be as straight with you as I know how."

"If I can't talk you into marriage, can I convince you to come with Nathaniel and me? It'll be fun."

"Larry, Nathaniel's journey to Ohio is terribly serious."

"Come on, lighten up. I understand the ramifications if he tracks down his wife. But the drive would be a lot more interesting with you in the car." He polished off his eggs, then bit into a strip of bacon.

"In a way I wish I were going, to look after my mother's interests. She'll be devastated ..."

"In that case, pack your gear."

"No, I'd better stay near home to make sure my grandmother's okay. Yesterday, when I left the house for an hour to take a walk, she and my mother had some sort of tug-of-war, and Mommy Anna ended up gashing her forehead."

"Don't I know it." He shuddered—I think, for my sake. "She's one lucky lady to only need stitches."

"You were wonderful the way you came to her rescue, Larry." His happening to show up when he did still seemed beyond phenomenal. Positively baffling.

"There's no need to thank me. Just throw caution to the wind and come with us."

"No, I need to stick close to home, for a number of reasons."

"I hope one of them isn't Armin."

I shook my head. "He's the least of my worries." I wouldn't admit I'd slept with the doll in my bedroom on the bureau last night. Mom had stashed it in her room, but I was on to her tricks. I was determined to track down the man who'd sent the doll and fabric; he could have been one of the last people to see Dad alive. I wondered if my mother had the same suppositions. My heart went out to Mom. And I missed Zach, in spite of myself. Would that I could banish him from my mind.

"Well, in that case, I'd better scoot," Larry said. "Not sure what Nathaniel and I will talk about, but we'll find common ground." He tidied up his mouth again with his napkin. He'd always demonstrated impeccable table manners, a habit my mother would appreciate. "By the way, I checked with the personnel department at the bank before I left and told them about you. There's a job waiting for you in Seattle if you want it."

"Really? I'm touched you'd go to all the trouble." He was a wonderful guy in many ways, for some other woman. "Thanks, Larry, but that's a long commute."

The back door swung open, and Armin sauntered in and removed his hat. "Any extra breakfast?" He plunked down on the chair at the head of the table.

"Holly and I are having a private discussion," Larry said.

"Go right ahead, pay no attention to me." Armin opened a napkin across his lap. "If Nathaniel's herd didn't need milking, I'd come along with you. I know Ohio like the back of my hand."

"I don't recall anyone inviting you," Larry said. "My rental car has a GPS navigational system. Do you know what that is?"

"You think I'm a country bumpkin, don't you?" Armin set his fist on the table like he was ready to arm wrestle Larry. In which case, I presumed Armin would easily win. "Just because we only go to eighth grade doesn't mean we're a bunch of hicks. Farming isn't easy. And I betcha I can drive a car as well as you. Not like an old lady."

"But you don't own a car, do you?" Larry's round cheeks glowed red; he looked ready to explode. "And I do. And credit cards to pay for gas."

"Don't go thinking Nathaniel's poor because he's a farmer. He paid top dollar for this house and is generous enough to let Anna and Esther live in it. And Holly, for as long as any of them want."

"Hey, you two, cut it out." I was half-amused and half-afraid the men would start a food fight. "If you can't behave civilly, please leave this kitchen."

"Sorry," they both said, in unison.

Larry glanced at his wristwatch. "I'd better pick up Nathaniel." Last night he'd slept in the bedroom behind the kitchen—my aunt and uncle's before they left—because my mother didn't think it proper for him to sleep on the same floor as I did.

Larry dodged into the sitting room. I heard him lope up the stairs to the second floor and down again. Then he returned to the kitchen.

"What were you doing up there?" I asked.

"Uh—nothing. I'll call you." He angled his torso away from Armin. "Not too late to change your mind, Holly."

"You too," Armin muttered, as if to rankle Larry. But Larry ignored his comment.

"Bye, Holly." He carried his overnight bag through the back door. I got to my feet to watch him out the window. I saw Rascal tied up to a hitching post. He lunged and barked at Larry as if Larry were unwelcome. Larry hustled past the dog and jumped into his rental, then nosed it out of the lane and onto the main road, heading south toward Nathaniel's. Away from Beth's.

In spite of the hubbub, and the comings and goings, I hoped to see Zach's pickup arrive. He owned a spot in my heart I'd yet to reclaim. I wondered why Victoria chose to marry another man and recalled Zach's telling me the same woman had dumped him twice. He could still be holding a candle for her, as Mom would say. I'd seen movies where couples remet and fell madly in love all over again, like I'd always thought Scarlett O'Hara and Rhett Butler would have done, if they were real people.

I brought Armin a plate. He helped himself to eggs and three rashers of bacon. "You're not going ta get yourself hitched to Larry, are ya?" he said.

"No, although he will make some woman a fine husband."

Armin scarfed down a mouthful of eggs. "Hah. I'll bet he hasn't done a real day's work in his life."

"That's not true. He's a successful banker." I served him coffee.

"Sittin' in a cushy office all day with his feet up, growing flabby. Yah?"

"He's kind enough to drive your brother to Ohio." I sent him a stern glower. "I thought you were joining the Amish church. Where's your humility?"

"Truth be known, I haven't made up my mind about joining. Now, if I were courting a woman in this district—" He whistled softly, and low. "There's no telling what might happen."

CHAPTER TWENTY

Esther watched Larry's rental speed out of sight, carrying her Nathaniel away. She waved, but neither he nor Larry waved back. She could make out Nathaniel's tall silhouette, and wondered if she should have tagged along. No, a ridiculous idea. Nathaniel's cousin wouldn't appreciate her presence, nor would the bishop deem it proper to have her interfere.

Waiting on Nathaniel's porch earlier, she hadn't kissed him good-bye or offered words of assurance. "I'll pray for you," she'd finally said as he got in the car, but he hadn't acknowledged her remark.

As she hiked along the roadside toward home, troubling notions wormed through her brain. In the past, Esther had wondered why Nathaniel's wife was never located. Had someone dragged her lifeless body to shore and buried her, or had the river's current swooped her under a logjam where she'd been devoured by wild animals and fish? Nathaniel must have envisioned these morbid scenarios a thousand times, just as she was tormented by her Samuel's disappearance in Vietnam. And now a doll and silk fabric had appeared, as if taunting her and prodding her once more to accept her role in his death.

When she became baptized into the Amish church, she would kneel before the bishop, ministers, and the whole congregation, and admit her multiple sins on bended knees. Then, maybe, she'd feel the weight of guilt lifted. She'd proclaimed to believe God forgives our sins, and had been assured by her pastor back home the Lord is all-merciful when we renounce our discretions and turn to him, yet Esther felt as if her foot were trapped in a snare, eternally anchoring her to another era.

A horse and gray covered buggy passed by, and the bearded driver tipped his hat as if he recognized her. She wondered if that same Amishman would wave at her once he learned how she'd beguiled Samuel during his *Rumspringa*—a time for young people to explore the world before joining the church. Most of the young folk their age had stuck close to home, but Esther had discarded *das alt Gebrauch*—the old ways. She'd had the gall to talk Samuel into hitch-hiking to California to see the Pacific Ocean with her. She'd unveiled her hair for all the world to ogle, he'd played a guitar, and they'd sung for change, dabbled with alcohol and marijuana—every segment of their vulgar escapade against the teachings of the Ordnung. Ach, Esther was the catalyst behind his demise.

She'd seen the People forgive atrocities, but wondered if they'd accept her. When Nathaniel heard every detail, would he still love her? That is, if he were free to marry. In the next couple days, his own nightmare might come to light, as if embers smoldering in a fire pit bursting into flames.

The chill morning air spurring her on, she rounded Mamm's house, entered the barnyard, and saw Armin leaving through the back door and meandering down the stairs as if he hadn't a care in the world.

"Hullo, Esther," he said, and his dog barked. "Quiet, Rascal."

The dog sat obediently, but pretty as it was, Esther didn't trust the animal around their chickens, not after what Nathaniel had told her.

She strode over to Armin. "What are you doing here, when you should have been wishing Nathaniel well and saying good-bye?"

"Nah, my brother doesn't like a fuss made over him."

She stood in front of Armin, out of the dog's reach. "Maybe you're right." Behaving as though she knew Nathaniel better than Armin did was ludicrous.

"And he'd get all over my case for not working." Armin transferred his weight back and forth. "Work, work, work is all he does."

"That's no way to speak about your brother the minute he's gone." Esther felt like a snapping turtle; a boy was prodding her with a stick. "Where's your respect?"

"I do respect him in many ways, but he's always griping at me for something. I've got to wonder if he really wants me around, since I'm such an irritant."

"I'm sure he appreciates your help." Nathaniel did seem a mite too hard on his younger brother. Apparently, Armin had broken their mother's heart, exactly what Esther had done. Esther wondered if Armin's on-the-fence behavior had instigated the animosity.

"He's got a funny way of showing it." Armin turned away from her and strode into the barn, his shoulders erect, his hat set at an angle. He certainly didn't lack confidence, even if Nathaniel had described him as mouthy when the two of them were alone. Maybe Mamm was correct when she suggested Armin would make Holly's ideal spouse. Neither Armin nor Holly had joined the Amish church, so at this juncture they could wed. On the other hand, Armin could easily take baptism classes, but Esther figured the chance of Holly's living a plain life and becoming baptized was slim indeed. Yet stranger things had happened.

She enjoyed the sensation of her thoughts waltzing through her mind until she identified Zach's pickup rolling closer and parking outside the barnyard. He shut off the engine but seemed to hesitate, not getting out.

She recalled Zach had promised Mamm he'd look in on Cookie. Well, he wasn't the only veterinarian in the county. If he jilted Holly, Esther and Mamm would hire another. Esther could tell him to never set foot on this property again.

Zach finally exited his pickup and headed toward her.

"Good morning, Esther," he said. He wore jeans, a navy-blue jacket, and lace-up work boots. "Holly around?"

"I see you don't have your bag. Did you come to treat Cookie or talk to my daughter?"

"I'm short on time—my own fault for sleeping in. I usually head for the clinic right off the bat, but today this is my first stop. May I speak to Holly?"

"Give me a minute. I'll ask her if she's receiving company."

Armin strutted out of the barn. "Zach, ya can go right on in. Cookie's waiting for you."

"I'll look in on Cookie another time. I'm here to speak to Holly."

Armin widened his stance. "You'll have to get in line. She asked me to take her on a buggy ride."

"That sounds fun." Esther recalled the day Nathaniel escorted Holly on an excursion. Esther chortled as she remembered the jealousy broiling within her chest; she'd assumed Nathaniel would be attracted to Holly, not her.

"I was just leavin' to hitch Galahad up and swing back here," Armin said.

The corners of Zach's mouth stabbed down. "Off for a joyride the minute your brother leaves?"

"Listen, I've been working since dawn and Galahad needs the exercise." Armin's voice blared.

"Nathaniel gave you permission to use his favorite horse?" Zach's volume increased to match Armin's.

"I don't need permission to use an animal I picked out, then trained to pull a buggy." A sneer flared across Armin's face. "And like I said, Galahad needs the exercise." He gripped his suspenders, lifted his chin. "You've got your nerve insinuating I don't work hard enough." He moved in on Zach. "And you're in no position to be courting Holly. Everyone in the county knows your Victoria came back bringing with her your child."

Esther agreed with Armin, but restrained herself from entering their squabble. Although the two were acting immaturely, she understood why Holly could be attracted to either man.

CHAPTER TWENTY-ONE

I glanced out the kitchen window and spotted Zach and Armin arguing, their mouths twisted, facing each other off like a couple of pit bull terriers. Zach targeted Armin with his finger, and Armin retaliated by tapping Zach's chest with his. For a moment I thought they might wrestle each other to the ground. Men could be so immature. Did I even want one in my life? The answer was a resounding yes, because I wanted children and companionship and love.

My gaze zoomed in on Zach's face and my heart seemed to sprout butterfly wings. Guess I'd started falling for him long before I even liked him. I'd always thought he was extremely good-looking, but when we'd first met I'd found him egotistical—because, I realized, I was at loose ends and jealous of his career and self-assurance and his great relationship with his mother. Then I'd discovered him to be humble, intuitive, and kind. I hoped with all my might he wasn't Justin's father.

I noticed Mom strolling toward the back steps, then heard her padding through the utility room.

"You have company," she said as she entered the kitchen moments later.

"So I see. Is it my imagination or are two grown men acting like belligerent teenagers?"

"Well, now, you and I have been known to behave childishly ourselves."

"That's the truth. But those two are making Larry Haarberg look pretty good."

"But you don't love him, do you?"

"No. And I can't imagine he loves me. He's got it in his head it's time to settle down and he picked me as his happily-forever-after. I'm not sure why, other than I don't drool all over him like other women."

Mommy Anna wandered into the room with a slight limp, her arm no longer in its sling, and wearing a Kapp, partially covering her bandaged forehead. She lowered herself onto the rocker in the corner. "Don't discount yourself, Holly," she said.

"Yah," my mother said, "just because you got your heart broken once doesn't mean all men are pond scum." I heard a tangle of conflicted emotions in her voice.

"Yeah, I know—"

"Now, if you married an Amishman you'd never have to worry about his divorcing you." Mommy Anna set the rocker into motion. "Simply isn't tolerated."

I saw my mother's lips straighten into two pencil-thin lines. She was no doubt agonizing about Nathaniel. How could she not?

"Are you still determined to marry Zach Fleming?" Mommy Anna slowed her rocking.

"I don't know." I pulled a chair over to sit by her. "You've known Zach all his life." I searched her grayish-green eyes. "Do you think he could have a son?"

"Any man could, if he's living wickedly." She stopped rocking. "You mustn't marry a man you don't trust. Your future husband should be like a compass pointing true north. Now, Armin is a bit ornery and carefree, but he's honest. What you see is what he is."

"If I didn't know better, I'd think you're playing matchmaker again." I cocked my head. "We know it didn't work last time, when you tried pairing me up with Nathaniel. That was a fiasco."

"It all turned out for the best," Mommy Anna said.

Her shoulders slumped; Mom turned away and started fresh coffee.

A rap-rap on the door brought me to my feet, but I paused for a moment, not wanting to seem too eager. I opened the door to find Zach. A delirious blend of joy and trepidation flooded my chest as I stared up into his face.

"Hi." It was all I could say as I restrained a smile, despite the circumstances.

"Can we talk in private for a few minutes?" An expression of worry warped his features.

"We could go outside."

"It's cold out," Mom said. "It could have dipped to freezing last night."

"That's okay." I reached for my jacket. "I want to walk down to the creek."

"I only have a few minutes," he said. "Not enough time to go all that way."

"You come in, Zach." Mommy Anna said. "We'll leave you two alone."

"No, I couldn't trouble you." He stared at her bandaged forehead.

I shrugged on my jacket, stepped into shoes. As soon as Zach and I were out the door, Zach said, "Is Anna all right? What happened?"

"Yesterday, while I was having the pleasure of meeting Victoria, Mommy Anna fell and cut her forehead. She needed eight stitches. My friend Larry drove her to the hospital." I wished I'd never taken Rascal for a walk; I'd still be living in blissful ignorance.

"Sorry to hear that." He expelled a heavy sigh. "I came to apologize. I should have come here for lunch with you instead of racing over to my mother's when she called."

"Or was it Victoria who pulled your chain?"

He frowned. "I didn't know she'd be there—especially with her child. My mother must have invited her. Mom's been in a tizzy ever since Victoria told her she's single again. She's wanted me to call Victoria, but I said, 'No way.'"

Sorrow invaded me like solidifying cement as I came to terms with the fact Beth didn't want me for a daughter-in-law. We descended the steps, and he followed me through the barnyard and across the lawn to the fenced-in flower garden at the far side of the house next to the clotheslines. Most of the garden's inhabitants—the geraniums and other annuals—were spent. The chrysanthemums, black-eyed Susans, dahlias, and daisies were wilted and droopy, like I felt.

"I don't get it." I recalled how zealous Beth had been to befriend me when we first met. "Beth told me my grandma practically raised her after her mother died. What's she got against me? My mother?"

"I have no idea." He covered his mouth to yawn. "Sorry, I got to bed late last night, then slept through my alarm clock this morning. After work, I'll go to my parents' and demand Mom fess up."

His feet pivoted away from me. "In fact, I need to get to my first appointment."

"You're leaving already?"

"I'm sorry. I came to apologize, but I have patients waiting." He pushed back his jacket sleeve and checked his wristwatch.

"But you had time to argue with Armin?"

"I didn't mean to make it sound like you're an inconvenience, Holly." He stepped toward his pickup, then stopped midstride and turned to face me. "Who's Larry?"

"A friend from Seattle who's doing Nathaniel a huge favor, driving him all the way to Ohio."

"Why did Larry come here? To see you?"

It seemed I'd finally gained Zach's full attention, but I didn't appreciate his aggravated tone of voice. He should be answering my questions, not the other way around.

"Yes, he did, as a matter of fact." I heard a tremor in my voice. "Not that I owe you an explanation."

"We're getting nowhere." Zach shook his head in a way that made me feel dismissed. "I need to check on a wounded goat down the road before I go to the clinic," he said. "I should have been there hours ago."

"Then leave, already."

"And the Schrocks' mule's sprained pastern isn't much better. They wanted me to stop by yesterday."

"So what are you doing here? It doesn't appear you have time to speak to me." My hands moved to my waist. "Maybe that's why Victoria married someone else."

"Hey, that's not fair. She—never mind about her." He inched closer to me. With gentle caution, his hands covered mine. "Holly, I don't know what to say other than I'm as serious right now as I was when I asked you to marry me."

The feel of his hands against mine made my knees go weak, like I was a swooning movie star in a silent film.

His cell phone rang, sounding obnoxious, persistent. He ignored it.

"Aren't you going to answer?" I asked. "What about the wounded goat?"

A starling perched on the clothesline belted out a succession of cackling trills as if imitating the phone.

Zach dropped one hand into his pocket, exhumed his phone, and turned it to silent. Then he glanced at the caller ID and shoved it back in his pocket.

The ambience had shifted, our moment of tenderness gone.

I moved away from him. "Better come back when you've taken care of your plateful of unfinished business."

"I do need to make tracks."

Moments later, as I walked back to the house, I heard his pickup's engine starting. Zach drove down the lane faster than usual.

CHAPTER TWENTY-TWO

Esther knew she shouldn't be watching Holly and Zach, but with Mamm's nose pressed against the glass windowpane, and Esther stabilizing Mamm's arm, she couldn't help but see.

She gave Mamm's elbow a small tug and guided her to the couch. "If Holly catches us spying on her she'll flip out," Esther said. She'd heard a cell phone ringing outside. She wasn't expecting to hear from Nathaniel until tonight, but hoped Larry was calling Holly to check in. But no, she'd seen Zach surveying his phone. Then his pickup's engine and spitting gravel on the lane filled the air.

Minutes later, as she was covering Mamm's shoulders with a shawl, she heard Holly speaking to someone outside and a dog bark.

"I'll be right back, Mamm. Please, don't you go anywhere." Esther dashed to the kitchen window to see Armin escorting Holly to Nathaniel's open buggy. He was using Galahad without Nathaniel's permission, she could almost guarantee it. But she had no right to say anything; she wasn't Nathaniel's wife yet, and might never be.

Esther trotted out the back door, down the steps, and over to the buggy. "Holly." She was glad to see both her daughter and Armin were wearing jackets. Ominous clouds hung over the horizon to the west, meaning rain might be approaching. "Do you have your cell phone?" Esther asked her.

"Yup. Larry charged it when he went out to find the nearest Starbucks last night." She guffawed. "Can you imagine Nathaniel going to the drive-up window at a Starbucks? He'd better get used to it because Larry can't live without his latte fix."

Armin chuckled, patted Galahad on the rump.

"What about—Nathaniel?" Esther's tongue felt too big for her mouth and garbled her words. "Have they arrived?"

"Mom, they just left. Larry said he'd call when they do."

"Of course. *Simbel mir*—silly me." Esther hoped Larry didn't drive like a maniac but wished he'd hurry up.

"I'll let you know the minute I hear anything concrete," Holly said. "Unless you want me to stay home and call Mommy Anna's doctor to reschedule her appointment."

"No, you go have fun. I'll use the phone shanty if I need it. I think after Mamm rests today she'll feel good enough to see Dr. Brewster tomorrow as planned."

"You want me to leave my cell phone?" Holly dug it out of a pocket. "Doesn't that make sense?"

"Yah, I guess, as long as Mamm doesn't see it. If it rings, she won't like it one bit."

"Here, Mom." Holly sounded testy. "I put the ringer on vibrate, so you'll feel it. I saved Armin's number to my contact list. You can call him to reach me for the next couple hours."

"Armin, you have a cell phone?" Esther said.

He shrugged. "Yah, I know Nathaniel wouldn't approve, so I keep it turned off most of the time."

"No, I don't suppose he would." If Armin got baptized he'd have to ditch it unless the bishop gave him special permission, for business use only.

She noticed one of the chickens on the loose again. "Armin, when you get back I want you to mend the chicken coop." She scanned the barnyard. "Where's Rascal?" Had the dog broken into their coop? At least he was the opposite of Samuel's parents' mongrel. A dog takes after its owner, she'd once heard. Armin's was naughty but good-natured, while the Fishers' was vicious and domineering.

"Rascal's at home," Armin said. "He'll be fine. If Nathaniel caught wind I had Rascal running at Galahad's feet, he'd have a conniption. And Nathaniel doesn't want dog hair in the buggy."

Esther was tempted to tell Armin his older brother would be peeved with his harnessing up Galahad under any circumstances, but stayed her tongue. She was glad Holly was taking off on a distracting adventure instead of pining over Zach. He'd certainly left quickly enough, but she'd ask Holly about their encounter later.

Galahad stretched his powerful neck and mouthed the bit. His ears bent forward.

"Someone's ready to rumble," Holly said, causing Armin to laugh. He was a fine-looking man, almost as *gutguckich* as her Nathaniel. Esther guessed many an unmarried young woman would snap Armin up in an instant should he come courting. She wondered if he attended Sunday Singings—occasions for young men and women to meet each other and pair up. If so, he could select the prettiest young woman to drive home.

Armin helped Holly into the buggy, then untied Galahad and got in on the other side. Galahad flicked his tail and tossed his head, but Armin steadied the horse like a pro.

Esther hadn't driven a buggy since her late teens, but figured she could handle Mamm's mare, Topsy. Or was Nathaniel fixing to let Esther use his buggy horse in the future? If they had a future.

A few weeks ago, when Holly was back in Seattle packing up, Nathaniel had chosen the docile mare to transport Esther and Anna to Sunday service—a three-hour mental ordeal for Esther, with so many gawking at her. Esther had avoided eye contact, sat in the back on the women's side, and attempted to blend into the walls of their neighbor's living room, all partitions removed and benches brought in to form a vast area to accommodate around two hundred.

Several had greeted her with reticence, but she also received a hug from one of her mother's oldest friends. Ach, they'd probably witnessed Bishop Troyer several weeks ago admonishing both the Gingerich and Fisher families to forgive each other as the Lord directed. Samuel's parents, Jeremiah and Beatrice Fisher, lived in a different district, but no way around it: she would run into them eventually. Had they really forgiven her, when Esther hadn't truly forgiven herself?

"See you later, Mom."

"All right." Esther watched the spirited gelding surge forward, like he was in the starting gate at the Kentucky Derby. Not such a bad life for a retired racehorse, thought Esther as she waved good-bye.

She returned to the house to look after Mamm. Entering the sitting room, Esther's hands were itching to knit. If only she had black yarn or the bishop's permission to proceed with the blue sweater. She supposed she should follow Mamm's advice, pull out the stitches, and make a lap blanket instead.

With the stretch of time ahead, she'd write Chap McLaughlin a letter and get it in the post box out front before the mailman arrived, that's what she'd do. With Mamm snoozing on the couch, Esther extracted paper from the small desk against the wall and found a fountain pen and stamps.

CHAPTER TWENTY-THREE

I glanced over to survey Armin's manly profile as he stopped Galahad at an intersection. Armin's gaze was glued to the road and his hands steadied the reins as Galahad's front feet pranced in place.

But Armin seemed to know I was watching him. "Where shall we go?" he asked, waiting for an opening in the traffic.

"To see a covered bridge?"

"A bridge doesn't sound exciting enough for a city woman like you."

"I'd like to see one, if only to make my grandmother happy."

"In that case, we'll have to cross the busy highway." He ran his tongue across his upper lip. "Nathaniel told me what would make your mother and Anna happy. For you to stay here forever."

"That's the plan."

"Yah? 'Tis the best news I've heard all year." He lifted the reins and clicked his tongue twice. Galahad took off at a canter onto a wider road, a pleasant three-beat gait. Every joggle and bump sent chills up my spine—a joyous sensation as the buggy swayed.

The wind swirled through my ears and fluffed my bangs. I hadn't paid much attention to the magnificence of the area this last week—I'd been distracted and weary—but today my senses sprang to life, the late autumn colors enriched by the mid-November sun lazing in the sky, casting long shadows. Towering maple trees, their few remaining leaves, blurred into a kaleidoscope of burgundy and umber.

When it came to driving, Armin was every inch as competitive as Nathaniel. He overtook a gray buggy carrying several women, and then another being steered by a bearded gent. Next, we tailgated a minibus packed with tourists; the passengers flew to their back window to snap photos of us. Working the reins, Armin slowed Galahad and made a right turn onto a narrow road.

Breathing in the pastoral aromas, my nostrils welcomed the heady fragrances of drying leaves mingled with damp grass. Layers upon layers, I thought, the leaves and manure had mingled with the soil, nurturing the earth since my ancestors first arrived to escape religious persecution. I wanted to find out more about our family's history.

I admired the expansive barns and silos, harvested fields, and a pasture dotted with grazing sheep. Everything I saw brought me joy.

"I think this might be where Nathaniel took me," I said.

Armin glanced my way. "What was that? *Mei Bruder* drove you in a buggy?"

"This very one. My grandma requested Nathaniel take me out."

"Yet he's marrying your mother?"

"Their engagement, what you call courting, took everyone by surprise. Mostly Mom, I'm guessing." My sight locked onto a stately three-story house adjacent to the grandest barn we'd passed. "That looks familiar." I craned my neck. "I think it's my grandparents' spread. I've only been there once, on a whirlwind visit one early morning." I sensed a panicky feeling in the back of my throat as I recalled the both calamitous and phenomenal event—like a suspense novel missing its last chapter.

"Jeremiah Fisher is one of my best customers," Armin said, enthusiasm fortifying his voice. "I found old Jeremiah his mules, so nicely matched—a beautiful sight to behold."

"I haven't seen my grandfather's livestock. I never got beyond the front door and kitchen."

"Why don't we stop and pay them a visit?" he said.

"The last time I came uninvited I wasn't exactly welcomed with open arms."

"*Puh*. Since we're here, let's give it a try. Jeremiah's always glad ta see me. He loves talking about *Geil*—horses." Armin piloted us into the driveway, lined with white picket fencing. On one side lay a field once dotted with pumpkins; on the other side, harvested corn. Up ahead stood the imposing three-story house with its wide wraparound porch I'd first seen at sunup several weeks ago.

I heard barking. His ears back, Galahad turned his elegant head and snorted.

Armin looked over his shoulder. "Oh, no, Rascal's followed us. I wonder if the Fishers still have that fierce *Hund*. It was getting up in years last time I was here."

"They do. I love dogs, but their Wolfie is hairy-scary." I turned around to watch Rascal bounding behind the buggy. "Maybe this is an omen." I gulped as I envisioned my freaky encounter with Wolfie, a black, shaggy beast the size of a Doberman pinscher. "We should take Rascal home."

"Nah, I can tie up Rascal when we get there. But not until he and Wolfie make their peace."

"What if they don't?"

"Have ya ever noticed how dogs settle their differences quicker than humans? Sometimes there's snarling and bared teeth, but eventually they come to an understanding."

"I hope you're right, for Rascal's sake." His tail raised, Rascal was already ahead of us. "Okay, even if my grandmother doesn't give me the red-carpet treatment, I'd like to see my grandfather and Uncle Matthew, who apparently looks like my father—were he still living." An unexpected feeling of despair crawled through my chest. When would I be able to talk about Dad without choking up?

"Don't ya worry about a thing, Holly. I can handle it."

"Thanks." A wave of fondness for Armin rolled over me.

"Nathaniel told me that at a nonpreaching Sunday, Bishop Troyer came to Anna's and straightened the Fishers out. Beatrice agreed to forgive your mother once and for good."

"A surreal scene if ever there was one." I felt on shaky ground again. "I guess most animosity was resolved. Still, a lot of questions were left unanswered." Like the letters Grandpa Jeremiah said he sent Mom and me. He was an old gent; maybe he'd meant to send letters but never did. Or most likely Beatrice never gave them to Mommy Anna to forward. Upon circumspection, a reasonable person, Beatrice included, would ask for our address and send them herself. I refused to allow the vision of Mommy Anna's discarding them to contaminate my mind.

"Nathaniel said the bishop didn't require them to make kneeling confessions," Armin said.

"They're rather old to get down on their knees."

"How are your knees, Holly?"

"Meaning?

"Would you ever attempt to join the Amish church, if the bishop allowed it?"

"Right now, sitting in this buggy in the most beautiful place on earth, my first inclination is yes. But how long would it be before I wanted to use the Internet and my cell phone? Although I wouldn't mind wearing a loose dress and apron and no makeup." Mom never wore makeup and looked pretty. I'd heard even Oprah went in public without it, but most days I hid behind a facade of liquid foundation and mascara.

Rascal's bouncing gait lurched to a halt as humongous Wolfie launched from the barnyard toward us with canine teeth bared.

"Whoa." Armin told Galahad, the horse rearing on its hind legs, then finally settling on all four.

The dogs—bug-eyed and hackles raised—circled each other. After much posturing and sniffing, Wolfie stalked over to a smallish elm tree and lifted his leg, then lumbered to the back stoop, where he sat growling.

"Rascal, you stay with us," Armin said, and jumped out of the buggy. He found a coil of twine behind the bench and fastened it to Rascal's collar. "Don't you dare get into mischief, ya hear me?"

Armin put out his hand to help me down. I hesitated, frozen with indecision. Wolfie wasn't the only contentious individual I dreaded tangling with.

"Armin, I want to tell you ahead of time, Jeremiah Fisher's wife, my Grandma Beatrice, doesn't accept that I'm their granddaughter.

Way back when I was conceived, before my dad got drafted into the army, my parents lived in a hippie commune in San Francisco." My voice grew faint. "Beatrice accused Mom of cheating on my father." Pinched brows, hollow cheeks, and a pointy chin is how I recalled my grandmother. I was glad my father hadn't inherited her looks and volatile temperament.

"Does Beatrice not see a family resemblance?" Armin asked, not dispelling my fears.

"My mother says my father's hair and eyes were the same color as mine. But how many other people have brown hair and eyes? Millions."

My thoughts cavorted back to my conversation with Zach. He'd claimed Victoria had refused to have a paternity test performed on little Justin. Did I dare ask the Fishers to participate in one to put a final end to Beatrice's skepticism about my being their granddaughter? I could understand why she didn't trust my mother if the past were the best predictor of the future.

"I don't get why your father wasn't exempt from serving in Vietnam," Armin said. "Surely he told the army he was nonresistant."

"I don't know the circumstances, but I guess he was arrested and then given a choice: enlist in the army or jail time. Apparently my father was last seen on the helipad during the evacuation of Saigon." I felt myself sinking into a quagmire. "Dad was the only living GI from his unit who didn't make it back to the States that day."

"I'm sorry, Holly, really I am." Armin tethered Galahad to a hitching post and brought the horse a bucket of water. Then he offered me his hand. "You wanna come in the barn with me?" he asked.

"Sure." I doubted I'd run into my grouchy Grandma Beatrice outside the house. I hopped down from the buggy and we moved toward the expansive white barn, twice the size of ours. Silos and a corncrib stood majestically beside the barn, and a lower structure appeared to be adjoining it, along with numerous outbuildings.

Armin slid open the barn door and stepped into the cavern, dark save a lantern casting an amber-hued glow. "Anyone home?"

"Yah, over here." I recognized my Granddad Jeremiah's crusty voice, then saw his crown of silvery white hair and his beard that I doubted had been trimmed since the day he got married. He wore a thick work jacket, boots, and hat.

"Hi," I said, my eyes adjusting to the dim light. "I'm back."

"*Gude Mariye*, Holly. What a fine-gut surprise to see you." His arms wrapped me like I was a priceless gift. I leaned into him and let the knowledge that I brought him happiness pour over me.

When he let go of his grasp, I said, "It's wonderful to see you. I hope you don't mind our stopping by." I patted my hair in place, trying to subdue it.

"Nee, I'm delighted. We should have invited you over weeks ago, but my Beatrice has been suffering from lumbago. I've been taking her to the chiropractor, and she's getting better. Still, I should have stopped over to Anna's ta see you." One arm encompassing my shoulder, he turned to Armin. "You got a *Gaul* picked out for me? I don't need another, but I'm always willing to look. You know me when it comes to horses."

"Fact is, I'm taking a vacation from dealing in horses." Armin's mouth drooped on one side, then he seemed to recover his gleeful spirits. "Instead, I brought you Holly."

"And I thank you." Jeremiah leaned back to better see me. "She's more valuable than any horse," he said.

As the men spoke, I canvassed the interior of the spacious barn, the vaulting rafters, bales of hay, stalls, and a potbelly stove with a couple chairs nearby.

"Matthew and I have been reinforcing the goat pen," Jeremiah said. "You might have heard, a coyote or a dog recently mangled a goat in your district. Tore her up pretty bad, which makes me doubt a coyote was the culprit. It would have taken its prey home to its lair, don't ya think? Not many animals kill for sport."

Armin smoothed his jawbone. "Maybe a bear?"

"I got ta tell you, Armin—as a friend—there's speculation your dog's the culprit."

"My Rascal? He never would."

Jeremiah put up a hand. "No one's accusing, mind you, but I thought you'd want to know."

"Yah, I'm glad ya told me. But I keep him locked up at night."

"Gut idea." Jeremiah shuffled to the potbelly stove, latched its door, then turned to us. "You two want to join me for Kaffi and pie? Rachel, my daughter-in-law, came out a few minutes ago to tell me she'd brewed up a fresh pot and cooked apple crisp."

I remembered gracious Rachel, Uncle Matthew's wife, who'd welcomed me weeks ago on an early morn and functioned as a buffer between Grandma Beatrice and me.

"I should get back home," I said. "Mom might need help fixing lunch."

As if reading my thoughts, Jeremiah said, "Beatrice and I live in the Daadi Haus, so you most likely won't see *mei Fraa* unless

I fetch her. Our son Matthew and his family dwell in the main house."

"A quick cup of coffee sounds too good to pass up," Armin said.

Grandpa Jeremiah led the way out of the barn, a serene place I planned to explore at length when I had more time. How would I get here? I'd have to break down and buy a car or learn to use Mommy Anna's horse and buggy.

"Where did you tie your horse?" Jeremiah asked Armin.

"What?" Armin let out a gasp.

CHAPTER
TWENTY-FOUR

Esther prayed to the Lord that her Nathaniel would someday be truly hers. She recalled, decades ago, begging fervently on her knees, night after night, for Samuel's return, but the Father Almighty had chosen to ignore her pleas. Why, she would never understand. But it must have been God's will.

She admonished herself for circling back into a past that could never be changed. Until recently, she thought her future was evolving like a brilliant rainbow after a storm. Apparently another pipe dream.

She felt like the caged leopard at Seattle's Woodland Park Zoo, pacing back and forth. She needed a job, something to occupy herself. If only Holly hadn't brought flamboyantly colored yarn back with her from Seattle, Esther would start up another knitting project. Although, why create a garment—even a lap blanket—for a man who might never be her husband?

With Mamm napping in the Daadi Haus, Esther searched for a project to keep her hands occupied and her mind from spinning in on itself. Her casserole for the noon meal—a medley of ground beef, grated cheese, chicken, tomato soup, and wide noodles—was already in the oven, and the Jell-O and fruit salad solidifying. Whether they needed it or not, she'd shake out the rugs in the front hall, that's what she'd do. She opened the front door and dragged several rag rugs that were as old as she was onto the porch, and left the door open a crack.

Holly's cell phone vibrated in her pocket. Esther was so excited she reached for it, even though she was outside, in full view of everyone. The bishop, a minister, or the deacon could come by, but Esther dare not let the phone vibrate very long. She had no idea when its answering service would take over.

"Hello, this is Esther Fisher." Out of habit, she recited her customary answer at the Amish Shoppe.

"Hi, it's Larry." His voice was as clear as if he were parked across the road.

"Holly's out and left her phone with me in case I need it." She wouldn't antagonize Larry by mentioning Holly was with Armin. After all, he hadn't asked.

"In that case I'll let you talk to Nathaniel. Don't want to get a ticket while I'm driving."

Ach, he was driving and talking on the phone, Holly's stunt when she'd hit a cow with her rental car. Thank the good Lord the animal survived without injury. Esther prayed silently for Nathaniel's safety whilst on the road.

"Esther, are you there?" Nathaniel's voice sounded flimsy as a thread of sock-weight yarn, like he'd already lost the battle, a shadow of the man she loved.

She felt her throat close around her voice box, but forced out the words, "Yah, it's Esther. Where are you?"

"On a highway. I haven't paid much attention, just eating my burger and biding my time."

She understood he couldn't speak what was on his heart with Larry sitting next to him.

"Is Larry driving very fast?"

"Ya. We're flyin' down the road like a rocket ship."

She heard Larry laugh, then his muffled voice say, "I'm only going five miles above the speed limit. Tell her we stopped for early lunch at a drive-through and took the burgers and fries to go."

"I heard that," she said, envisioning Larry dipping French fries in ketchup with one hand while his other steered the wheel. She wished Nathaniel would ask Larry to slow down, but it would be difficult to tell a man how to drive when you couldn't drive yourself. Especially when he was chauffeuring you all that way. Still, she wished Nathaniel would make his thoughts known.

If she could fault her deceased husband, Samuel, for one personality flaw it was that he didn't stand up for himself enough.

She remembered her dat saying, "Too soon old. Too late smart."

Anyway, if Samuel had stayed, he might have married Beth—

A buggy clip-clopped down the road in her direction. Esther pivoted toward the house so the occupants wouldn't see she was using a phone.

"I s'pose I'd better hang up," Nathaniel said.

"Yah. I—" She heard a click, then a block of silence filled her eardrums before she could say good-bye. No matter. She had nothing else to tell him. Her letter to Chap sat in the mailbox, but Nathaniel didn't know about the correspondence, or the doll and cloth. She didn't wish to complicate his life; he had worries aplenty of his own.

She jammed the phone in a pocket and grabbed up a rag rug. She shook it over the railing as hard as she could. The breeze kicked up a cloud of dust and blew it into her face. A sneeze seized her, followed by another.

The phone vibrated again, and her heart skipped a beat. Nathaniel was calling her back to tell her he would find a way for them to be together no matter what.

"Hello?" The expectation in her voice made her blush.

"Hi, Esther, it's Zach."

"Oh." She wiped her nose with a Kleenex.

"Is Holly there?"

"No, but she should be back soon. It's almost time for the noon meal, not that anyone's paying attention to time." Her day had stopped when Larry's car jetted away.

"Where is she?" he asked.

"On a buggy ride." A truck clattered past.

"Who took her?"

"Well, now, Armin did."

"For heaven's sake. She actually went with him?"

Esther hated being caught in the middle, but held tightly to her commitment to be honest. "He said he'd get her back around now, and knowing his appetite, I think he'll keep his word."

"He's such a mooch, you're probably right."

Again, the phone went dead. Esther was getting tired of being hung up on, but knew she'd keep answering it until Holly returned.

CHAPTER TWENTY-FIVE

I spotted Wolfie sitting stoically on the back stoop as if he hadn't watched Nathaniel's horse and Armin's dog wander away, when in fact he'd probably instigated a fight with Rascal and frightened Galahad.

Armin loped over to examine the broken tether, hanging from the hitching post.

Both Galahad and Rascal had vanished.

"I once owned an escape artist," Jeremiah said. "Maybe Nathaniel's horse nibbled at the tether and undid it, then moseyed 'round to our vegetable garden." He pointed to the side of the house and Armin jogged ahead.

"No sign of hoofprints in the dirt," he said, when we caught up with him.

"Headed back to Nathaniel's barn?" Jeremiah said.

Armin slapped his thigh with his hat. "I surely hope so."

I stared at Nathaniel's lifeless buggy. "Now what?" I asked Armin. A flush was creeping into his cheeks and turning his ears red.

"Looks like you two will need a ride home." Jeremiah seemed amused, wrinkles cresting at the corners of his eyes. "I could lend you a horse, Armin. I've got a spunky standardbred gelding you could borrow."

"Thanks," Armin said, "and do ya have a saddle? Or I could ride bareback. Once I find their tracks, I might need to cut through a field."

"I do have an old saddle. I'll find it and brush off the cobwebs."

"Point out the horse and I'll fetch him," Armin said.

"He's solid black—save a star on his forehead," Jeremiah said, and went in the barn while Armin trekked out into the pasture.

Five minutes later Armin saddled and bridled the horse. He took hold of the reins, then positioned his foot in a stirrup and hoisted himself up onto the saddle.

"Sorry to leave you like this, Holly." Armin adjusted the stirrups, lengthening them.

"Is it true horses always head for the barn?" I asked.

"I'm hoping that's what will happen." He patted the horse's neck and spoke to him in Pennsylvania Dutch.

"Then doesn't it make better sense to take Nathaniel's buggy home?" I asked.

"No time."

"Yah, you go ahead," Jeremiah said to Armin. "Make sure that dog of yours is tied up before nightfall too. I'm betting a few farmers will have their shotguns loaded."

"Hey, what about me?" I felt marooned. "Some buggy ride."

"Sorry," Armin said, "but the sooner I track Galahad down the better."

"Before Nathaniel finds out?" I asked, then regretted my remark. Armin must have felt bad enough without my badgering him.

"I'll make sure Nathaniel's buggy gets home," Jeremiah told him. "My grandsons will help us."

"I can't thank you enough." Armin jabbed the horse's sides with his heels, and the animal took off like a slingshot down the drive.

"Holly, I'll take you back to Anna's," Jeremiah told me.

"Thanks, I'd appreciate it, if it's not too much trouble."

"Nee, I'll ask your Uncle Matthew to hitch up our carriage. Like I said, my grandsons can bring Nathaniel's buggy to his house in a bit, or maybe in the morning." He glanced at the buggy and shook his head. "Now, why don't ya come on in for Kaffi?"

I checked my watch—an item none of the Amish seemed to wear—and noticed it was almost time for lunch. I wished I'd borrowed Armin's cell phone to call Mom, but too late now. And I doubted Armin would use it in front of my grandfather.

"I can only stay a few minutes and then better get back home." I wanted to see Matthew's wife, Rachel—my aunt, but only about five years my senior.

"Sure," Jeremiah said, "we don't want Esther and Anna worrying about you."

He must have picked up on my angst, because he said, "Don't ya worry, Holly. *Alles ist ganz gut*—all will be well."

"Matthew," he called, and my bearded uncle came out of the milk house wearing rubber boots, a work coat, and a hat. I studied Uncle Matthew's face as he strode toward us, and was struck by his resemblance to me: the bridge of his nose, the set of his eyes, his full lips. Too bad he'd never met my dad.

"Gut ta see you, Holly," he said, then his gaze took in the dangling tether on the hitching post.

Jeremiah explained Galahad's getaway to Matthew, and asked him to hitch up his buggy. "Give me ten minutes," Uncle Matthew said, smirking to Jeremiah as if they shared an inside joke.

"In the meantime, Holly, let's have Kaffi and Rachel's apple crisp," Jeremiah said. As we approached the back stoop, the aromas of roasting apples, warm cinnamon, and baking dough wafted our way. Even Wolfie was too distracted by the scrumptious scents to snarl at me. He tried to follow us into the house, but my grandpa kneed him out of the way, thankfully. I still didn't trust that mongrel.

"Look who I have here," Jeremiah said as he escorted me into the kitchen.

Rachel's lips blossomed into a smile. "*Kumm rei*—come in, Holly," she said. "I'm ever so glad ta see you." Her hands in hot mitts, she hugged me, then hurried to the stove, removed the apple crisp, and set it on a cooling rack. "Are ya staying for dinner?" she asked. Strands of her butterscotch-colored hair peeked out from beneath her traditional heart-shaped prayer cap.

"Thanks, but I only have time for coffee." I scanned the large kitchen: grander than Mommy Anna's, with a bigger refrigerator, a double sink, and a sizeable counter. In the center of the room stood a rectangular table covered with green-and-white checkered oilcloth, ten chairs hemming its perimeter.

Rachel wore an amethyst-colored dress and dark apron. Seeing the fabric's smooth texture gave me a desire to ask her to lend me one. She'd be generous enough to do it. I appreciated her life on this fabulous farm with a loving husband and several children. Except Rachel must endure her mother-in-law's presence, I reminded myself.

My Grandma Beatrice swooped into the kitchen. "I see Wolfie caught a prowler lurking about." Her arms folded across her flat chest. Even Mommy Anna had called Beatrice a *schtinker*, which couldn't be a compliment.

I tried to view my sudden arrival through her wire-rimmed Coke-bottle glasses. "Sorry to show up again without an invitation," I said.

"Holly may stop by anytime," Grandpa Jeremiah said.

"You're always welcome, Holly." Rachel took off the mitts, set them beside the stove.

"At least she isn't trying to dress Amish," Beatrice said. As she inspected me, her beady pupils seemed to shrink to dots.

"Please, have a seat," Rachel said, and placed cups on the table. She brought a pitcher of milk from the modern-looking refrigerator. The stove appeared contemporary too; I figured all their appliances were generated by gas.

"What was that ruckus outside?" Grandma Beatrice's cement-gray hair was parted with severity, and her prayer cap strings were knotted under her pointed chin. "I heard a horse galloping by, and then another, like a bandit."

Jeremiah tugged on his beard. "I lent Armin Midnight to catch up with Nathaniel's horse."

"You let Armin use my favorite *Gaul*?"

"I thought you favored Ruby," Rachel said, in a good-natured manner.

"I wouldn't lend Armin any horse," Beatrice said. "He might sell it. Bartering is in his blood, and he's not to be trusted." She glared at Jeremiah, who narrowed his eyes at her.

"Armin was giving me a much-appreciated buggy ride," I said, hoping to defuse the conversation.

"Your Mudder let you go out with Armin?" Beatrice scowled. "He's a vagabond, a loose wheel who'll roll away any old time he pleases. He should be looking after Nathaniel's farm, not pussyfooting around the county when his Bruder is out of town."

So they all knew Nathaniel was searching for his wife—and no doubt that my mother hoped to marry him. I clamped my lips together; I was not going to speak about Nathaniel and Mom in front of Beatrice. I wondered whether Beatrice had really forgiven Mom for stealing my father away.

I swigged down my coffee. "I really should be leaving," I said.

"Aw, I wish you'd stay longer," Rachel said. "She turns in early," she whispered in my ear. "Come back after supper some evening."

The floor looked squeaky clean, but Beatrice picked up a broom and commenced to sweep around the stove as if she'd like to whisk me out the back door.

"Thanks for having me," I said to her, but she kept her gaze fastened to the linoleum flooring. If she'd made the slightest move, I might have kissed her cheek, but she quickened her sweeping, avoiding me.

Minutes later, Grandpa Jeremiah helped me into their gray carriage. He slapped the reins, and their reddish-chestnut mare pulled us at a leisurely trot.

"Is this buggy new?" I asked.

"No, but recently polished. And we keep it under cover at night." His eyes twinkled. "You come over more and I'll teach you everything you need to know about driving a carriage. You want to try now? This mare is a pussycat. She'll obey you."

"I suppose." Anxiously, I scooted over to him and took the reins, adjusting my fingertips to the feel of them. I enjoyed a pleasant sensation traveling up my arms. After all the years of make-believe in the old buggy on the Amish Shoppe's front porch, I was driving a real one!

"Yah, that's the way," he said.

All around me the world moved at half speed, but doubts about Zach, my fuzzy-thinking Mommy Anna, Nathaniel, and Galahad's whereabouts still somersaulted like acrobats at a circus in the back of my brain. No wonder I felt *verhoodled*, as Mommy Anna would say.

"Your father would be proud of you," he said, garnering my attention.

"Then you do believe I'm your granddaughter?" I kept my vision fixed to the road for fear the horse would wander into oncoming traffic.

"Absolutely, I do." He reached over and gave one rein a gentle tug, and the horse turned onto another road. "My Beatrice had such a difficult time getting pregnant, only the Lord took our Samuel from us. It must have been God's will, but she turned bitter." The corners of his mouth tipped up. "As you know, we were blessed with two other children. And now we have you, *Grossdochder*. Beatrice will come around, just wait. You should see her with her other grandchildren. Sweet as chocolate-covered cherries."

He had more faith in Beatrice than I did. I bet if I ever had children, she'd spurn them. Unless they were Amish.

"I don't blame her for harboring some resentment toward my mom," I said.

"We must forgive others if we expect God to forgive us." He adjusted the reins, covering my hands with his for a moment. "Says so in the Bible."

I realized I didn't need to grip the reins as tightly as I was, and allowed my fingers to relax—a little. How cool was this? I was driving my grandfather's horse and buggy!

"Do you mind if I ask about my dad?" I said. I wanted to riddle him with questions, but didn't want to seem pushy.

"We don't talk about him much. But I wouldn't mind a few questions."

"This might sound weird, but do you think he had a crush on Beth?"

"Ya mean Beth Fleming? I doubt it, although I do recall her coming by every so often. But I should tell you, it isn't our way for young people to speak about such matters. Sometimes parents are the last to know."

"But you knew about my mother."

"We suspected. And then the two of them hightailed it to New Holland one night and moved into an Englischer's basement. People reported seeing your mother working at a tourist-type restaurant up there. Then they left for California without a word." He seemed to be having difficulty breathing and his hand moved to his chest.

"Are you okay?" I pulled on the reins, and the mare came to a halt.

"Yah." He sniffed, wiped his nose with a handkerchief. "Truth is, for many years I was too hard on Samuel. We had just one son and such a large farm. I misused him, like he was one of my hired farmhands. If I had to do it all over again, I'd have treated him with kindness and patience."

"But you're so nice."

"I'm as flawed as any man, but I learned from my mistakes."

"You seem perfect to me. I've always wanted a grandfather."

"You should call me *Doddy*, Holly."

"Okay, *Doddy* Jeremiah."

A car honked, and my grandpa steered the mare off to the side of the road to let the automobile pass us. He and I sat in silence for a moment as I repeated his words to myself. Mom had told me Dad's parents were too strict with him, meaning some of what she'd told me was true. Her assessment of Beatrice seemed to be right on. Still, my mother had no right to deprive me of Mommy Anna. And the gentleman sitting next to me was a gem.

I was determined to find out what happened to Jeremiah's letters to my mother, if they existed. Beth had once mentioned Jeremiah's writing to Samuel, but she would have been a teen at the time and that memory forty years old. Maybe Jeremiah had said he intended to write but hadn't actually followed through. And maybe she was lying to make my mother look bad.

Grandpa Jeremiah took the reins from me. "Any other questions?" he asked. "We're almost there."

"Yes, one more." For now, anyway. "Are you absolutely sure you wrote my mother letters?"

"Yah, I penned them myself for ten years or so. I've lost track."

"And you gave them to your wife?"

He nodded, his beard moving down, then up. "She put them in an envelope and took them to Anna's house. I asked Beatrice to get

Esther's address, but Beatrice said she didn't want it. And she told me visiting Anna was always pleasant."

I imagined a mathematical problem gone awry: two plus one did not equal four. Someone was fibbing.

CHAPTER TWENTY-SIX

Since Esther had Holly's cell phone at her disposal and the endocrinologist's telephone number in the kitchen, she saw no reason to wait until Holly got home to call to reconfirm her mother's appointment for tomorrow. Mamm was in the Daadi Haus; Esther would lower her volume so her mamm wouldn't hear her speaking.

Moving into the kitchen, Esther tapped in the numbers. "Dr. Brewster is so pleased your mother's coming in," the woman said, with a tinge of urgency. "We keep time slots open for emergencies. Not that this is an emergency—but we could even fit her in this afternoon."

"No, I want to give my mother another day to recuperate from a fall." And then Esther would need to find a strategy to talk Mamm into going, even if it meant offering to stop for dinner and pie at Bird-in-Hand Family Restaurant on the way home.

"Tomorrow morning is fine, thank you," Esther told the receptionist, and took the address in the outskirts of the city of Lancaster. The distance to the office was too far for a horse and buggy, not that she'd ask Armin for assistance. He was maintaining two farms until Nathaniel's return—or at least Armin was supposed to be. He seemed lackadaisical, the kind of fellow who might get distracted and forget. After all, where was he now?

The words *Judge not lest ye be judged* came to mind. She reprehended herself for being critical, when in fact Armin was a likeable fellow and hadn't perpetrated half her sins. And he was her Nathaniel's brother. She allowed her imagination to spiral into the future and considered an unlikely occurrence: Holly's falling in love with Armin and becoming baptized. Holly had adored dressing Amish, and now that Esther thought about it, her daughter hadn't rushed out to buy or rent a car, charged her laptop computer, or lamented that she'd lost her job at a Seattle stock brokerage firm. Esther imagined Holly and Armin having children, providing Esther with grandchildren right next door! What could be better?

Esther shook her head. She was being ridiculous and wasting precious time when she should be looking after Mamm. Like it or not, her mamm was going to the doctor's office tomorrow. Esther would need to call a driving service to make arrangements and must find the number. She recalled seeing a business card in a kitchen drawer among a stew of papers, pencils, rubber bands, and a couple pairs of Mamm's glasses. Mamm used to be so organized when Esther was a child, but not anymore. When Esther last opened the drawer she'd unearthed a paring knife and a shriveled-up radish.

She noticed movement out of her peripheral sight and glanced out the window to see Zach's pickup coming to a stop at the side of the house. A minute later she heard feet plodding through the utility room, then knuckles rapping on the kitchen door. She was tempted to pretend she didn't hear him. He'd come to see Holly, after all, not her.

He knocked again, and Esther finally opened the door. "Hello, Zach. Holly isn't here."

His features sagged; his crestfallen demeanor reminded her of Nathaniel when he'd left earlier—like a deflated basketball.

"She should be home any minute," Esther said. "I thought she'd be back by now."

"I'll come in and wait, if you don't mind." Zach had no doubt visited Esther's mamm his whole life, sitting in this very kitchen with his mother, Beth; it made sense he'd feel at home. Still, Esther wished he'd skedaddle until Holly returned. No matter what Esther said to him, her words could be taken wrong. Holly would not appreciate her meddling in their relationship crisis. And with Mamm's incoherent thinking and memory, there was no way of knowing how she'd greet him.

But he looked so forlorn, she said, "Where are my manners? Please have coffee and a cookie." She poured him a cup, brought cream from the refrigerator, and set the cream and a plate of snickerdoodles on the table, next to the sugar bowl. "There ya go."

"Thanks." His voice sounded flat.

The kitchen smelled of her warming casserole, a sign she was preparing the noon meal. But she dare not invite him to stay without consulting Holly.

His weight on one foot, Zach leaned against the counter. "I assume Holly told you about Victoria and her son."

Esther licked her lower lip to keep from wading into the subject; Holly would see it as her butting in where she didn't belong.

"I was blindsided yesterday," he said, and sipped his coffee black. "My former girlfriend Victoria had the audacity to show up with her little boy at my mother's house. Victoria claims the child is ours, not her husband's, who has apparently run out on her."

Esther wanted to say, "How appalling," but pressed her lips together.

"He's a cute little tyke, but he's not mine." He set the cup on the counter. "Your mother, Anna, never liked Victoria when we dated, but my mother was crazy about her and encouraged me to marry her at every turn."

"Zach, you don't owe me an explanation. I've made plenty of mistakes." Holly and Beth must have filled him in. And he'd heard the bishop on the nonpreaching Sunday last month.

"As Holly's mother, you have a right to know." He raised his chin, but it lowered itself, as if his neck had lost all strength. "Years ago, I asked Victoria to marry me twice and she kept hedging. Then without a word, she eloped with a guy I considered a close friend. Turns out, she'd been seeing him on the sly for months. She made me feel and look like a chump."

"I can understand you'd be disillusioned. " Esther paused, knowing Holly wouldn't appreciate her interference. "Sometimes those horrid situations turn out to be a blessing in disguise." She summarized Genesis 50:20 in her own words. "What was intended to harm you, God intended for good."

"Yes, that's what I came to realize. I'd been all set to marry a two-timing cheater. After she moved to Philly and I got over the shock and bruised feelings, I realized it was a blessing in disguise." His face was chalky, his motions listless. "But now she's back, claiming I fathered her son. He's not mine. Although my mother wants a grandson so much she won't listen to reason."

"Shouldn't you be telling this to Holly and not me?" Esther wished her daughter would get home and put an end to this awkward situation. What was taking her so long?

"I tried to explain," he said, "but I don't think she believed me. And now she's out with Armin? Am I getting the shaft again?"

"It's best I don't say a thing." Even though he was Beth's son, Esther's heart went out to Zach. If he longed for Holly half as much as she ached for Nathaniel, he was miserable.

She brought out the cell phone and Zach's eyes widened. "Zach, Holly left me this. I wouldn't ordinarily use it, but I need to set up a ride to take Mamm to the doctor's tomorrow morning."

"I'd be happy to drive you. I own a Ford sedan, so we'll all fit in. Tell me when to be here."

"But you're so busy." He had as much chaos in his life as Esther did. She wondered if he'd heard about Nathaniel's missing wife. No doubt one of the local farmers had mentioned it, if not Nathaniel himself.

"I'll make the time," he said.

Her casserole smelled delectable, meaning it was most likely done. There was no way around it; she'd have to crack the oven door and take a peek so she didn't overcook it. Sure enough, the macaroni noodles on top were browned to perfection. She breathed in the aroma of melted cheese, sautéed onion, green bell peppers, and ground beef. How impolite to bring it out and not invite Zach to join her and Mamm. But what if Holly had invited Armin to dine with them?

Esther slipped her hands into mitts, lifted the casserole, and placed it on a cooling rack on the counter. Zach's gaze locked onto it, his nose raising to inhale its succulence.

"I'd better go so you can eat," he said, not moving.

Esther put her schnitz pie in the oven and turned the oven's temperature from 350 to 450. She set the timer for fifteen minutes. "I might bring Mamm her meal on a tray. I don't want any more accidents before tomorrow." She mulled over his offer to drive them. "Zach, I thank you for your kindness. I'll take you up on your offer if you can be here at nine thirty." She knew she was being doubly rude, but added, "I'm assuming you won't bring Beth with you."

"Absolutely not. I'm steering clear of my mother. I don't know what's gotten into her since I announced my intentions to marry Holly. Right away, she battered me with reasons why Holly and I shouldn't act hastily."

"I don't want to cause a riff between you and your mother," Esther said.

"Too late to prevent that." He glanced at the casserole, then stood and took a step toward the door. "I'll see you tomorrow morning."

"Thank you." Esther understood why Holly found Zach so attractive, beyond his handsome appearance. Be he Beth's son or not, the man was hard to fault, even if he'd fathered a son. Why, Esther would have a grandson to coddle!

She glanced out the window and saw a chestnut mare and a gray covered carriage enter the barnyard. A white bearded Amishman emerged. "Jeremiah Fisher? What in the world is he doing here?"

Zach moved to Esther's side. A moment later, Holly glided out of the buggy as if she'd ridden in them her whole life. Esther chuckled to herself; her daughter had been practicing out front of the Amish Shoppe.

"Would you please wait in case Mamm wakes up and trundles out here looking for me?" she asked Zach. And in case Holly didn't wish to speak to him in front of Jeremiah. Esther didn't want Jeremiah witnessing a lovers' quarrel, fodder for Beatrice's gossip.

"Sure," he said, staring out the window.

Esther shoved her feet into shoes, and strode through the utility room. Her mind struggled to put together a logical reason Holly would be with Jeremiah, but could make no sense of the situation.

CHAPTER
TWENTY-SEVEN

I saw Zach's pickup parked outside the barnyard! My heart blipped into high gear the moment my grandfather's buggy passed by it. But Zach was probably in the barn checking on Cookie, I reminded myself. My mother was the only individual tentatively exiting the house and descending the back steps.

"Hello, Jeremiah," Mom said as she came over to us.

Jeremiah tied the mare to a post, then turned to her. "*Gude Mariye*, Esther."

"Where's Nathaniel's buggy?" Mom laced her fingers. "And Armin?"

"Armin's horse ran off," Jeremiah said. "Nathaniel's buggy is at our place."

"Ach, ya don't mean it."

"Yup, Galahad flew the coop," I said, and let out a huff. "Rascal, too."

"Armin's dog's name is Rascal?" Grandpa Jeremiah gave his head a slight shake. "You can tell a lot about a dog by its name."

"Like Wolfie?" Mom said.

"I can't argue with you there." Jeremiah tipped back his hat. "Wolfie isn't the friendliest *Hund*, but you won't find our goats getting attacked at night. Now Armin's dog—"

"Do ya think Rascal is at fault?" my mother said.

I moved closer to her. "Mom, did you see Galahad trot by?"

"No. But I wasn't keeping an eye open for him." She clasped her hands under her chin. "I'm glad I didn't know about it when I spoke to Nathaniel earlier."

"He called?" I said.

"Larry did—" Mom covered her mouth with her fingertips for a moment, then spoke to Jeremiah. "It's a long story, but Larry is Holly's Englisch friend from Seattle who is kindly driving Nathaniel somewhere."

"I heard all about Nathaniel's predicament," Jeremiah said. "Such a jumbled mess. Good to know God's in control."

"Yah, God is in control." Mom's brows furrowed. "But we can pray, can't we?"

"Yah, sure, that his will be done."

I felt sorry for Mom—she reminded me of myself—but I thought we should wait until we were alone to discuss Nathaniel and her iffy future with him.

"Is that Zach's pickup?" I knew it was, but I tried to act blasé by directing my gaze to Jeremiah's mare.

"Yes, he's in the house. I didn't know if I should invite him to stay for dinner."

A kaleidoscope of emotions and questions bombarded me, including bewilderment, foreboding, and dejection. But my desire to see him overpowered my negative thoughts. "Please do," I said, "and invite Jeremiah, too."

"We've got plenty of food," Mom said, "but I didn't know if Armin and Zach could sit peacefully at the same table together."

"If Armin shows up, I'll make sure the young men are at their best behavior," Jeremiah said, the corners of his mouth lifting.

Mom slipped her hand under my arm. "I need to tell you, I accepted Zach's offer to drive Mamm to her doctor's appointment tomorrow morning. We need a ride, and I was about to hire a driver. But they can be costly."

I recalled our measly financial state. "Okay, I suppose."

"You could sit in the backseat with your grandma," she said, as if that would solve our problems. "He seemed mighty downhearted in the kitchen just now."

"Sometimes a person can seem to be one thing—" I didn't want to rehash the past in front of my grandfather.

"I could drive you in the buggy." Jeremiah tilted his head toward his carriage. "Glad ta do it. The ride would take longer, but I'm an early riser, and my grandsons handle the milking."

"That's kind of you." Mom sounded hesitant, her eyes wary. "But it's so far for your horse, not to mention dangerous with all the traffic."

"Matthew could do the driving if it would ease your anxieties," Jeremiah said. "I know I've gotten on in years."

"Thank you, but we'd better stick to our plan," Mom said. "Zach has a sedan and told me he has the time."

"Humph, what if his office calls?" I glanced up at the window and saw Zach watching us. "What's he doing in there?"

"I asked him to stay in the kitchen in case Mamm wakes up." My mother turned to Jeremiah. "She's been having—uh, problems with her balance."

I guessed she didn't want the details of Mommy Anna's forgetfulness brought home to Beatrice, who might have a field day yacking
about my grandma at the next work frolic. Which I might just attend
with or without Mom.

"Well?" I said, not wanting to be the first to enter the house. "Are
we inviting Jeremiah to dine with us?"

"You're most welcome to stay, but won't Beatrice worry about
you?" Mom asked him.

"*Mei Fraa* can be persnickety, but Matthew and Rachel will feed
and reassure her." He patted his tummy. "Yah, I accept your invitation."

"Great." My guess was Beatrice would not approve.

Mom led the way up the steps as Zach opened the door.

"Holly—"

My first impulse was to fling myself into his arms, but I needed
to be cautious. "Hi, Zach."

Ushering us through the utility room and into the kitchen, Mom
asked him, "Would you like to join us?"

"Yes, if Holly doesn't mind."

"Sure, stay." I glanced at the table; it needed to be set. "Mom says
we have more than enough."

Jeremiah removed his hat and shook hands with Zach. "Gut
seeing you."

Zach hung the hat on a peg, then helped my grandpa remove
his jacket. Zach hung up the garment, then turned to me. In spite
of my bruised ego, I wanted to sink into his embrace, to abandon all
rationality. But I steadied myself.

Mom breezed over to the oven and turned down the temperature, then reset the timer. The room smelled scrumptious, of baking

apples—what I figured she had in the oven—and of the casserole she'd made for me many times. But my stomach felt like it had shrunk to the size of a dime.

Mommy Anna toddled into the room no longer wearing her ace bandage. "What's happening?" She yawned; one side of her face was creased, as if she'd just awakened. Her cap had slid back and its knot come undone. I could see Zach and Jeremiah were assessing her bandaged and discolored forehead.

"Looks like we're having a party," Mommy Anna said. "Welcome, Jeremiah! It's fine-gut to see you."

"*Ich bedank mich*," Jeremiah said. The two sat at the table— Jeremiah at the head—and fell into Pennsylvania Dutch and laughter. I could make out bits and pieces having to do with Armin's horse running off. Which I didn't find funny, because Galahad or Rascal could get hit by a car or stolen.

Then, as if Jeremiah had seen a ghost, his face blanched as white as his beard. He turned to my mother. "What's Anna talking about? Did our Samuel send you a doll and a letter recently? How can that be?"

I could recognize my mother's every facial expression—I knew her so well. Her mind was grappling for the right words to explain the unexplainable. "In part Mamm's right, but she's got her facts a little mixed up," she said.

"I do not! Don't make me sound *narrisch*—crazy!" Mommy Anna pointed at her forehead. "How else did I get these stitches? You and I were both wanting to hold the silk and doll when I fell and hit my head."

Telling me that my mother was wrestling the doll away from my ailing grandma! Mom was taking out her frustrations about Nathaniel on a defenseless old woman. I abhorred violence. I knew the Amish were nonresistant, meaning they were taught to turn the other cheek and to never strike back. How could Mom possibly hope to join the Amish church while acting aggressively?

"Let me get this straight," Zach said, breaking into my thoughts. "Holly's father sent you a doll?"

"No, a former soldier from Vietnam sent it." My voice quivered.

"And a letter," Mom said, pulling out a chair for Zach. "A man claiming to be a wartime friend of Samuel's. But we have no proof he has the right Samuel Fisher, or if he's even telling the truth."

"I could get the man's telephone number," Zach said, sitting. "I'll call my clinic and have my receptionist look it up."

"I wrote him a letter today." Mom opened the cupboard and extracted dishes.

"A letter will take days," Zach said.

I gathered cutlery from the drawers and set the table. "I'm sure the doll was meant for me."

"It's quite fancy," Mommy Anna's eyebrows met in the center, pulling on her bandage. "You won't believe it when you see it."

"Hold on, everyone, you're talking about my son." Jeremiah's voice sounded indignant. He placed his elbows on the table, leaned forward. "I don't believe our Samuel would have bought a fancy doll. Unless Esther asked him to."

Mom's hand grasped a chairback. "No, I didn't. I was as shocked as everyone."

"Why didn't you inform us?" Jeremiah asked.

"It arrived yesterday, and I wanted to get the facts straight." Mom's cheeks looked sunken. "We still don't know if it's a hoax or a case of mistaken identity."

"I do. My dad bought the doll for me. Somehow he knew Mom was carrying a girl. Don't you believe in divine providence?" I asked everyone in the room.

"Where is this doll and letter?" Jeremiah said, his mouth severe.

"Mom has the letter, but I'll go get the doll."

"Are ya sure you wouldn't rather have dinner before my casserole gets cold?" my mother said. "Let's thank the Lord and have our meal."

Zach rose and pulled out a chair for me. He had the most beautiful eyes, like deep pools of water. I couldn't shake my infatuation; he'd cast a spell over me. But I kept my face from exposing my feelings.

"How can I eat now?" Jeremiah's posture became rigid, his fists on the table. "Was my Beatrice right about you, Esther? All along she said you can't be trusted."

"It only just arrived." Mom sat next to Mommy Anna, across from Zach and me. "I never asked my Samuel to send a doll so I think it's a mistake."

"I'll get it if you like." I pushed my chair away from the table.

"Gut idea," Mommy Anna said.

My doll, I told myself as I climbed the stairs to the bedroom. I was amazed to see the blue Tiffany's box sitting next to the doll. What a beautiful color, enhanced with white satin ribbon. Larry had apparently left the box for me, or maybe he was worried about losing it on the trip to Ohio. I hoped that was the case.

Lifting the doll, I felt a wave of indecision encapsulate me. What if Jeremiah tried to take it home with him to show Beatrice? I wouldn't let him.

"Did my dad buy you?" I asked the doll; she stared back at me
with vacant eyes. Jeremiah and Beatrice would dislike it as much as
Mommy Anna did.

I recalled Mommy Anna's declaration about Dad's perhaps buying the doll for someone else's daughter, and the fabric for a woman
he'd met overseas. I'd also heard that in adverse circumstances men
were capable of making unconscionable decisions, contrary to their
fundamental beliefs. But I couldn't accept that my father would do
such a thing, no matter the situation.

I heard a block of silence resonating from the kitchen as I
descended the stairs. I played several scenarios in my head, none of
them good.

CHAPTER TWENTY-EIGHT

With her daughter lollygagging upstairs, Esther dipped the serving spoon into the casserole.

"What's keeping Holly?" Mamm buttered a slice of bread. "We'd better go ahead without her."

Esther noticed Mamm taking a bite. Never had Esther seen her mamm eat before praying.

"Jeremiah, would you lead us in prayer?" Esther hoped he hadn't noticed.

"Honored to." He lowered his head for the silent prayer, followed by an amen, then raised his head. "Kind of you to have me over, Anna and Esther."

"Our pleasure," Mamm said. "'Tis too quiet since my sons moved away. One day, when I'm feeling better, I'll visit them in Montana and see my grandchildren."

"I didn't realize you'd been ill."

"I feel fine today, just a little achy. But don't all old people have that complaint?" Mamm favored her good hand but was using both of them.

"Mamm's been avoiding her doctor," Esther said, then wished she hadn't. Not that he wouldn't notice Mamm's erratic behavior on his own soon enough. She was eating her buttered bread upside down!

"Maybe your physician will have your answers tomorrow morning," Zach said.

"Ach, tomorrow?" Mamm grimaced at Esther. "You made another appointment?"

"We went over all this. Your lab results have been in for weeks." Esther placed the casserole in front of Jeremiah, and gave him an ample portion. Next she moved to serve her mother. "They had an opening this afternoon, but I thought you'd prefer to wait until tomorrow."

"I'd prefer to wait until never. I was just at the doctor's." She pointed to her forehead.

"Yah, they did a good job stitching you up."

"You fell?" Jeremiah said.

"Lost my balance, nothing serious." Mamm smoothed grape jelly on the other side of her bread.

Holly entered the room empty-handed. All eyes pivoted to watch her perch next to Zach, who immediately stood to help her into her chair. "That looks delish, Mom," Holly said, and scooped a small amount onto her plate.

Jeremiah nodded. "Yah, 'tis *abbeditlich*—delicious. But where's that wretched doll?"

"Upstairs in my bedroom," Holly said. "Why ruin everyone's meal speculating over it when we don't even know if the sender has the right Mrs. Samuel Fisher?"

"I'd like to have a look at it, anyways," Jeremiah said.

"Okay, after dessert." Holly filled her mouth, and Esther guessed she didn't want to continue the conversation. Esther was relieved the doll wasn't standing on the counter or table. Maybe Jeremiah would become tired and forget about it. Or Esther could distract him with the letter from Chap McLaughlin.

As Esther swallowed a mouthful of carrot-raisin salad, she noticed Zach glancing fondly at Holly. He was leaning her direction, but she seemed to be tilting away from him. He spoke in her ear and she whispered in his, too quietly for Esther to hear.

"I could drive you there," he said, using full volume.

Holly shook her head, but the corners of her mouth lifted. "I need the exercise after all this food."

"May I walk with you?" Zach looked like a ravenous puppy waiting for a biscuit.

"Okay." She gave a one-shoulder shrug, as if she couldn't care less, but Zach seemed elated.

"You going to see if Armin got Nathaniel's horse back?" Mamm asked. If nothing else, her hearing was still in good shape.

"Yes, I thought I would." Holly nibbled on the casserole.

"Why he took that feisty Galahad out in the first place is beyond me," Jeremiah said, and patted around his mouth with a napkin. Then a realization seemed to bloom in his eyes. "Armin must have been showing off for Holly."

"Yah," Mamm said. "I bet he's hoping—"

"Mommy Anna!" Holly half stood and bulged her eyes in Mamm's direction. "Please, let's not continue this line of conversation."

Esther agreed. "It seems there's too much speculation going around. It's akin to gossip."

"Let's not forget to respect your elders," Mamm said.

"All the more reason to emulate the teachings of the Good Book," Esther said, "and set a good example for the young folks."

For several minutes, everyone concentrated on eating, passing bowls around and helping themselves. Esther wondered if their thoughts were on their meal. Unlikely. Each was orbiting his or her separate universe. When they'd polished off their meals, the timer dinged. "May I tempt you to a slice of schnitz pie or a snickerdoodle?" Mom said, and got up to remove her pie of mashed apples with brown sugar from the oven.

"Smells yummy, but I couldn't eat another bite," Holly said, and everyone else echoed her statement. Even Jeremiah. Ach, she missed Nathaniel, who would have accepted.

Esther realized she should return Holly's phone to her, or maybe she'd better hang on to it. Especially if Holly were going over to Armin's to check on the lost horse. Esther would miss her chance to speak to Nathaniel. Good or bad news, she ached to hear the sound of his voice.

She supposed the best news to most in the community, even Nathaniel, would be the pronouncement his wife was alive. Wishing someone dead must surely be immoral. Something else to admit before the bishop and beg for God's mercy. She envisioned Nathaniel bringing his wife home with him, then the two arriving at church Sunday, his sitting with the men and her with the women. Worshipping in the same room would be intolerable.

Holly cleared the table in record speed. She set the plates in the sink and filled it with sudsy water. "I promise to wash these when I get home," she said. "Don't anyone do my job for me. Promise?" She tilted her head. "You coming, Zach?"

"Thanks for the delicious meal," he said, standing, "and the good company." He pushed his chair against the table. "I'll be back at nine thirty tomorrow morning."

A look of confusion crossed Mamm's face, as if she'd forgotten about her doctor's appointment. Good.

But would Jeremiah forget about the doll?

CHAPTER TWENTY-NINE

"Pretty slick maneuver," Zach said to me the moment the two of us were outside in the cool fresh air.

"What?"

"The way you managed your departure without showing your grandfather the doll. Although I must say my curiosity's piqued. And the letter has me intrigued."

"When Mom opened the carton yesterday she and I were stunned, to put it mildly." I felt a knot growing in my throat. "And there were several yards of gorgeous silk. A vivid fuchsia no Amish woman would wear. Of course, Mom wasn't living a plain life back when Dad was in Vietnam. Still, none of it feels right."

We crossed the barnyard and headed to the road. No way would I take the shortcut to Nathaniel's without Armin, although Zach was probably as capable at handling farm animals.

"I hope you don't intend to use that stunt when we're married," Zach said, and took my hand, his fingers entwining mine. A tingling rush like sparkling cider seemed to bubble up my arm, filling my chest with warmth.

"You'd want to marry a woman your mother's snubbing?" I said, and felt a sinking in my chest. I couldn't erase Victoria's and Justin's faces from my memory either.

"Mom's had her chance to select a spouse," he said. "Now it's my turn."

"But you picked Victoria."

"Thank the good Lord she jilted me." In the past, he'd told me a woman turned him down twice and then ran off with his friend. At least my former cheating fiancé had chosen to marry a stranger. To me, anyway. Who knows how long the two had carried on their clandestine affair?

"I'm sorry you were hurt," I said.

"By our age, hasn't everyone?" His hand covered mine like a supple glove.

"You're probably right." I watched two vultures glide in wide arcs above Nathaniel's harvested field. "I've been burned, and I still don't trust my instincts when it comes to men."

Almost to the road, he paused and said, "Want to tell me about it?"

"Zach, one of our problems is we hardly know each other."

"I want to know you better." He lowered his face, then his lips brushed mine. I felt passion igniting as his arms encircled me.

I heard hooves clopping. "Holly!" Armin called.

"Ignore him and he'll go away," Zach said in my ear.

I stepped back from Zach to see Armin atop the black gelding Jeremiah had lent him, headed in our direction. The animal was not as energetic as it had been a few hours ago. I wondered how many miles they'd traveled.

Armin reined in the horse several yards from us. He'd shed his hat and was wearing cowboy boots, of all things; I guessed he kept them hidden from Nathaniel, because they'd be considered fancy.

"Can't you see we're busy?" Zach said, sounding huffy. "What are you doing with Midnight? Trying to ride the poor animal to death?"

"Nee, I stopped at Nathaniel's and gave him water and feed. He's still got plenty of fire in him."

"You're nuts. He's obviously fatigued." Zach pointed to a trickle of blood on the lower half of the horse's rear leg. "Look, he's bleeding."

"Just a nick from a bramble. I thought I'd cleaned it off."

"Jeremiah's at Anna's. You'd better not let him see his horse until you do a better job than that. I could clip around the area, cleanse it with Betadine solution, and apply antibacterial ointment."

"Listen, Dr. Fleming, I know ten times more about horses than you do, no matter how long you went to school. That little cut is going to dry right up on its own."

"I take it you've had no sign of Galahad or Rascal," I said, trying to distract the men and deflate their tempers.

"Not yet." Armin ran his fingers through the horse's damp mane. "I was hoping he and Rascal would have returned to Nathaniel's by now. Lizzie's over there, waiting and watching."

"She'd be able to handle Galahad?" I asked.

"Sure, Lizzie can coax Galahad with a couple sugar cubes," Armin said.

Zach folded his arms across his chest. "How is it Galahad got loose in the first place?"

"He broke a tether over at Jeremiah's," Armin said. "I'm thinking the Fishers' dog scared him."

"Or perhaps you didn't tie him up correctly?" Zach said.

"You've got your nerve. I know how to tie a horse better than you do." In an instant, Armin hopped out of the saddle and stood facing Zach. "Look at your hands, Doc, like ya just had a professional manicure. You've never done a lick of real work your whole life."

The horse, its reins falling to the ground, started nibbling grasses and dandelions growing at the side of the lane.

"I think your big brother would disagree," Zach said, sounding as if he were suppressing a mouthful of barbs. "And last week I split a half cord of wood for my parents."

"Stop it, you two." I stood between them. "While you're arguing, Galahad is still on the loose."

I could tell by their expressions and the rigid set of their jaws; they had plenty more to say to each other. "Aren't Amish and Mennonites nonresistant?" I said as a last effort to tame their flaring tempers.

"He started it," Armin said.

"Okay," I said, "since you two seem to know so much about horses, where would Galahad head?"

"And don't forget dogs," Zach said. "The Millers nearly lost a goat to a predator. It's barely hanging on."

"That has nothing to do with my Rascal." Armin plucked off a tall reed of grass and chewed on its end.

"Can you prove that?" Zach narrowed his eyes at Armin. "Tom Miller told me they saw a dog running along the road earlier today."

"It could have been Rascal trying to catch up with me."

"Well, Tom thinks it's the same dog he's seen hanging around his farm."

"Maybe he has a female dog in heat. Rascal is all male."

"He wouldn't attack goats, would he?" I tried not to envision the grisly scene.

"Nee. Don't ya see? Zach's putting these ideas in your head so you'll steer clear of me. He's afraid you'll decide you prefer the Amish life to his."

"Holly would never become Amish," Zach said.

"That's not what I hear." Armin tossed the grass away. "Nathaniel told me she wore his daughter's dress and apron, and even figured out how to secure the pins. And he said she relies on her computer less and less."

"We don't have Internet set up at my grandma's," I said. But Armin was speaking the truth. And I'd neglected to put on makeup today. Not to mention, I'd all but given up driving.

"She loves riding in the buggy," Armin said. "I can tell that. 'Tis plain as the pout on your face, but you're too *dickkeppich*— thick-headed—to see."

"How do you know so much about my future wife?"

"You ain't married yet, Zach. And I hear tell you come to the table with a child you've neglected to mention."

"Because I only found out yesterday—"

Armin shrugged, palms up. "Either way, I still think Holly would be happier spending the rest of her life with me."

"Huh?" Was I being pursued by two men at once? No, make that three. My mind scrolled back to high school; I'd been a wallflower at dances, waiting and hoping a cute guy would notice me. Even during college, I'd tried to emulate the popular young women but could never pull off giggling at every mundane statement a date said. And now three eligible bachelors claimed they wanted to marry me. Or were they stringing me along or in some masculine Men-are-from-Mars competition?

"She would not be happy living Amish." Zach's statement rubbed me the wrong way. "Holly, tell him to get back to finding Galahad and to stop hitting on you."

"I've never appreciated people ordering me around." My hand moved to my hip. "I can think of dozens of characteristics about the Amish I find appealing. Like Amish children playing board games with their siblings instead of vegetating in front of the TV set or being mesmerized by video games, and having fathers who stick around home when they can." Zach could never pull off that feat.

Armin set his hat at a jaunty slant. "We farmers stay on the farm most of the day helping raise and working alongside the children. Amishmen make the best husbands in the world. Not boasting, just telling the truth."

"Could you live without electricity, Holly?" Zach's strident voice reminded me of a mathematics professor I didn't like in college. "No computers or cell phone? No air conditioners on sweltering days or central heating in winter when the thermometer plunges below zero?"

"Modern conveniences are not what warms a girl's heart," I said.

"How about the convenience of sleeping in past four thirty?"

"I wouldn't make Holly wake up early when I milk the cows," Armin said. "I could brew my own pot of coffee, as I have for many a year."

"What about children?" Zach asked, which seemed too personal a subject to be bandied about.

"All mothers get up when the children rise, don't they—Amish or Englisch?" Armin bent and took hold of Midnight's reins.

I wondered once more why my mother and father had left Lancaster County. I presumed my dad would have returned home, if he'd lived. Yet Mom chose to abandon her family and lifestyle.

I ruminated on Mom's *Rumspringa*; she'd declared it was the worst mistake of her life.

Well, I was too old for running around. I wanted to settle down, and soon.

CHAPTER THIRTY

Holly's cell phone vibrated in Esther's pants pocket. She glanced across the kitchen table. Good: neither Mamm or Jeremiah seemed to notice.

Esther stood abruptly, scudding her chair's legs across the linoleum floor. "I've got to take care of something. Sit right there. I'll be back in a few minutes."

Seeking refuge and privacy, she dove into a jacket and fled from the kitchen through the utility room. "Hello?" she whispered into the phone.

"Holly, is that you?" Larry said.

"No." Esther opened the back door with her free hand and stepped outside. The sky was overcast but bright, the air brisk—she guessed in the low fifties. "I'm sorry, it's Esther. I still have her phone."

"Oh." His buoyant voice sank. "Would you get her for me, please?"

"Holly went out." Esther shut the door behind her as quietly as she could. "The minute she returns I'll give her the phone. In fact I'll track her down right now. Can you hang on?"

"Thanks, Mrs. Fisher."

"Please call me Esther, Larry. I'm sorry to keep you waiting like this. You've been so very kind." She descended the steps. "May I speak to Nathaniel while I'm looking for her?"

"No can do. Nathaniel just went into his cousin's house."

"You're there already?" Esther's thoughts were so scattered she had no idea what hour it was.

"Yes, we made it in record time. I'm calling from the car because Nathaniel asked me not to use my cell phone in their home."

"Are you staying with his cousin too?" She considered asking what the house looked like. She knew little about Nathaniel's in-laws, only that they were farmers. "Is there room for both of you?"

"Yeah, there is, but I don't know yet. After I take Nathaniel wherever he needs to go I might check into a motel with a TV and Internet."

Esther's mind juggled a hodgepodge of considerations: Nathaniel had gone into his cousin's house; he'd opted not to call her first to let her know they'd arrived safely; he hadn't left a message for Larry to give her.

She didn't understand Nathaniel's motives and didn't want to think about them, but they hovered in the periphery of her brain like mosquitoes just out of reach. All she could do was be patient, which made her feel powerless. The words of Psalm 27:14 came to mind: "Wait on the Lord: be of good courage, and he shall strengthen thine heart: wait, I say, on the Lord."

But this waiting was draining her to a shriveled prune. She bet she looked ten years older; if she glanced in a mirror, she might not recognize herself.

"How's Nathaniel holding up?" She was unable to stifle her curiosity.

"Not well. Comatose might describe him. Except for giving me directions every now and then once we reached Holmes County, he's hardly said a word, just read that Amish magazine *Family Life* or stared out the windshield, his hands in his lap. Although he does seem to like those lattes."

"Larry, you do know what he's facing, don't you?"

"Yep, I get the picture. His suicidal wife, who supposedly snuffed herself fifteen years ago, might still be alive. I'd be freaked out too."

The saying *sometimes the truth hurts* mingled with her other chaotic thoughts. Esther had to hang up before she broke down and started crying right here in the barnyard.

"Why don't I ask Holly to call you when I find her?" she managed to get out.

"Hold off for a bit," Larry said. "I'm heading into the house. I'll call her back later."

"Thank you, and please keep us updated."

With the phone in her pocket, Esther should return to the kitchen, but she wasn't in the mood for chitchat. Jeremiah and Mamm probably hadn't even noticed her absence yet. Using what she knew was paltry logic, Esther told herself this space of time might be Jeremiah and Mamm's one chance to converse about the good old days without Beatrice's interrupting them.

Zach's pickup was still parked alongside the house. Esther thought she heard voices, sharp and abrasive. She wandered out of the barnyard. As she proceeded along the lane leading to the road, the voices grew in volume. Up ahead stood a black, saddled horse, chomping grass. Next to it, Holly, Zach, and Armin were using hand gestures, the men's voices rough. None of them seemed to notice Esther's approach.

Esther wished she were invisible. Now was not the time to give Holly her cell phone and explain about Larry's call. None of them would like having his name brought up. Too bad Esther couldn't pass right by and go somewhere for a good cry.

Esther upbraided herself to return to the kitchen, but she couldn't face Mamm and Jeremiah in her flummoxed state. She felt herself drawn toward Nathaniel's as if she were a kite being reeled in. Would it be idiotic to meander over to his place for what might be her last visit to see his farm? She mulled over the fact that Nathaniel had lived in a large house by himself ever since his two daughters moved out when they married; Esther felt sure Nathaniel had intended to make her the mistress of his fine home. She sighed as she imagined his arm around her shoulder after they wed—should their union be God's will.

Keeping a wide berth from the horse and threesome, Esther said, "Holly, would ya please check on your grandmother and Jeremiah? Tell them I'll be back in ten or fifteen minutes to serve up schnitz pie if they want some."

Holly finally noticed her. "Okay—sure, Mom," Holly said. "In a second."

The two men, their faces flushed, tipped their heads but said nothing. Fine, Esther wanted no part of their tiff.

She scurried to the two-lane road, took a right, and continued along the path next to the pavement. Minutes later, she reached Nathaniel's white clapboard house. The shades on the front windows were halfway up and at odd angles, as if raised hurriedly. He'd either wished to leave them that way or Armin hadn't bothered to open them properly. Although both men were fine-looking and intelligent, the two couldn't be more different. Nathaniel was humble, gentle, and kind, while Armin was pompous and arrogant. Still, he held a certain appeal that might captivate Holly—like Mamm said. Esther needed to come to grips with the fact that sometimes Mamm was right—perhaps most of the time, if not for her forgetfulness. Holly might choose Armin in the end, but Esther couldn't fathom her daughter becoming baptized Amish. Holly's and Esther's upbringings were like night and day. Esther's first sixteen years she'd lived on the farm with her parents and siblings. She'd spoken only Pennsylvania Dutch and German until she started school, when she learned English, and her education ended at eighth grade. At the other end of the spectrum, Holly was raised in the city by a single mom, was an only child, had graduated from college, and until recently had aspired to work in a downtown brokerage house.

Esther stood for a moment gawking at Nathaniel's front door, freshly painted forest green to match his window shades. To greet his future new spouse—meaning Esther—or to welcome his former wife? Ach, Esther had once held such high hopes: a second chance at happiness. The reality that Larry might be carrying another passenger—a female—with them made Esther feel like she'd been skewered with a pitchfork.

"All is in your hands, Lord," she said, sotto voce, watching the spinning blades of Nathaniel's windmill.

Once, Nathaniel had explained that over the years since she'd left, many of his neighbors had switched to gas-powered windmills to pump water, but his worked fine and cost him practically nothing to run. "Why fix what ain't broke?" he'd said, causing her to laugh. If he were her husband, she'd always wear a smile. She'd never complain again, she promised the Lord.

November and December were wedding months for the Amish—on Tuesdays and Thursdays. So far this year, Mamm had been too wobbly to attend any. If only Esther and her Nathaniel were already married—but not if his former spouse were still alive.

Esther felt exhaustion penetrate her, running bone deep. Her head was so heavy she could barely stand erect. She could not imagine surviving another day without Nathaniel. But she would; she had in the past when her Samuel hadn't returned from Vietnam. Caring for Holly had kept her alive. But Holly didn't need her anymore. Her daughter was about to embark on her own adventure. If Esther were ripped in half again, she doubted she could mend.

She moved around the side of his house, and breathed in the after-the-harvest fragrances she loved: corncobs in the crib and dried hay. Since Nathaniel left this morning, her world had shrunk into a dense, constricting tunnel, but in truth the sun shone, pushing back the clouds, illuminating his white barn and other buildings—a cooler color than a week ago, the shadows longer. The breeze carried with it a clean crispness like no other time of year.

"What are you doing here?" Esther recognized Lizzie's voice and whirled around to see the comely woman in her early twenties at the back door.

Lizzie charged outside; her compressed lips hinted of disdain. "Nathaniel didn't mention guests, so I'm assuming you're here uninvited." Lizzie sounded *griddlich*—cranky. "Under the circumstances, your being here is inappropriate."

Lizzie was right, but Esther tried to stand tall and appear at ease. She scrutinized the young woman's flawless complexion, her precise part, her pristine Kapp, her ironed aquamarine blue dress and dark apron.

"Has Galahad returned?" Esther said, to regain a foothold. She felt so weak a gust of wind could blow her over. As could Lizzie's diatribe.

"No," Lizzie said, "not that Nathaniel's horse or property is any of your business."

Again, Esther braced herself against Lizzie's blistering words. Esther tried to dismiss the vision of Lizzie making herself at home in Nathaniel's kitchen, preparing a fine array of treats, awaiting his return. She wondered how Lizzie would behave should Nathaniel come back with his wife in tow. Set her sights on Armin?

CHAPTER THIRTY-ONE

I wanted to tag along after Mom, but she'd asked me to go back to the kitchen to keep an eye on Mommy Anna and to entertain Jeremiah.

I felt empathy mingled with embarrassment for my mother if she were indeed snooping over at Nathaniel's home, especially if she ran into Lizzie. I hoped Lizzie was taking the day off and that Mom wouldn't do anything kooky like write him a love note and affix it to his back door. As long as she had my cell phone, Nathaniel could contact her through Larry. I wondered if he'd called with news. Part of me wished I'd gone with the men to Ohio to be Mom's advocate and to watch the drama evolve.

Zach glared at Armin. "Don't you have a horse to find? Galahad could have crossed the Canadian border by now."

"Real funny, Dr. Wannabe. Couldn't make it into dental or medical school?" Armin held tight to the reins when Midnight stretched his neck to nab a dandelion.

"I'll have you know, being accepted into a good veterinarian program is as tough as getting into medical or dental school. My phone would ring twenty-four hours a day if I didn't have an answering service."

"Well, la dee da. Ain't you special?"

Zach worked his jaw. I'll give him this: he didn't retaliate to Armin's baiting. Zach could have pointed out that Armin hadn't gone past the eighth grade, if he were a typical Amish youth. But for all I knew, Armin had furthered his education and wouldn't mention that fact for fear his brother might find out.

"Can we talk about something else?" I said. "For instance, Zach, how's your new receptionist?" I'd met the young lady twice. "Is she working out?"

"I'm not sure. She's come to work late three times."

"She seems awfully young."

"She's nineteen and is saving for college next year. Holly, the job's still yours should you want it."

"You'd make Holly sit at a desk all day talking on the phone scheduling patients?" Armin's voice turned as sugary as Mommy Anna's shoofly pie when he spoke to me. "Holly, I'd never ask you to work outside the home. Unless you wanted to set up a roadside stand selling baked goods or vegetables from the garden. Only if that's something you'd enjoy."

"Give up, Armin, footloose and fancy-free," Zach said. "Your track record of following through with commitments isn't stellar."

"I'm not going to be your audience, Zach Fleming. I've got better things ta do than listen to you put me down in order to build yourself up." Armin gathered Midnight's reins, inserted his foot in a stirrup, and hoisted himself onto the saddle. The horse came to life and swished its tail. Armin rotated the animal in a tight circle; its front legs raised and its rear hooves carried its weight like a ballet dancer.

"You'd better not let the bishop see you gallivanting around in cowboy boots," Zach said, sounding preachy.

"You've got your nerve bringin' Bishop Troyer into this conversation—the man who will someday marry Holly and me."

"Give me a break!" Zach shot him a look of disbelief.

A moment later, Armin and the horse sped away like a jet on a tarmac. Although I knew Armin was showing off, I admired his dexterity and skill in the saddle. I could use some of his moxie. And so could Zach when it came to dealing with Victoria and his mother. I felt dizzy just thinking about it.

"That idiot." His eyes protruding and his teeth bared, Zach looked livid. He took a deep breath, held it in.

"Don't be so hard on Armin," I said.

"I've watched his shenanigans most of my life, except for when I was in school and he was off doing the good Lord knows what. Armin's never matured."

"How do you know so much about him?"

"Keep in mind, as children, we lived down the road from each other."

"You're not implying you've never made a mistake." I ran my hand through my hair; my fingers caught in a snarl.

"I've made plenty of mistakes, Holly, but if you're referring to Victoria, I don't know why this is happening. I will not let her propaganda ruin my life or allow Armin to turn you against me."

I tried to make myself seem half-amused, when in fact I felt like a sinking rowboat. "If I were Justin's parent I'd want to know. Isn't paternity easy to prove or disprove with a DNA test?"

"But she won't let me."

"All of a sudden you're a helpless victim?"

"In this case, I am, because, as I've told you, I'm not the boy's father."

"Then what's Victoria's goal?" Her name clogged in my throat like a wad of chewing gum. "She wants you back in her life? Child-support money? Revenge? Why the melodramatic scene at Beth's in front of an innocent child? She must have a motive."

"I asked her the same questions, but she evaded answering. Not that I'd believe her." Zach glanced toward the road as a pair of draft horses pulling a wagon stacked high with baled hay plodded past, then turned his gaze to me. "She's stayed in contact with my mother. Mom mentioned Victoria and her husband had a child. But I didn't ask or care if it was a boy or girl."

"Even after this woman cheated on you, Beth kept her for a friend? Why would she, unless a grandchild were involved?"

"I don't know why my mother does a lot of things. All I care about right now is you and me. If you had a child, I wouldn't hold it against you. I'd accept him or her as my own."

"So you admit it's a possibility—"

"I admit nothing. I'm not perfect, but in this case I'm innocent. If you don't trust me, maybe we aren't meant to be together."

He sounded two clicks from instigating our breakup. An icy slice of fear ran through my chest as I realized I could lose him forever. Maybe I already had. "I'm not refusing to trust you," I said, "but I need to know. If I weren't in the picture, would you take Victoria back?"

"No. She's the last woman I'd turn to. You recall the saying 'Fool me once, shame on you; fool me twice, shame on me'?"

I was hoping he'd say, "No, because I love you, Holly, and only you." I examined his blotched face, his pale mouth. I wondered if I was being fair with him. I imagined my parents arguing and then clinging together with increasing love and loyalty.

Heat steamed out from around my neck. The temperature was coolish, but I unzipped my jacket. I figured neither Zach nor I was going to back down until our tempers deflated. Maybe I'd have to come to grips: my knight in shining armor had stayed single as long as I had because he was as messed up as I was.

Zach pulled out his cell phone and tapped in a number on his contact list. "Hello, Rich? It's Zach Fleming. Nathaniel's dappled gray gelding, Galahad, is on the loose. Armin's been searching for him, but so far no luck."

I heard a man's voice on the other end, but couldn't make out the words.

"And Rich?" Zach said. "Armin's dog has gone missing too. Yeah, the one we were talking about. Better warn your deputies."

"Thank you," I said, recalling why I cared for Zach. "I should have thought to call the authorities myself, even if it's not the Amish way to reach out for law enforcement." I felt my ire ebbing, my distrust subsiding. "Surely somebody's noticed Galahad."

"Unless he took to a forested area. Or someone unscrupulous caught him and decided to make some extra dough."

"Why did you mention Armin's dog?" I asked. "I figure Rascal will stick with Galahad or stop at a house with a food bowl on the back stoop."

"Because—you're not going to like this, Holly. But you didn't see the mangled goat."

"You mean a farmer might shoot Rascal?"

"If the dog's pestering his stock, yes. And for good reason."

"Because you're jealous of Armin you'd have Rascal executed?" I was flooded with outrage.

"Holly, once a dog has tasted blood, it's never the same. Their instincts can kick in, like a cat after a bird. We can't blame animals for doing what comes naturally."

"But you have no proof it was Rascal. I can't believe your attitude. You're a veterinarian. Don't you even like dogs?"

"Of course I do, but I'm a realist. If Rascal isn't the culprit, he's got nothing to worry about." Zach inched toward me. "I wish you wouldn't take this so hard."

"I wish a lot of things."

His hands moved out to me, but I hid mine behind my back. "Do you remember my mother's dog, Missy?" he said.

I nodded as I recalled the gregarious border collie, her ribs extended with a litter of pups.

"Missy's due any day," he said. "I'm planning to take one home with me, when it's old enough."

My negative reaction took me by surprise. I was the woman who'd wanted a dog most of her life—except for a brief period, as a child. Call me overly sentimental, but thinking about my cuddly terrier-mix Maxwell's early and sudden death still made me feel glum.

"How could you possibly raise a puppy when you don't even have time to spend with me?" I asked.

"These last few weeks have been gruesome—the worst in years," he said. "I won't always be so preoccupied. Hiring and training the new receptionist, twice the number of midnight emergency calls than usual, that conference last weekend, and then Victoria's theatrics. I wanted to be spending time with you, Holly, honest."

A chorus of unanswered questions chanted in my inner ears, echoing through my mind like rocks ricocheting down a well. I needed to gain distance.

"I've got to find Mom. I shudder to think what she's doing." I moved away from him. "Since your pickup is next to the house, when you leave would you ask Jeremiah to stick around and keep my grandmother company until we return? Mom and I will clean the kitchen."

"Sure, I'll see you tomorrow morning at nine thirty," he said to my back as I trotted toward the road, wishing I'd worn running shoes.

"Thanks," I said over my shoulder. By then, Nathaniel might have found his wife, leaving my mother too bummed out to take Mommy Anna to her doctor's appointment.

I needed Zach's help in more ways than one.

As I hastened toward Nathaniel's, I reminded myself of my many blessings: Mommy Anna, Jeremiah, and even crotchety Beatrice, the house and farm that felt like home. I tried to reinforce my positive thinking as best I could—I'd read self-help books and had counseled friends to look on the cup-half-full side. But in reality, Mom's future teetered on the edge of a cliff, and my storybook romance was crumbling. Life was not fair!

CHAPTER THIRTY-TWO

After dodging Lizzie's snipes, Esther fled Nathaniel's place and hurried toward home. She never should have come here, let alone left Mamm in Jeremiah's care; he could have gone by now.

Esther saw Holly jogging along the side of the road toward her. Esther had never seen her daughter jog in this lopsided, disjointed stride, her arms and fists held to her chest, her mouth open, gasping for air.

Esther braced herself, the way she would if she saw a tree branch falling, but didn't have time to escape.

She reminded herself: Larry couldn't have called Holly, because Esther had the cell phone. But Nathaniel could have called the phone shanty and left a message. A ream of possibilities spun through her mind like a school of minnows, but Holly's demeanor grabbed hold of her attention, dismissing her thoughts about Nathaniel.

"What's wrong, daughter?" Esther said when Holly was within earshot.

Holly halted a couple yards away and bent at the waist, as if she had a stitch in her side. Then she straightened up and inhaled a lungful. "I was worried about you," she said, panting. "Everything okay?"

"Yah, I'm fine. Let's get home." Esther started them toward the house along the path at the side of the road. She heard a siren in the far-off distance and a dog yipping, but not Rascal's deep bark.

"Did Galahad and Rascal return?" Holly's face reminded Esther of a child on her first day of school—expectant, but insecure.

"Nee, neither of them. Lizzie's over at Nathaniel's. I should have known she'd be there and be grateful, but if I never see that young woman again I won't miss her." Esther's hand covered her mouth, but too late to detour her mean-spirited words.

I'm sorry, dear God, Esther told the Lord in her mind. I'll try to love my neighbor—God's second greatest commandment, according to the book of Matthew. But could Esther love Lizzie as she loved herself, as the Bible instructed? If she wanted to embrace the Amish church, she must tackle her sins one by one.

"You got in an argument with Lizzie?" Holly asked.

"It was my own fault for going to Nathaniel's. I don't know what possessed me."

"Unrequited love?"

Esther quickened her pace. She didn't want to talk about her and Nathaniel's ill-fated courtship. She faked a cough, then sputtered. "I was checking to see if Galahad returned. But it was rude of me to leave Jeremiah and Mamm sitting at the table."

"I asked Zach to tell Mommy Anna and Jeremiah we'd be right back." Holly slipped her arm in Esther's, an uncharacteristic move. Maybe Holly thought one of them would fall. Her daughter was sure-footed, but seemed ready to topple.

"Did something happen while I was gone?" Esther asked, and glanced into Holly's beet-red face.

"Zach and I quarreled after Armin showed up. Or was it the other way around? In any case, Zach and I—" Her upper lip trembled.

"I'm sorry you're hurting." Esther's own tribulations would take second place to her cherished Holly. Esther deserved whatever hardship the Lord Almighty sent her way, but she couldn't imagine Holly had displeased God.

Esther tried to ignore the cars passing by, one slowing down then speeding up again, and a carriage teeming with children, driven by a young woman—their mother, Esther thought.

She heard multiple clopping sounds and saw Armin atop the black horse, headed toward her and Holly. Galahad trailed behind them, tied with a rope.

"Look, Armin found Galahad!" Holly's voice expanded to one of happiness. "Thank you, God."

Galahad whinnied and pranced about, his head held high and his ears pointed toward Nathaniel's farm.

"Yah, that's good," Esther said, holding her tongue. If Armin hadn't taken Nathaniel's prized gelding to begin with, none of this difficulty would be happening.

Armin was missing his hat and his hair was tousled. "I told you I'd find Galahad." He stopped before them.

"You look like you're stepping out of another century," Holly said to Armin, and his lips curved into a grin.

"You're the one livin' in the wrong era here on this road. You should join up with us." A horse and buggy clip-clopped by, as if proving his point.

Holly seemed impressed with him. Esther supposed Armin was an imposing figure atop the black horse; he reminded her of

Nathaniel. Ach, she wondered what he was doing this very minute in Ohio. Most likely still speaking to his cousin or possibly the deputy assigned to the case.

"Where was Galahad?" Holly asked.

"Having the time of his life in an Englischer's pasture not far away. I wouldn't be surprised if someone opened the gate and invited him in."

Galahad pulled on the lead, tossed his head, and tried to get the bit between his teeth as a car motored by.

"You're lucky," Esther said, noticing Armin's boots. "Nathaniel would have been mighty displeased if you lost Galahad. Or worse, if he'd been struck by an automobile."

"But my brother's not here, and no harm done. Yah?" Armin propelled Jeremiah's horse and Galahad into Mamm's lane a few yards as a van whirred along the road.

Esther and Holly followed. "Where's Rascal?" Holly asked.

"You haven't seen him?"

"No, and Mom was just down at Nathaniel's house." Holly wrapped her arms around herself. "Armin, I'm worried. When Zach called the authorities to ask them to keep an eye open for Galahad, he mentioned Rascal was running free."

"That blabbermouth," Armin said. "Sticking his nose where it doesn't belong."

"Zach was trying to help." Holly's statement went up at the end, as if a question.

"Nathaniel wouldn't want the police called." Armin patted the black horse's sweaty neck. "Am I right, Esther?"

"Yah, probably." She hated being caught in the middle of their spat. Esther doubted it was a lovers' quarrel, but when speculating on her daughter's desires, too often Esther had been wrong.

"'Tis not our way to involve law-enforcement agencies." Armin glanced back to Galahad, who seemed to be growing more impatient and was jerking on the lead. "Now I've got myself in a pickle," he said. "Nathaniel's buggy is at Jeremiah's. Let's see, if I bring both these horses over to the Fishers' I can leave Midnight and have Galahad take the buggy home."

"No, I won't hear of it," Esther said. "I can see Galahad is exhausted. Jeremiah's horse needs a rest too. Take Nathaniel's other buggy horse with you later. Or in the morning."

"I s'pose you're right. As it is, Lizzie will give Nathaniel an earful."

"Lizzie's a regular chatterbox," Holly said to Esther. "She'll fill Nathaniel in on every detail."

"Yah, she's a storyteller—" Armin whistled under his breath.

Esther figured Lizzie would twist the plotline to suit her.

"Is Jeremiah still here?" he asked.

"I assume he is." Holly glanced to the house. "I haven't seen his buggy leave."

"Then I'd better come with you and ask his opinion."

"Aren't you worried about Rascal?" Holly lifted her chin to speak to Armin.

"Nee, he'll show up when he's ready. God will protect him."

Esther knew the rain fell upon the just and the unjust. "I hope you're right."

CHAPTER
THIRTY-THREE

"Before we go in, may I have my phone back?" I asked Mom as the two of us straggled into the barnyard following Armin, who led the horses into the barn.

"Could I keep it?" she said. "I'm hoping Larry will call with news of Nathaniel."

"Me too." I put out my hand palm up. "When he does, I'll let you know right away."

Mom's bun sprawled down her back and looked like a robin's nest after a windstorm. "Never mind," I told her, "you hang on to it. Your needs outweigh mine tenfold."

"Actually, when you were talking to Zach and Armin, Larry did call," Mom said. "That's what brought me outside. I was looking for you."

My head jerked. "Why didn't you tell me earlier?"

"I meant to," she stammered, "and I should have informed Armin. He must be concerned about his brother—and his sister-in-law." Mom looked bedraggled, one click from a meltdown. "I'm so *verhoodled*, and you three seemed deep in discussion."

"What did Larry say?" I asked. "Are they in Ohio yet?"

"Yes, and Nathaniel had just gone into his cousin's home. Larry was about to join him, and said he'd call back. Nathaniel asked him not to use his phone in the house, so Larry may not call for a while."

"Or they could all jump in the car and go looking for the woman. If Amish prefer not to involve the police, wouldn't they search for her themselves?" I felt like texting Larry, but wouldn't disrespect Nathaniel's cousin.

"You're right." She slowed to a halt. "By the way, Zach reconfirmed he'll be by at nine thirty tomorrow morning to drive Mamm to her doctor's appointment. Will you be up to going with us?"

"I don't have much choice. We've got to get Mommy Anna to Dr. Brewster's, and I want to hear what the doctor says."

"Gut. I appreciate Zach's willingness to drive, since you've had a dispute and all."

"An impasse is more like it." My voice came out a whimper. "Mom, is there something wrong with me? My dream of finding my grandma came true, but my love life is a mess, like Mommy Anna's cluttered kitchen drawers."

"Daughter, there's nothing wrong with you. I hurt our whole family—stunted our relationships. Nothing good ever comes from deception." Mom spread her arms around me like a mama bird. She stood several inches taller than I did, her shoulder a cushion for my head. "I'm so sorry, Holly, dearest girl. Maybe that's why God is punishing me now."

I felt her trembling and leaning back. "Hey, Mom, doesn't it say in the Bible that if we come to God and confess our sins we'll be forgiven—washed from scarlet to white?"

She gave me a teensy smile, probably all she could muster. "Are you referring to Isaiah 1:18? 'Though your sins be as scarlet, they shall be as white as snow; though they be red like crimson, they shall be as wool.'"

"Yes. I'm going to write that verse down and memorize it." It was pathetic how little scripture I knew by heart. "I might go to church with you and Mommy Anna next Sunday, if Mommy Anna's up to it." I purposely didn't mention I wouldn't attend Zach's Mennonite church with him and his family again unless a miracle happened.

I started us walking toward the stoop. "If I go to the church service, how will I understand what the minister's saying?" I asked.

"Study up on your German?"

I placed my foot on the bottom step, then paused. "I wish I'd brought one of my old college textbooks here with me."

"We can get you another. If you don't understand, we can come home and look up the scripture in an English Bible."

"And Mom, don't worry, I won't wear an Amish dress and apron."

The corners of her mouth curved up. "You looked pretty dressed that way."

"Really? Thanks." Her positive opinion of me mattered more than I'd expected. "I thought you found me ridiculous," I said.

"I wonder if I saw you through my brother's critical eyes, but he's living in Montana now. And maybe I felt regret for losing all those years I could have been dressed plain myself, like I should be doing right now. In any case, I treated you unfairly."

Her words were a balm to my ears, soothing my anguish about Zach. Were we still engaged? Neither of us had officially broken it off, but then he hadn't pursued setting a date either.

"I've got to tell ya, you'd be a great comfort Sunday if you went with me," Mom said. "With my future so uncertain, I don't know how I'll make it if Nathaniel—" Her eyes turned glassy. "I've never been so fearful." She blinked in rapid succession. "No, that isn't true. I'll never forget when your father was missing, or just last month, when you and I came here, and I saw Mamm, after decades."

"You made it through those adversities, and no matter what happens, I'm here for you," I said. "I'll go to church with you. I've wanted to, but felt too self-conscious. And I was so infatuated with Zach, and wished to be with him every minute." Mom and I climbed the stairs.

At the top she took my hand, and I turned to face her. "Holly, do you love him?"

"I thought so, but maybe I wanted to be married so much I let myself believe I did. I'm beginning to think arranged marriages have their merits. Which man would you choose for me?"

"None of us is perfect. And I'm not the woman who would live with the consequences of the choice."

"As it's turned out, Zach's too busy to spend time with me. And now, I find he's got a secret life of his own."

"You don't know that for a fact."

"You're sticking up for him?"

"I've had my reservations about you and Zach, for selfish reasons. But we shouldn't condemn a man before he's found to be guilty, yah?"

"I suppose you're right. How did you get to be so wise, Mom?" I guessed she always was.

"I'm not so smart," she said. "*Es Sclimmscht vun Narre*—the worst of fools is what I was."

I scanned the barnyard, hoping to spot Rascal. I wondered if a domesticated dog was capable of taking care of itself in the wild. I silently prayed for his safety. If God saw every sparrow and every hair on my head, surely he'd watch out for Rascal as he had Galahad.

"Let's check on Mommy Anna." My hand grasped the doorknob to the utility room.

"Yah, we don't want her cooking while we're out here." We both chortled, distraught as we were—each in our own realm of uncertainties, but united in a new way. Mom and I were gradually moving closer, like the tide rising imperceptibly to meet the shore in a quiet cove.

As I turned the knob, an unsettling thought tunneled through my mind, reminding me of elementary school bullies shooting rubber bands at substitute teachers, when they weren't teasing me. "Mom, before we go in, is there anything else you want to tell me about Jeremiah's letters?"

She raised a hand, as if on the witness stand. "I never received any, if he really wrote them. I'm still not convinced he did. Ya know, he's an old man whose memory might be failing. Maybe he thought about writing to me, but never did."

If I were prudent I should let it go, I told myself, but inconsistencies needled at me. "We have both Mamm and Jeremiah in the same room, without Beatrice to interrupt them. Should we ask for more details?"

"We could. But would knowing the answer help either of us? It seems like a dangling carrot—a temptation best left alone."

"If Mommy Anna has the letters, we probably would have run across them when we moved her into the Daadi Haus last month."

Although I'd never noticed my mother's letters—not that I had reason to open her shoe boxes, stacked on the top shelf of her bedroom
closet in Seattle.

"We have an attic …" Mom patted her hair, removed a few pins,
and rolled her bun back into place. "But would looking through
another's personal belongings without their permission not be wrong?"

"You're right," I said. "Still, I do want to bring up the subject. If
you don't mind."

She refastened her bun with several hairpins. "If you mention it
naturally."

"Okay." My stomach knotted as my mind replayed last month's scene
with the bishop and my extended family on a nonpreaching Sunday in
fast-forward. "I've acted abominably, but it won't happen again."

Mom and I passed through the utility room. I heard Mommy
Anna and Jeremiah chattering in Pennsylvania Dutch. I could
make out a few words like Mommy Anna's saying, "*schrecklich*"—
terrible—and Jeremiah replying, "*Des is en schlechdi Sach*!—this is a
nasty matter!"

Mom and I entered the kitchen. My mouth gaped open when I
saw the doll on the kitchen table.

The room fell silent, as if we were all figures in a wax museum—
as inanimate as the doll.

"How did she get downstairs?" I asked, and glanced to Mom,
standing next to me.

She shrugged. "I didn't bring it down."

"I did." Mommy Anna grinned. "Jeremiah wanted to see the doll
for himself." She and Jeremiah must have been talking about it and
hypothesizing about the letter from Chap McLaughlin.

Mom moved to the table. "You could have fallen, Mamm," she said. I figured my mother was uncomfortable having Jeremiah in the same room with the doll. I was thankful Mom had Chap's letter, unless Mommy Anna had dug it out of Mom's purse. Never mind; according to Mom, she'd already written to Chap McLaughlin.

I recalled my one photo of Dad, taken at age eighteen. Mom hadn't exactly given it to me, but she'd left the faded black-and-white photo on her bureau in Seattle instead of shredding it or stashing it in a file drawer. I couldn't resist taking it. Why shouldn't I own a photograph of my own father? I wondered if Jeremiah would want to see it, but dismissed the idea. My mother had told me portraits were against the Ordnung. But that didn't mean I couldn't display it at some time. Or I might keep it just to myself so Mom wouldn't be forced to see it.

"Good news, everyone," Mom said, I assumed to draw attention away from the doll. "Armin found Galahad. He's feeding and watering the horses right now, then he'll come in to speak to you, Jeremiah, so you two can figure when's the best time to pick up Nathaniel's buggy."

"The horses looked tired," I said.

"But the men know a hundred times more than we women do." Mom sent me a message with her eyes to keep quiet.

Jeremiah shook his head. "Armin always loved horses, but his own horse-sense, it wonders me. To think of all the time he wasted gadding about when he could have settled down here like his Bruder Nathaniel."

The room filled with silence again; it seemed like the world had stopped revolving.

"Armin's a fine-gut man," Mamm said, bringing the room back to life. "He should get baptized and married as soon as possible."

"'Tis not too late." Jeremiah gave the doll another looking over and squinted his hooded eyes. "I'm sorry you've been deceived, Esther. No way would our Samuel buy that doll."

My mother winced, then seemed to marshal herself. "Jeremiah, may I get you more coffee and a slice of schnitz pie?"

"No pie, thanks, but I'd take Kaffi."

"Holly has a question before you leave, if you're willing to speak of it."

"What's on your mind, Holly?" he asked.

"It's about the letters you wrote to my mother." I fetched the coffee and topped off their cups.

Jeremiah added sugar and a splash of milk. "Yah, I remember penning them."

"And then?" I persisted.

"I gave them to my Beatrice to give to Anna." He stirred his coffee, swallowed a mouthful.

"Nee, Beatrice never gave me letters," Mommy Anna said. "Not that I recall, anyways."

I set the urn on the counter and came back to the table. "I don't understand why you didn't ask Mommy Anna for my mom's address."

"My Beatrice thought Esther wouldn't like it. She said Esther had been rude to her, in the past."

My mother's chin dipped, a tip-off that Beatrice might have told the truth. I reminded myself I'd often sassed Mom during my teenage years and well beyond. Who was I to condemn a single woman who had raised a self-willed daughter? I wished I could retract every smart-alecky statement.

"I finally gave up writing Esther when I received no replies." Jeremiah yawned, revealing crooked teeth. "*Ich bin mied wie en Hund*—I'm as tired as a dog." Using his hands, he pushed himself to a standing position, his spine curved like a barrel. He looked fatigued—in a benumbed state. "I best be on my way before Beatrice starts fretting."

"Of course." Mom lifted his hat from a peg. "Holly, why don't you accompany your grandpa outside and down the back steps? They're mighty steep. Make sure he holds the railing." She gave Jeremiah his hat, then helped him with his jacket. "Thank you for bringing Holly home," she said. "*Ich bedank mich*."

"*Gem gschehne*." He raised a hand as a farewell to my grandma. "Gut seeing ya, Anna."

"You're welcome anytime," Mommy Anna said.

I slipped my hand under Jeremiah's elbow. Mom was giving me an opportunity to be alone with him, but what should I say?

CHAPTER THIRTY-FOUR

Esther felt the cell phone vibrate once, the moment Holly was out the door. She couldn't leave Mamm alone. Not with the doll.

"I have to answer this call," Esther said. "It could be Larry or Nathaniel."

"You have a phone in the house?" Mamm's mouth narrowed. "What next?"

In her haste, Esther's hand fumbled as she extracted the phone from her pocket. She dropped it. "Oh, no!" She picked it up, praying she hadn't broken it. "Hello?"

She grabbed the doll and stood it on the refrigerator, then dashed to the back door. Holly and Jeremiah were at the bottom of the steps in conversation. "The cell phone," Esther said, ignoring Jeremiah's look of concern. Esther descended the stairs. "I dropped it, then tried to answer, but no one was there."

Holly reached out, took the phone, and slid it in her pocket. "Don't worry, Mom, probably a text from Larry. I'll check his message later. I'll be in soon."

Esther hesitated, then mounted the stairs. She heard Jeremiah invite Holly to ride home with him, but Holly begged off. "I'll visit you again next week."

"You could spend the night if ya like," Jeremiah said. "We'd have plenty of time for talking."

Esther was tempted to dawdle outside the back door, but didn't dare. Sure enough, when Esther reentered the kitchen she saw Mamm had gotten to her feet and was reaching for the doll, inches out of her grasp.

"Can't I leave you alone for a minute?" Esther said, then was sorry for her snippy tone of voice. "Please forgive me, Mamm, I'm taking my frustrations out on you and have no right." Esther should have asked her mother not to move the doll or taken it outside. But then Mamm might have followed her. Esther was reminded of when Holly was a toddler; her daughter had needed constant supervision. Esther was mothering Mamm, making Esther feel as if the generations had leapfrogged.

Mamm's lips pursed and she thumped back onto her chair. "How do you expect the bishop to let you into baptism classes if he finds you with a cell phone?" She hunched over her empty coffee cup.

Esther refilled it. "You're right, I shouldn't turn it on in the house."

"Or ever use one," Mamm said.

"I'm waiting to hear from Larry and Nathaniel."

"That's no excuse."

"I was wrong, Mamm. And wrong to grow impatient with you just now."

How and why Mamm had brought the doll downstairs was a subject Esther didn't want to tackle. She felt a dull headache establishing itself at the edges of her cranium.

"Well?" Mamm mixed three tablespoons of sugar into her coffee. "Since you have a phone, tell me who called."

"I don't know. Holly will fill us in." Esther tried to bolster herself into acting bravely, but she was tired of pretending to be courageous—a lifetime of putting up a false front.

Minutes later, Holly came in. "Larry texted. They're on their way to this woman's cabin. Larry's driving Nathaniel, his cousin, and a minister." Holly's gaze latched onto Esther's. "And Larry said he ran a make on Chap McLaughlin through Larry's office at the bank and has the guy's phone number. Chap came out clean and he served in the army in the early seventies."

"We owe Larry a lot," Mamm said. "It's a shame he ain't Amish."

"Yah, he's acting as a family friend," Esther said.

"And someone else texted." Holly held the phone up to Esther to read the screen: "Thinking of U, Z." Holly gave a one-shouldered shrug and stowed the phone in her pocket.

"I wasn't eavesdropping," Esther said, "but I heard Jeremiah inviting you to his farm."

"I accepted," Holly said. "But I told him next week would be better."

"And Nathaniel's buggy?"

"He and Armin have that switcheroo figured out for tomorrow morning, after milking. Hopefully Armin will be gone when Zach arrives."

"Zach's coming to check on Cookie tomorrow?" Mamm said.

"Yes, I'm sure he'll look her over." Esther put her index finger to her lips to signal Holly not to mention Mamm's doctor's appointment the next day. It seemed Mamm had forgotten about it.

"No sign of Rascal." Holly's arms flopped to her sides as if her hands were too cumbersome to use.

Esther crested an arm around Holly's shoulder. "He might be at Nathaniel's. Maybe Lizzie broke down and let him in the house, or shut him in an outbuilding."

She knew her daughter would be devastated if anything happened to Armin's dog, but Esther was too worried about Nathaniel to spare energy on Rascal. And should Jeremiah's letters be found, Esther wasn't sure she wanted to read them. Maybe it was best to let sleeping dogs lie.

"From what Jeremiah says, Armin had better find Rascal quick." Mamm added more sugar to her coffee until the cup almost overflowed. She leaned forward and supped off the top, lapping like a horse at the water trough. Never had Esther seen her mother use such uncouth manners.

Armin entered the kitchen sock-footed, hat in hand. "Anna, I'm going to take your cow, Pearly, down to Nathaniel's until he returns. Otherwise she'll have to wait too long between milkings."

"I'll milk Pearly," Esther said. All heads whipped around to evaluate her facial expression. "I'm serious. I can milk a cow. And gather the eggs too."

"Would you teach me?" Holly asked, surprising Esther.

"I guess, why not?"

Armin's thumb moved up and down his suspender. "I could show you myself, Holly, but cows require milking mighty early. And I told you you'd never have to milk cows while I'm around. 'Tis man's work."

"How about you learn to quilt instead, Holly?" Mamm said.

"That's a great idea," Esther said.

"I started a sunshine shadow—I think, but can't recall." Mamm fidgeted with her napkin. "I have pieces already cut, but you could do anything you wanted with it. Holly, will ya please get my wicker basket in the Daadi Haus? It's on the floor by the easy chair."

Holly strode through the front room and returned with a handled basket. She peered into a variety of fabric scraps. "This looks too complicated."

"How about a nine-patch?" Esther said. "That's what my mamm's mamm, Emma Mae, taught me, when I first learned to quilt."

Holly set the basket on the table. "Only if you'll help me every step of the way."

"Sure, in fact, you and I can work on a quilt together. Or if you prefer, I could start one too."

"I love the quilt you made for me when I was a girl," Holly said. "I should have brought it with us. Maybe Dori will send it."

Esther envisioned the burgundy birds perched on wreaths of tulips applied to an off-white background—ten to twelve even stitches per inch—each sewn by her hand. Appropriate for Holly's bed in Seattle, but perhaps not in Mamm's house. The image of Holly and her working side by side brought Esther a feeling of tranquility, then her thoughts transferred to her and Nathaniel's future wedding bed—but she banished the image. She'd make a quilt for Holly or send it to her in-laws in Montana instead.

"Let's go to the fabric store tomorrow, after that other appointment." Esther winked at Holly.

Understanding seemed to bloom in Holly's warm brown eyes. "That's a super idea. I'll need Mommy Anna's help choosing the right colors, and I don't know how much yardage to buy or which threads and needles."

"I've got plenty of scraps around the house," Mamm said.

"We'll need muslin and new backing," Esther said. "Mamm could help us pick the right weight. And I wonder how old Mamm's thread is. It might need to be replaced."

"Please come with us, Mommy Anna," Holly said. "A ladies' morning out. And maybe eat lunch somewhere after."

"I haven't been to a restaurant—well, now, I can't recall the last time. I'll have to wait to see how I feel tomorrow."

"Okay, we'll see how the day unfolds."

Armin broke into the conversation. "In the meantime, what about Pearly?"

"Leave her here. I'll come milk her right now." Esther felt a distant yearning in her chest for her youth. "If three women are to live in this house, one of us will have to do the milking."

"As soon as Nathaniel comes back, I will," Armin said, but Esther knew her life might never be the same after Nathaniel's return. And Holly? She seemed to be treading water at the deep end of the swimming pool.

CHAPTER THIRTY-FIVE

I had Chap McLaughlin's telephone number entered in my cell phone. But I couldn't call him with Mommy Anna in the kitchen and my mother out in the barn. I'd have to wait until later.

I glanced up at the doll on top of the refrigerator and felt an influx of uneasiness. I'd need to put it out of sight so Mommy Anna didn't do what a girlfriend's grandmother had: the aged woman stood on a chair, fell, broke her hip, and contracted pneumonia. I was determined Mommy Anna would see Dr. Brewster tomorrow. Zach had better show up. If he didn't, I'd call a professional driver and be done with Zach forever!

He'd texted to say he was thinking of me. It sounded like a message to a friend, not his future wife. He'd shortened his name to Z, as he always did. No reference to his looking forward to seeing me tomorrow. No "I can't live without you!" or "I love you!" I longed to hear the words.

I could text him back, but didn't know what to say. He needed to straighten out his life before I became a part of it. But deep down inside me, like an underground river, flowed a current of desire for him.

"I still want to learn to milk a cow," I said to Mommy Anna, trying to substitute my thoughts for another topic.

"Why would ya want to milk old Pearly?"

"For fun. And, who knows, Mom could be right about we three women living together."

"I doubt that will happen. Anyways, Nathaniel promised he'll supply us with milk."

I wondered if she recalled where Nathaniel was or the repercussions of his quest. "Still, I want to master everything he and Armin do for us. Including driving a buggy." I was determined to overcome my gut-fear of horses. Armin would help me.

"You want to learn to bake bread instead?" Mommy Anna flapped up her hands. "Ach, I forgot to start the dough today. Where's my memory up and gone to?"

I wanted to tell her Dr. Brewster might help fix her in a jiffy, but didn't wish to spook Mommy Anna if she'd forgotten about her appointment.

"We have plenty of bread," I said. "Mom baked two loaves yesterday."

Like a homing pigeon, my mind orbited back to Zach. I relived our first luscious kiss on the way home from the airport, which had seemed like an impetuous act. But he'd said he wanted to kiss me since first we met. My mind replayed his out-of-the-blue proposal. Nothing else about him seemed to be reckless. When I'd first met him I'd found him off-putting, probably because my nerves had been jangled and he was so relaxed. I'd been a jittery mess and had turned to Zach's mother, Beth, for support. I'd spoken openly and given Beth my confidence. In doing so, I'd possibly jeopardized my mother.

Relentless questions heaped up like a stack of uneaten pancakes gone cold. I recalled: Zach told me he'd gladly raise my son as his stepchild, if I had one. Would I not embrace his little boy in the same fashion? Yes, I would. Of course I would. And Justin was a cutie if I'd ever seen one. But after I'd learned how deceitful my mother was—like having a rug pulled out from under me—I wasn't sure what to believe anymore.

I felt a shift inside, as if regaining my equilibrium after disembarking a merry-go-round at a carnival. The thought of losing Zach didn't shake me down to my core, as it had before. Maybe his stalling was for my benefit, a sign from God, the Holy Spirit tapping me on the shoulder—I should pay heed. Was I supposed to break off with Zach and join the Amish church like Mom?

I would have considered becoming Amish an absurd option only last month, but today the idea seemed reasonable. I'd always longed for an extended family and a sense of belonging. Here it lay right in this very community.

I'd make a mental list of the pros and cons and speak to Bishop Troyer. When I'd met him I'd been impressed with his wisdom and fairness. I was pretty sure the bishop would not pressure me to join. It wasn't very often that an Englischer chose to become Amish, but I'd heard several in the area had been baptized into the church. I should seek them out and discover the pitfalls and benefits. I'd been told the Amish population continued to grow because of large families, not through evangelizing. Most—up to 90 percent—of the young Amish chose to join the church after their running-around period. Quite impressive. Even Armin was coming back to roost and had in essence proposed to court me. I wondered if he were entering the marriage arena only to irk Zach. Or was Armin serious?

Mommy Anna yawned without covering her mouth.

"Come on, let's get your feet up," I said, and guided her into the Daadi Haus for a nap. She had a busy day ahead of her tomorrow.

As we passed the doll, she didn't glance up at it or comment. And my seeing its flashy dress, high heels, and intricate hairdo didn't appeal to me as before. Even if Dad had purchased it, the doll didn't fit in this house or in this county. Thinking about it only bogged me down.

I helped Mommy Anna ease onto her bed; her eyelids slid shut and her breathing slowed to a sleeping state. I took the doll upstairs and stuck it in my mother's room next to the folded silk.

I was itching to call Chap McLaughlin. If I were Amish, I'd wait for his letter. On the other hand, if the letter, doll, and silk were a prank or an honest mistake, I didn't think my mother could endure another disappointment, not to mention my own anxieties. I needed a resolution—enough of this free-falling like an acorn and hoping the ground beneath me was soft and cushy instead of a slab of cement.

I heard a rapping on the kitchen door. I dismissed Mom and Armin; they'd stroll right in. I glanced out a window and saw Beth's minivan parked outside the barnyard. My mind had been so entrenched in thought I hadn't heard her tires roll up. Beth was the last person I wanted to see. I was tempted not to answer the door. But then I heard another rap-rap, followed by, "Yoo-hoo, anyone home?"

Her saccharine voice made me cringe. I guessed Beth was used to entering the house; she'd been Mommy Anna's surrogate daughter for decades during my mother's absence.

I descended the stairs and went into the kitchen to see the tallish blonde, her long hair parted on the side and held back by a clip.

"Hello, Holly." Her gaze didn't quite meet mine. She wore a camel-colored midlength skirt and a matching quilted jacket. "Good to see you."

"Hello, Beth." Venomous verbal missiles did a tango on the tip of my tongue, but I pressed my lips together to curtail them.

"Zach asked me to stop by and apologize." Beth's gaze finally met mine.

"In other words, Zach requested you come or you wouldn't be here?"

"Not entirely. I've been inhospitable the last few weeks and I owe you an apology." Beth unbuttoned her jacket, revealing a small-flowered blouse. "I've had my hands full."

"My hunch is ever since you heard Zach planned to marry me I've turned into a pariah." And that Mom had Beth sized up right.

"I was surprised." She fingered her wedding band. "Zach and you seemed hasty, especially since you'd never demonstrated affection for him. In front of me, anyway."

"But now that I do care for him, you're horrified to have me for a daughter-in-law?" My voice sounded brittle, like a sheet of ice ready to splinter.

"No—"

"Because I'm Esther Fisher's daughter? You and Mom will continue your competition over my dad even though you're happily married and my father's dead? Do you hold Mom responsible for Dad's death?"

"To be totally honest, I still harbor some resentment, for which I ask God's forgiveness. But that's not my reason for wanting you and Zach to delay getting married."

"Last month, you invited me over and even divulged he was fond of me. It seemed like you wanted nothing more."

"I shouldn't have, knowing Victoria might resurface. She'd told me her husband left her a few months ago, and that he didn't even visit his son or pay child support."

"I don't get why you kept in touch with her in the first place." I stepped nearer, in-her-face close. "How long have you known about her little boy?"

"I knew Vicki—what I call Victoria—had a child, but it wasn't until I told her Zach wanted to marry you did she tell me he was Justin's father."

"And you believe her over your own son?" I felt compelled to defend Zach when I didn't know the truth myself.

"I've always hoped Zach would have children, but I've acted atrociously. I was wrong to interfere. Will you accept my apology?"

"Why should I?" I recalled skinning my knees as a child—the stinging, raw pain of her rejection was worse.

"I'm asking you for forgiveness."

I folded my arms. "Doesn't forgiveness follow repentance? And don't give me a ration of Christian platitudes. The truth is you hope Zach dumps me so he and Victoria can get together again. A ready-made family."

"I can see I've hurt you, Holly." Her hands rose as if to hug me, but I recoiled out of her grasp.

"You said you loved my grandmother, but you haven't visited her in weeks."

"I have been neglectful, what with Vicki and Justin, and Missy expecting her pups any day." She fastened one of her jacket buttons. "In fact, I should get back to her. Missy has been acting restless and nesting. Zach said she'll most likely deliver the pups tonight or in the morning."

Using tactile memory, I recalled the border collie's luxurious coat. I wondered how the dog was doing—her ribs must be extended and her middle hanging low—but I resisted asking. I kept my face an aloof mask, while my brain weighed the specifics. Zach had promised to be here in the morning at nine thirty, knowing he might be needed to help deliver Missy's litter. Would he simply not show up? Half of me could understand, but he should have warned me and offered to find us another ride. Certainly not Beth, but I knew there were drivers-for-hire in the county.

"Is Anna around?" Beth asked, moving toward the sitting room.

My hands akimbo, I barred her way. "She's asleep and I won't let you disturb her."

"All right." Beth looked crestfallen. "Please send Anna my love." She receded toward the back door, and I shut it behind her.

The words from the Lord's Prayer, which I'd recited at church my whole life but never given ample thought, came to mind: "Forgive us our trespasses as we forgive those who trespass against us." Exactly what Jeremiah had mentioned to me in the buggy.

I thought of examples of how readily the Amish offered forgiveness, like after the shooting in the one-room schoolhouse in 2006. I remembered watching the footage on TV after the atrocity, how blown away I'd been that the Amish extended forgiveness to the assassin. Some had attended the shooter's funeral and reached out to his grieving wife. Bishop Troyer would urge me to follow Beth and offer forgiveness.

But feeling the way I did, anything I said to Beth would be an empty cliché.

CHAPTER THIRTY-SIX

Standing in the barn, Esther watched Armin brush off the cow, then wash her udder with a rag dipped in disinfectant and water. Ach, he was still wearing those ostentatious cowboy boots.

"You want me to tie her back legs so she doesn't kick the bucket over?" he asked Esther. "Pearly weighs over a thousand pounds."

"Has she ever kicked anyone?"

"Nee, never, but she don't know you. Cows can be funny that way."

"She looks gentle enough." After scrubbing her hands, Esther sat on a low stool next to the cow. "Hello, Pearly." She stroked the Holstein's udder and felt the animal relaxing, her milk letting down. "Gut girl," Esther said, wondering if one of her brother's kids had named the Holstein.

Using her thumb and first fingers Esther pinched, then squeezed. Success! A stream of milk flowed out, landing in the galvanized bucket. Pearly munched on feed and seemed grateful to have her load lightened, even if by a stranger.

"You're a natural," Armin told Esther. "Like you've been milking cows by hand your whole life."

"I used to help Dat." Esther relished the aroma of Pearly's warm milk and the pinging sound as the spurts of ivory-colored liquid hit the bucket. "I guess ya never forget how."

"Are you sure you want to get up at four thirty to milk her again tomorrow?" Armin squatted next to her. "I could take her to Nathaniel's. We use modern equipment, powered by a gas-run generator—just like Isaac's operation, before he sold it."

"Yah, I'm sure. You go ahead."

"Do you remember how to strain the milk? It needs to be refrigerated right away."

"Yah. I saw filters and clean glass containers in the house."

Armin stood, but seemed to be stalling. "Pearly will need to be put out to pasture tomorrow morning after milking."

"I'll remember."

"And you saw how I brushed and washed her?"

"Yah, and dried her udder with a paper towel."

"If you're sure you're okay, I'd better skedaddle on over to Nathaniel's." Armin straightened his hat. "Someone's comin' to Nathaniel's to help with the milking," Armin said. "I don't want him telling my big brother I'm goofing off." His feet pivoted toward the door. "I'll return and muck out the stall later."

"*Denki*—thanks," Esther said. "But, wait, you could answer a question, if you have the time."

He turned to face her. "Ya need help with something?"

"In a way." She knew she was being meddlesome, but plodded ahead. "It's regarding your intentions toward Holly. If I'm not putting the cart before the horse."

He tugged his ear. "There ain't much to tell ya."

She knew Armin was skirting the issue, as most Amishmen would. "Because you don't know, or because you won't let me in on it?" Esther said.

He opened his mouth, then clamped his lips together and sauntered toward the door. "You should ask Holly," he said over his shoulder, and was gone.

Esther kept to her milking. As she squeezed on the cow's teats, random thoughts of Nathaniel dovetailed, but they didn't bring waves of desperation as violently as before. She wondered if she'd already adjusted somewhat to the concept that Nathaniel and she might never be together.

All was in God's hands.

Esther enjoyed the rhythmic motion of her arms. She figured she'd be tuckered out by the time she was finished, but was too pleased with her success to care. It felt satisfying to be busy, concentrating on her task.

After thirty or forty minutes, Esther had finished milking Pearly and was preparing to carry her heavy bounty to the house to store in the refrigerator. Now she wished she had Armin to help her. Surely Holly had heard back from Larry by now. Ach, Esther should be preparing dinner. What would they eat? Esther had been transported while milking, but reality was returning. She hoped Holly could manage Mamm's erratic behavior.

"Esther?" Beth said.

Esther's arm twitched, but she didn't spill a drop of milk, thank the Lord. She imagined herself through Beth's condescending eyes. Beth had always been a head-turner. Although they were almost the same age, Esther couldn't compare to the stunning, willowy blonde. But what did it matter? Esther admonished herself for her vanity.

"Hello, Beth."

"I passed Armin and he told me you were out here." Beth moved closer. Her gaze scanned the barn's interior as if she were stepping into a parallel universe. Esther wondered if Beth had ever ventured into this lofty structure that smelled of silage and manure. Most likely she'd stuck with Mamm in the house, or helped in the vegetable or flower garden.

Esther fabricated a skimpy smile. "What brings you out here?"

"Anna's sleeping." Beth's voice sounded guarded. "And Holly gave me the cold shoulder."

Esther noticed new lines around Beth's eyes and lips, and her skin was pallid. Esther's mind spun back to the tempestuous night she and Holly first arrived in Lancaster County last month. Raindrops had hammered the roof of their rental car, cascading across the windshield. She and Holly had ended up staying with Beth—a scene out of the old TV show *The Twilight Zone*.

"Are you all right?" Esther asked her.

"No—" An expression of dread blemished Beth's glamorous face.

"Is your husband okay?" Esther figured Beth wanted to talk about Holly and Zach's relationship, but Esther vowed not to discuss her daughter behind her back.

"Roger's fine." Beth's hand rose to the base of her throat; her fingers detected her collared shirt wasn't tucked in properly. "There's nothing wrong with our marriage, other than he travels so much." She unbuttoned her jacket and straightened her blouse's collar, but still looked untidy. "When he called last night I told him what a mess I've created. He was furious."

Esther felt an unexpected round of sympathy for this woman for whom she'd held almost a lifetime of well-rooted envy. But she didn't trust Beth; she must have a scheme in mind to bring her out to what Beth would consider a grubby barn. Esther had never seen Beth with mud on her feet—she was wearing beige flats today, unlike Esther, who'd stepped into a pair of rubber boots. Beth wanted something or she wouldn't stoop to speak to Esther.

"Anything I can do for you?" The bucket's weight caused Esther's shoulder to throb; she set the milk down on a bench. What a fine quantity Pearly had provided, more than three women needed.

"I was always jealous of you, Esther." Beth's words sounded like gobbledygook. No way could Beth be jealous of her.

"I don't understand," Esther said in all sincerity.

"You had two loving parents, and a house full of brothers, while I had one parent, my dad—a good man, but he worked all the time—and no siblings." Beth rubbed her hands together as if she were freezing. "Before I went to college and lived in a dorm, many nights I was left at home by myself. I used to get scared and wished I lived with you. And you had Samuel, who adored you."

"You want to discuss Samuel?"

"No, the past is the past. I have no right to bring him up." Beth stabbed her hands into her jacket pockets. "I could never compete with you in any way. You were more beautiful and forthright, while I was run-of-the-mill and timid." Was Beth baiting a trap or toying with her the way a cat might an injured chickadee?

"You had Mamm eating out of your hand," Esther said, wanting to put a stop to Beth's babbling.

"No, I didn't. Anna was most kind, and I'll never be able to thank her enough." Beth's voice sounded scritchy, as if coming down with laryngitis. "But I knew I was a stand-in for you. She longed for her real, flesh-and-blood daughter. And I wasn't Amish, although I gave joining the church some consideration, so I'd fit in. But I didn't fit in. Ever. Like I've been floating along Mill Creek, but never sinking my feet into the silt."

Esther didn't think she'd ever been so dumbfounded. Beth was envious of her, the wayward daughter who'd skipped town and missed her own father's funeral?

"You came home and it was like you'd never been gone," Beth said. "Look at you—still Anna's favorite. And you're as beautiful as ever. You don't need makeup or to touch up your hair."

"Are you being straight with me?" Esther didn't feel attractive, what with her brown hair graying at the temples, nor did she feel worthy of Mamm's love.

"Anna remained faithful to you, praying for your return." She scrunched up her mouth as if swallowing baking soda. "I'm ashamed to admit, I'd hoped you and Holly would leave after a week."

"We hadn't intended to stay more than a few days." Esther massaged her fingers—they'd begun to ache. "Beth, what can I do for you? I need to get the milk into the refrigerator." And she needed to keep dust and debris from its steaming surface.

"I'd better get back home too. My dog, Missy, is expecting her litter. I want to have Zach there in case something goes wrong."

"We're counting on Zach for a ride tomorrow morning."

She blinked several times. "But I might need him. I'm afraid of the sight of blood."

"Can't your husband help you?"

"No, Roger's out of town. I'm on my own again."

In her mind, Esther saw Beth at age fourteen, watching her mother wither away, her lungs racked with cancer, then living with a devastated and distracted father. She envisioned Beth crying herself to sleep at night. No wonder Beth feared death and being alone with a dog whelping its first litter. Compassion for Beth replaced Esther's resentment. She felt tears pushing at the backs of her eyes.

"Beth, if you need your son tomorrow, I understand. We'll find another ride."

"Thank you. I don't deserve your kindness. I've botched things up royally."

In a spontaneous move—before she could think—Esther reached her arms out and hugged the woman she'd wasted a lifetime envying.

As Beth clasped Esther in return, Beth wept.

Minutes later, Beth stepped away, found a hankie in her pocket, and dabbed her eyes. "Can you find it in your heart to forgive me, Esther?"

"Yah, I've judged you harshly, Beth, and held on to bitterness. Please forgive me."

And Lord, she thought, that request goes for you, too.

As Esther and Beth embraced each other again, Esther reflected on her transformation since her return to Lancaster County, and came to the realization she would become baptized Amish, with or without Nathaniel.

CHAPTER
THIRTY-SEVEN

I fished my phone out of my pocket and read Larry's text message:

Found woman's house—a hovel. No sign of her. Will try again later or in AM.

I contemplated dashing out to the barn to tell Mom about the text, but decided against it. Why spoil her fun? If she was having fun. I wondered if she'd find milking Pearly as entertaining as she'd hoped. I might just get up early one morning and ask her for a lesson. And I'd collect eggs, and learn to bake bread and whoopie pies too. About time I became proficient in an Amish farm and kitchen. And soon, I'd start my first quilt. No more standing on the sidelines.

As I proceeded to set the table for supper, a slideshow of my days sitting behind a desk at work skidded by in the back of my brain. Did I miss my job following the roller-coaster stock market from a computer screen? Nope. Did I adore living here in this house? Yup!

Footsteps clomped up the back steps and hinges creaked. I opened the door to the utility room and saw Mom lugging a galvanized bucket and setting it on a counter. She lit a gas lamp, illuminating the room with a warm yellow glow that made her look younger. I came over to see what she was doing.

"Look!" Her face glowed with joy as she showed me the white foamy liquid, its sweet creamy aroma embellishing the air. "Holly, I've had a fine-gut time."

She bustled into the kitchen and I tailed her. She brought three gallon-size glass jars down from the cupboard. They looked clean, but she washed them with sudsy water, rinsed, and dried them, then brought them into the utility room. I followed Mom to observe her strain the milk with dexterity, using a stainless steel strainer with a cotton pad, as if a natural everyday chore.

"And I had a fruitful talk with Beth." She spoke over her shoulder as she poured strained milk into the containers.

I felt my stomach tighten into a knot. "Now what?"

"Her dog's whelping its puppies soon, so Beth needs Zach with her."

"I don't want to dampen your spirits, Mom, but I'll scream if he doesn't show up tomorrow to drive Mommy Anna."

"But darling, he may not. And I told Beth it was okay, we'll fend for ourselves." She screwed on the lids and beckoned me to help her carry the jars of milk into the kitchen and set them on the counter next to the refrigerator. She rearranged the refrigerator's contents to accommodate the jars and set one inside.

My hand moved to my collarbone. "I've already decided if he doesn't drive Mommy Anna to the doctor's as promised, it's over between us." Mom's smile collapsed. "It's not your fault," I said. "I need to get realistic. Zach doesn't have time for a wife, and he's nowhere close to resolving his paternity issues."

She deposited the second jar in the refrigerator. "Holly, do you hope to marry him?"

I stored the third jar, its contents still warm. "I don't know anything anymore other than I want my grandmother to get better." I closed the refrigerator with my hip.

She slipped into the utility room and returned with the empty bucket.

"In the past—before this *greislich* scandal—Zach has been a fine-gut man." Mom moved to the sink. "Mamm told me he never bills her to treat old Cookie. And remember when you hit the cow with your rental car, how supportive he was?"

"That's one collision I'll never forget." A judicious reason not to own an automobile right there. "I've been skittish about driving ever since."

"Thank the Lord, the cow recovered." Mom put the bucket in the sink.

"Okay, I agree, Zach is a generous and kind human being, and a wonderful son, and a skilled veterinarian. But that doesn't make him good marriage material. Maybe next year he'll be ready, but not now. He's up to his neck—"

"You could be the woman to help him through his trials." She poured liquid soap and flushed hot water into the bucket. I stepped to her side and watched the bubbles burst.

"Mom, I don't know where all this charity is coming from. What's gotten into you?"

"For one thing, I've truly forgiven Beth, not that I had a right to resent her to begin with. But I've carried a grudge. With that burden lifted, I feel a hundred pounds lighter." As she talked she washed the bucket, inside and out with a long-handled scouring brush.

"When did you two speak?" My shoulders lifted.

"Fifteen minutes ago. She came into the barn."

"To duke it out?" I imagined two cats hissing at each other.

"No, quite the contrary. She asked for my forgiveness." Mom repeated the washing process using disinfectant.

"Is the sun now rising in the west?"

"Now, I'm serious." Mom rinsed the bucket, flipped it over, and set it in the drying rack. "We talked our differences out. I had no right to feel bitter toward her to begin with."

"Humph, I have to wonder what Beth's after," I said.

"I think she feels genuine repentance." She dried her hands on a towel.

"I'm glad, Mom. I really am, if it's true." I needed to update her on Larry's message. I paused, my mind attempting to phrase the next sentence in an encouraging manner. "While you were in the barn, Larry texted me." My news might launch her into a nosedive, but Mom deserved the truth. "The men apparently found the woman's shack, but she wasn't there."

"I see." Her complexion turned a grainy white. She flung the towel on the counter.

"They'll keep going back until they find her. It's probably some mixed-up mistake we'll all laugh about someday." No, we'd never joke about the situation, whatever the results.

Mom tilted her head back and closed her eyes as if repulsive images were assaulting her.

I took her hand, and she blinked her eyes open. Her shoulders trembled and a sob escaped from her mouth. I hugged her, but her arms were unresponsive.

"Mom, I have the feeling it's going to be okay. You, Mommy Anna, and I will be fine." But giving her false hope might only make her letdown more heartrending. "In the meantime, let's contact a driving service, the guy who brought your sisters-in-law last month. Do you have his number?"

She drifted across the kitchen to the row of drawers under the counter by the refrigerator. "It might be here." Mom opened a drawer, pawed through a mishmash of papers, pens, and doodads, then handed me a business card.

"Thanks." I stuck the card into a pocket of my slacks, then handed her my cell phone. "You hang on to this in case Larry texts again, while I run to the phone shanty and call the driver. Even if Zach turns out to be available tomorrow, I'll bet he doesn't want to hang around when we're at the doctor's and then go to a fabric store for quilting supplies."

"I suppose you're right," she said. "Do you know where the phone shanty is?"

"Yes, and it's about time I got used to using it if I'm going to live here without electricity."

"Please don't make any rash decisions, Holly."

"I'm not. I'm placing a simple telephone call so we won't be stressed in the morning wondering about a ride to Dr. Brewster's. And I need some fresh air." Solitude is what I craved. I punched my hands into the sleeves of my jacket. "Are you okay by yourself?"

"Yah." She brought out a couple of platters from the cupboard, I assumed for items now buried behind the milk.

"I'll be right back." I grabbed a flashlight and trod outside to find darkness shrouding the sunset, leaving only a slice of apricot-orange glow on the horizon. I inhaled a trace of smoke. I hastened to the phone shanty, set apart from the houses, tucked amid bushes and a tree. The air was turning nippy, but I built up heat as I hurried to the one-windowed, weather-beaten shack.

Pulling the card out of my pocket, I remembered the driver, a middle-aged man wearing modern clothing and long sideburns, who'd delivered and picked up Mom's sisters-in-law last month. I shone the flashlight on the card and noticed the bulb flickered and produced a minimal light. I should have tested it before I left.

I dialed his number on a vintage black telephone as old as I was. Next to it sat an answering machine and a telephone book.

"Sure, you betcha," Mel, the driver, told me. "We know where Anna Gingerich lives. I'm driving to Philadelphia tomorrow, but my wife, Cheryl, will be there at nine thirty sharp."

"After the appointment, we want to go shopping," I said.

"No worries. Cheryl will take care of everything."

Since I was here, I decided to call Zach to tell him he was off the hook. His phone rang half a dozen times, then switched to his voice mail. Annoyance brewed, but I reminded myself Zach wouldn't recognize this number on his caller ID. He hadn't answered because he was busy with a patient or away from his phone.

"You don't need to drive us tomorrow, Zach," I said, after the beep. I was determined to keep derision from souring my voice. "We have alternate transportation arranged. Mom told me your mother needs your help delivering Missy's pups. Mom and I would prefer you do that. Really."

Maybe Missy was having her puppies right now. I sighed. Someday, I did want a dog of my own. I thought of Rascal and wondered if he'd found his way to Nathaniel's. But I didn't have time to zip over there to find out.

I imagined coquettish Lizzie fixing Armin a sumptuous meal after he'd finished milking and doing his chores. I didn't know what he liked to eat, but in her charming way she'd have found out. She'd probably baked him his favorite pie too. I couldn't roll out dough—another skill to be mastered.

Armin could be removing his hat right now, breathing in the enticing aromas of stewing chicken, vegetables, and newly baked bread, and then sitting at the table. He might ask Lizzie to join him. For some oddball reason, this lovey-dovey scene grated on me. I doubted Armin would return to our house tonight. What man could resist hot food fresh from the oven, when all we were serving was leftovers: cold sliced meat, cheese, pickles, applesauce, and day-old bread.

I stepped back out into the night and felt disoriented. While I was in the phone shanty, the sun had sunk behind the hills to the west and stars populated the sky. The flashlight flickered. I tightened the aluminum cylinder to no avail; it cast a dim, feeble light.

An owl hooted in a stand of maples. A breeze rustled the treetops; dried leaves scattered to the ground, giving the illusion of movement. Or were they bats?

A sliver of a moon showed itself, but moments later vanished along with the stars behind a mattress of clouds. My flashlight cast elongated shadows as I crept alongside the road. A branch snapped off to the left and I shone my flashlight into the thicket.

An animal had been attacking livestock. I wondered if cougars and bears lived in this county.

"Rascal?" A spike of adrenaline prickled my arms.

The air resounded with silence, save a car's motor ebbing—miles away.

"Lord, protect me." Like opening a floodgate, I was besieged with prayer requests about what I should do with my life, about my grandmother, and Mom and Nathaniel. Maybe both Mom and I were destined to live our lives as spinsters. Was that God's plan for me? I hadn't thanked him for my blessings in ages. Why would he respond to my pleas?

A raindrop splatted on my forehead, then another. Thunder roared in the distance.

"Holly, is that you?" Armin said, trotting up behind me.

I spun around. "What are you doing out here?"

"Lookin' for Rascal. How about you?"

"Using the phone." My musings about him and Lizzie were way off base.

"The phone shanty's not so bad, is it?" His voice seemed cautious, not its usual easygoing cadence.

"Now that you're here to protect me it isn't. I thought I heard a noise."

"Probably a raccoon or an opossum. You'll get used to the area and the sounds of the night soon enough."

"Has anyone reported seeing Rascal?"

"Nee, and I'm worried." He shouted out Rascal's name. "I can't blame a farmer for protecting his livestock. Rascal will be hungry, unless a kind soul fed him. He might skulk around a chicken coop …"

Thunder volleyed across the valley and the breeze gathered velocity. I suspected Rascal couldn't hear Armin's voice calling him.

"We'd better get you home," Armin said to me, and took my free hand. He grasped it firmly. He was just shepherding me home, I told myself, but felt a tingly warmth traveling up to my throat.

"It could be pouring in a minute." He started us walking back. I saw the faint glow of a gas lamp in Mommy Anna's window in the Daadi Haus.

Lightning illuminated the sky—too close for my comfort. I glanced up at Armin's shadowed face and realized I'd grown comfortable with—make that fond of—his looks. And him.

Electricity pulsated through the air, making my senses come alive. A bizarre thought unfurled its wings in the back of my mind. Were Armin's kisses as sweet as his talk? Once he grew a beard, would I enjoy the feel of it against my chin?

."Tell me about Lynnea, this young lady you were so fond of," I said. He slowed to face me. "You have a good memory."

"How about you?" I said. "Do you have good memories of her?" "I do."

"Then why didn't you marry her?"

An automobile, its headlamps on bright, sped toward us.

"I can't quite say. Each time I was fixin' to propose, I got cold feet and couldn't get the words out." He moved closer to shield me when the car zoomed by. "Afterward, I was always relieved." Still clasping my hand, he commenced walking again. "We weren't meant for each other like you and I are."

I didn't know what to think. Was he sincere? "Maybe she's pining over you, waiting for your return," I said, keeping in stride.

"Nee. I recently got an invitation to her wedding in New York State. She's getting married next week."

"Isn't that rather short notice?"

"Not for us. The invitations don't get hand delivered or sent until the couple is published at a Sunday service."

"Do you feel sad about it?"

"Not in the least." He chuckled. "Maybe relieved. When she hears about you and me, she'll have nothing to complain about."

"Hey, wait a minute, Armin—"

"Armin King," he said. "Don't ya like the name King better than Fleming? And don't you like me better than Zach?"

I came to a halt and swiveled to face him. "Are you actually proposing to me?"

"I'm suggesting we court."

As the thunder and lightning increased I tried on the name Holly King for size. "Would we both have to join the Amish church?"

"I can think of a thousand worse things." A gray carriage rolled past us, but Armin didn't seem to notice.

"Are you leading me on?" I said.

"Not in the least. I wasn't going to attend Lynnea's wedding, being as it's so far away, but I would if you came with me. We could take the train or bus. You'd see for sure and certain 'tis no longer anything between the two of us."

"Someday I would like to go to a real Amish wedding, but I don't think that would be proper etiquette. And my mother and grandmother need me. How about you? Are you going?"

"Not without you. Anyway, my brother needs me. Well, who knows what he'll need when he gets home. Or what he'll do."

I tried to imagine how I'd proceed if I were in Nathaniel's shoes. The Ordnung did not allow divorce, but that didn't mean a man couldn't act like a downright scumbag—although I'd yet to hear a story of such an Amish husband. Mom made her own father sound like a petty dictator at times, but she was fifteen or sixteen when she'd made that assessment. When her age, I'd thought the same thing about her. If an Amishman left his wife, she'd have the community to support her. She'd never be alone. My biggest fear—abandonment.

A patrol car swerved to the side of the road, stopped, and the window lowered. "Armin King, is that you?" the uniformed driver said.

Armin let go of my hand and strode to the car. "Hullo, Stewart. How ya doin'?"

"Just got a call from a farmer who reported there's an animal prowling around his sheep. Said he's got his shotgun out. Want to come?"

"You bet." Armin turned to me. "Sorry, Holly, I'd better check this out. Can you get home by yourself or we could maybe give you a lift?"

"No time," the patrolman said.

"I'll be fine," I said.

"Okay." Armin slid his fingertips across my cheeks, then slipped his hands around to the back of my head, and kissed me right on the mouth!

Before I could react, he withdrew and hopped into the car. If he was trying to shock me, he'd succeeded.

I stood in a daze, watching the patrol car's rear lights diminish as it sped away.

CHAPTER
THIRTY-EIGHT

Esther felt like a balloon with a pinprick hole. After speaking to Beth, Esther had entered the kitchen feeling ten feet tall, but she'd shrunk since Holly mentioned Larry's text.

Nathaniel had located the woman's abode.

Esther chided herself; what did she expect? The men had traveled to Ohio with a sole purpose. Nathaniel wouldn't leave until he found the woman even if Larry Haarberg gave up and drove back to Lancaster County by himself.

She hummed, then sang, "To everything—"

Her voice cracked; she swallowed the lump in her throat. "Turn, turn, turn. There is a season, turn, turn, turn." The oldie she and Samuel had performed on street corners decades ago.

She'd believed a new season had arrived and that her life was changing for the better. But perhaps her time for healing, laughter, and embracing was not meant to occur until she met the Lord in heaven.

A torrent of excruciating thoughts churned through her mind like shards of broken glass. Even if the woman in Ohio was a complete stranger, Nathaniel might return a changed man and find Esther drab, her bottle-green eyes faded like Mamm's.

She noticed the saltshaker needed filling. Esther couldn't remember where the extra salt was stored, and she felt light-headed and clumsy, as if her legs had abandoned her. Was Mamm's condition contagious? Ach, she wondered if her mousy brown hair was falling out too.

Listening to raindrops tap the window and a tree branch lashing against the side of the house, Esther walked into the counter and smacked her hip. She gasped from the searing pain. No matter, it was nothing compared to the aching in her heart.

The back door opened and closed, and light footsteps pattered through the utility room. Holly entered the kitchen looking disheveled, her cheeks flushed, her damp hair mussed.

"I secured us a ride for tomorrow." She removed her jacket, its shoulders a shade darker. "And I left a message for Zach, who didn't answer his phone." She hung her jacket on a peg. "It's just as well. One less argument."

"I'm sorry you got caught in the rain." Esther said, rubbing her hip.

"It doesn't matter." Holly's lips parted and she glanced to the ceiling as if contradictory thoughts thrummed through her mind—but she didn't share them with Esther.

"I'll see if your grandma feels good enough to come to the table," Esther said. "Unless there's something you want to talk about."

"No, not really." Holly brought glasses out of the cupboard and poured water into them. As she carried two glasses to the table, a blaze of lightning, followed by a booming crash, made her flinch.

———

The next day, at the one-story clinic on the outskirts of the city of Lancaster, Esther and Holly helped Mamm climb onto the exam table in the endocrinologist's office. The small room's air was laden with bleach and pungent cleaning agents, but Mamm hadn't seemed to notice. Nor had she complained about the glaring overhead lights.

Mamm must have slept through the storm that raged across the county last night. Lightning had spiked the ground with vengeance, striking trees and whitening the sky, followed by deafening roars, sounding like fighter-jets on takeoff. Esther had wondered, as she tossed fitfully, if the tempest were an ill omen, a sign they should stay home today. But this morning, when she rose to milk Pearly, Esther saw violet rays splaying through the fog and the sky clearing. And Mamm had awakened in a cheerful mood. However, when the passenger van showed up, Mamm had balked and refused to leave her house. Esther and Holly had resorted to bribing Mamm with promises of a shopping spree at Zook's Fabric Store, followed by lunch or a dish of ice cream smothered with chocolate sauce, whipped cream, and a maraschino cherry.

Dr. Brewster entered the exam room. "Good morning, Mrs. Gingerich." She put out her hand to shake Mamm's, but Mamm clasped her hands together, her knuckles whitening. She ordinarily insisted people use her first name, but not today.

"Uh—good morning." Mamm had sounded lucid while speaking to the endocrinologist's nurse a few minutes ago, but now her voice quavered, and she seemed to be staring past the doctor.

Dr. Brewster was in her late forties, with angular features and her auburn hair bobbed short—a pleasant, efficient type. She greeted Esther, who introduced Holly.

"Mrs. Gingerich, I've reviewed your blood tests and your symptoms, and spoken to my colleagues." Dr. Brewster logged into a computer, sat on a wheeled stool, and rolled over to Mamm. "I believe you have hyperparathyroidism."

"Her thyroids are working overtime?" Holly asked. She stood at the foot of the examination table, while Esther sat on a chair.

"No, hyperparathyroidism is an excess of parathyroid hormone in the bloodstream due to overactivity of one or more of her four parathyroid glands." Dr. Brewster spoke methodically, her words enunciated.

"I've never heard of it," Holly said.

"The parathyroid glands are four pea-sized glands located on the thyroid gland in the neck." Dr. Brewster pointed to a colored chart on the wall of the interior of the human throat. "If the parathyroid glands secrete too much hormone, as happens in primary hyperparathyroidism, the balance is disrupted. Blood calcium rises, as it has in your case, Mrs. Gingerich. This high level of calcium in the blood is sometimes what signals an abnormality in the parathyroid glands."

Mamm's speckled hand wrapped her neck. "Is it cancer?"

"No, you do not have cancer."

"Praise the Lord," Esther said.

Dr. Brewster looked into Mamm's eyes. "But 85 percent of people with primary hyperparathyroidism have a benign tumor called an adenoma on one of the parathyroid glands, causing it to become overactive. Benign tumors are noncancerous."

Esther stood, her hand moving to Mamm's arm. "'Tis gut news, Mamm, yah?"

"Nee. That hyperpara—whatever she said—is not what's wrong with me."

"Let's hear the doctor out," Holly said. Esther was grateful for her daughter's assistance, even if she'd seemed distracted since sunup and had not helped Esther strain and store Pearly's milk.

"Mrs. Gingerich, leaving your blood tests aside, let's go over your symptoms, shall we?" the doctor said. "You mentioned you're tired all the time, that you forget things, and that you feel more irritable than you used to."

"Nee, I don't feel irritable!"

The doctor sent Esther a sly smile and continued. "Mrs. Gingerich, I've noticed your hair is thinning on the front of your scalp."

Mamm straightened her Kapp, pulling it forward to conceal the balding spot and bandage. "I'm an old woman."

"You have heart palpitations." Dr. Brewster glanced at the computer screen. "And I've noted your blood pressure is high."

"Why, this hyper … parathyroidism doesn't sound so bad, Mamm." Esther stumbled on the word and was glad the doctor didn't toss her a condescending look. "Dr. Brewster, is there a medication Mamm can take for it?"

Dr. Brewster's eyes turned serious, but her voice remained calm. "Surgery is the most common treatment for hyperparathyroidism."

"Nee, I won't have surgery!" Mamm hopped off the exam table. Holly's hands flew out to steady her landing.

"But Mommy Anna," Holly said, her arm linking with Mamm's to stabilize her, "if Dr. Brewster is right, you sound like a textbook case."

"I don't care. I certainly will not have surgery. 'Tis a waste of time and money. Ya know we don't have medical insurance."

"We'll figure a way to pay for it," Esther said. Although she couldn't imagine how. Perhaps take a loan out at the bank, using the house as collateral. Nathaniel had told her he would put the house in Mamm's and her names, but she had yet to see a legal certificate. And he'd made that commitment before Armin's return and before word of his wife.

"Even so, I won't go under the knife." Mamm inched toward the door. "Ach, no cutting on my neck. I can't think of anything worse."

"Even if it makes you feel good enough to visit your sons and your grandchildren in Montana in the spring?" Holly said.

"Well—" Mamm's hand swiped her mouth. "I'll have to pray about it." She turned to Dr. Brewster. "Are you sure that's my problem?"

"Yes, I am."

"Isn't that wonderful news?" Holly said. "You could have something ten times worse."

"I suppose." Mamm seemed unconvinced, and Esther felt lightheaded herself. And guilty for not forcing Mamm into the doctor's office weeks ago. Why had she allowed Mamm to delay? All because she didn't want to accept a ride from Beth. Yes, Esther had been headstrong and unyielding, like a stubborn mule on a sweltering day.

Esther spoke to Dr. Brewster. "We'll talk about it later."

"There's nothing to talk about." Mamm reached for the doorknob and swung the door open.

"On your way out, would you set up another appointment?" the doctor said. "Say, in two weeks? Or sooner would be better."

"I won't be back." Mamm tottered into the waiting room.

"Sure you will," Holly said.

Esther noticed Holly discreetly checking her cell phone. The corners of Holly's mouth dragged down. Esther was disappointed Holly hadn't heard from Larry. Yet, Esther had an inkling something else was troubling her daughter.

CHAPTER THIRTY-NINE

I waved at our hired driver, Cheryl, the heavyset woman sitting behind the wheel of the minivan out front of the clinic. While we were inside seeing Dr. Brewster, the parking lot had filled with cars and a horse and buggy. A busy, thriving practice, I figured—a good sign.

Cheryl hustled out to open the doors. She guided Mommy Anna to the seat behind hers, and helped fasten Mommy Anna's safety belt.

I slid in from the other side and landed in the center of the bench seat. "Mommy Anna, are you sure you're up for shopping?" She looked beat.

"Yah, I can rest on the way there." She sagged against the seat-back and closed her eyes. I imagined she was weighing Dr. Brewster's words. I considered them good news, but my grandma might be terrified.

"We could go straight home if you like," I said, my upper arm resting against hers.

"Nee, I haven't been out of the house all month."

Mom climbed in, sandwiching me between her and Mommy Anna. A nice, cozy nest.

"Where to?" asked Cheryl, and Mom mentioned Zook's Fabric Store in Intercourse.

"You bet, one of my favorite places. And it's on the way." She ferried us onto the main road and pointed us east. "Do you mind if I listen to music?" she asked.

"Not a bit." I figured the background noise would keep Cheryl from hearing our conversation.

"How do you know where Zook's is?" I asked my mother, noticing a sign for 340.

"Greta took me there in their buggy while you were in Seattle." She set her purse on her lap, fiddled with the handle. "Greta didn't want to arrive in Montana empty-handed in case there wasn't a fabric store nearby. We boxed armloads of quilting supplies and material for clothing, and sent them ahead to my brother Isaac."

My phone vibrated several times. I saw Zach's name and number. "It's Zach," I whispered to Mom, and her shoulders slumped. I knew she'd hoped to hear from Nathaniel by now. "I don't have to answer," I said.

"No, go ahead."

I placed the phone to my right ear, nearest Mom. "Hi, Zach. We made it to the doctor's office without a glitch." I kept my volume low. Mommy Anna didn't seem to hear me; her breathing was slow and her head tilted toward the door. But I assumed Mom caught every word.

"And Anna?" Zach said. "Did the doctor have a prognosis?"

"Yes. Not as serious as we'd feared, but I'd rather explain later. We're all in the van."

We slowed as we followed a gray carriage that soon turned onto a smaller road. Then our driver accelerated until she reached a slow-moving truck. She drummed her fingers on the steering wheel to a bluegrass melody.

I glanced out the side window and saw a substantial farm I hadn't noticed on the drive out. Mommy Anna had fidgeted and fretted the whole way to Dr. Brewster's office, but she seemed at peace. For now, anyway.

"That's great," Zach said. "Guess what. Missy had six pups this morning. I'm still at my mother's. You all want to stop by on the way home and see them?"

"We're going to buy quilting supplies right now, and then I think Mommy Anna will be too tired."

"I could come over later and pick you up."

"I don't think so," I said, not wanting to step into an unfriendly environment. "Maybe tomorrow."

Mom smooshed her lips together. "We could go to Beth's with you," she whispered to me.

I shook my head. "Zach, I need to hang up, but I wonder if you know anything about an animal attacking sheep last night."

"Yes, I heard a farmer tried to shoot a dog or coyote that was harassing his herd, but the man thinks he missed the culprit."

"Could the animal be injured?" I imagined a dog lying in a ditch in agony, bleeding to death.

"Yes. Not a good situation if someone comes upon it. You're not alluding to Rascal, are you?"

"No, because I don't believe he's a savage beast." But deep in my heart, I understood anything was possible. I said a short prayer in my head, pleading with God to bring Rascal home safely.

"Holly, promise me you won't go looking for him," Zach said. "If he's hurt he could be dangerous. Please call me right away if Armin needs me to treat him."

"You'd take care of Rascal?"

"Of course I would."

"Thanks, Zach. I'd better say good-bye now."

After I disconnected and handed Cheryl the phone to charge, Mom asked, "Why won't you go see the puppies? Beth and I have made up. I could go with you."

"What if Victoria arrives with her son? And who would look after Mommy Anna?"

"She could come with us or we could hire Lizzie to look after her."

"Now, that's an outlandish idea if I've ever heard one. You're a bundle of surprises, Mom. Don't we have enough to contend with?"

"We can talk about all that later. I promised Mamm we'd go shopping, and I could use a distraction. What better entertainment than selecting fabric for a quilt? Wait until you see Zook's. Plain on the outside, with a spectacular selection of fabrics at reduced prices."

"There's a lot I don't know about you," I told her. "My fault." Over the years Mom had hand-stitched quilts to sell at the Amish Shoppe, but I didn't realize she loved quilting as much as knitting. Did all children pretty much ignore their parents and assume the world revolved around them? I'd been self-absorbed, fixated on building a career I didn't give two cents about anymore.

"Aren't you looking forward to starting a quilt?" she asked me.

"Yes, I want to, but my mind is spinning like a top." I spoke into her ear. "Did you hear what Zach said?"

She nodded. "You're growing fond of Armin, aren't you?"

"Why would you say that? Because I'm concerned about Rascal?"

"Come on, I can tell." Her green eyes searched my face. I felt like I was under a microscope. "Mamm said Armin was sweet on you, so no big surprise," she said.

"I can't be enamored with two men at the same time, can I?" I hoped the driver couldn't hear me above her radio.

Mom leaned against the door to get a better look at me. "They say all's fair in love and war," she said. I assumed she was joking to keep our spirits lifted.

"That doesn't sound like an Amish quote." I tried to sound cheery.

"I suppose not." Her features became solemn, her eyes losing their glimmer. I surmised her thoughts had writhed back to Nathaniel.

"You're getting a text," Cheryl said. She handed me my phone over her shoulder.

"It's from Larry," I told Mom in a subdued voice, and read aloud. "Dropped Nathaniel off at woman's place, in case car was scaring her. Holmes County is a beautiful area, but not as beautiful as you." I felt the heat of embarrassment staining my cheeks.

"Can you write him back and ask him what their plan is?"

"Sure." I texted: *When are U going to pick Nathaniel up? Anyone told U what the woman looks like?*

Returning in 2 hours. Several descriptions. Age could be right. Nathaniel said she sounds too short, but can't women shrink w/age?

Mom read my phone's screen and sighed. I bet alarming possibilities were crisscrossing her mind. I visualized a bag lady like I'd seen in Seattle, living in filthy rags and talking gibberish. Or maybe Nathaniel's former wife was a stylish, foxy lady who'd become Englisch and didn't want to face being shunned.

"Please tell him how much we appreciate him," my mother said, and swallowed.

My mom says Thanks! I wrote.

Glad to help.

"Larry has been a blessing, that's for sure," Mommy Anna said. She'd awakened as we came to a fork in the road, then rolled past Zook's Fabric Store, a pale yellow two-story structure that looked like it could have once been a home.

Cheryl took a left into a parking lot and stopped near the entrance to Nancy's Notions and Clothing, part of the same building. Only a couple other cars were parked in the center of the lot; at the far end stood a goat pen.

"Three stores under one roof, so you can enter here," Cheryl told me. "This parking lot was jam-packed last month, but the bulk of the tourists have gone home. You may have the stores mostly to yourself and locals."

A gray carriage pulled up to the building in front of a sign that said "No Parking." Two young Amish women got out, tied their horse to the hitching post, and entered the store. I admired their graceful dresses and aprons, their delicate white prayer caps.

"I need hooks and eyes and thread from Nancy's Notions," Mommy Anna said.

"Sure you're up to this?" I asked her.

"Yah. I just had a *wunderbaar* dream while I was sleeping." Her eyes brightened. "Esther and I will make you a quilt for a wedding present. We can work on it together. The women in Zook's will help us select everything we need. The staff is excellent."

"Hold your horses, who says I'm getting married?"

"Are you joking, Holly?" Mom snickered. "You have suitors coming out your ears."

"Yah, three of them," Mommy Anna said, her voice animated. "Only one is Amish, but who wouldn't want a quilt as a wedding gift?"

Cheryl tipped her ear back, probably to listen to us, not that I could blame her.

"I'd love to make Holly a quilt, whether she marries or not." Mom looped her arm through mine.

"Thanks, Mom." From watching her, I recalled the hours and meticulous care for details required to complete a hand-stitched quilt. "I'm grateful to both of you, but, Mommy Anna, don't your hands hurt too much?"

"Dr. Brewster said she's going to make me better." She readjusted her glasses and set them on the bridge of her nose. "Unless you think her diagnosis is incorrect."

"No, I believe her," I said.

Mommy Anna's elbow tapped mine. "First, Holly should choose a husband," she said. "Then I'll decide if I want the surgery."

I could see it all now: my grandma would delay the surgery exactly as she'd delayed today's appointment, until it was too late. And I lost her.

A wacky idea came to mind. "I will choose a spouse, Mommy Anna, after you commit to the surgery," I shot back. "Once we schedule the date with Dr. Brewster."

"Holly, what are you thinking?" Mom gaped at me. "Marriage is not to be trifled with lightly."

I winked at Mom, who stared back with huge eyes.

"It's not fair." Mommy Anna crossed her arms, jamming her thumbs under her armpits. "You're trying to trick me."

"I want what's best for you," I said. "Both of us have monumental decisions to make." I did want to get married, someday.

Cheryl got out and stood near Mommy Anna's door, but didn't open it. Several minutes passed. We three in the van stared straight ahead until Mommy Anna finally smoothed her apron.

"Yah, okay, I'll agree, Holly, if you'll dress Amish for a week, before you choose your future husband." Mommy Anna grinned, the first genuine toothy grin I'd seen in weeks. "And that includes a Kapp."

"Say you'll do it," Mom whispered. "She'll probably forget."

"No, I won't," Mommy Anna said, proving her hearing was excellent.

"You promise you'll do what Dr. Brewster wants?" I said. "I'm not going to trek around wearing Amish garb, then have you tell me you forgot this agreement." I undid my seat belt.

"I won't forget. You want me to put it in writing?"

"Not a bad idea," my mother said.

I turned to Mommy Anna. "In other words, I could call Dr. Brewster's office right now and set up a pre-op appointment?"

"Yah, I agree to do it. You place the call." Her lower lip tightened. "But I won't go unless you fulfill your half of the bargain. I mean it."

"Where will I get a dress that will fit me other than at Nathaniel's?" I regretted bringing up his name for Mom's sake.

"Mine would be too big in the middle," Mommy Anna said. "But I think I have a couple in the attic that were Esther's."

"They'd be so old," Mom said. "Why did you hang on to them?" She leaned forward to look at Mommy Anna.

"I'd hoped for another daughter," Mommy Anna said, "but the gut Lord gave me five sons, so I'm not complaining." She reached across me and patted my mother's knee. "And the best daughter there ever was."

Mom's eyes grew moist. "Guess I have the best Mudder in the whole world too."

"Holly, what's your favorite color?" Mommy Anna tossed me a wry smile.

I glanced down at my teal-blue jacket. "Any shade of blue."

"Then we'll sew you a blue wedding dress, too."

"Now, wait a minute. Let's stick to one everyday dress, okay?"

"Yah, for now."

CHAPTER FORTY

While Esther and Mamm walked toward the front of Zook's, past a plethora of patterned fabrics Esther was pining to explore, Holly stepped outside with her phone to call Dr. Brewster's office. Esther was astounded Holly had cajoled Mamm into committing to surgery, but she knew Mamm could change her mind. Her decisions wavered like wet noodles these days.

"May I help you?" an Amish saleswoman said to Esther. Save one Englisch shopper, Esther and Mamm were the only customers in the store.

"Yes, I want to sew two Amish dresses and aprons," Esther said. "One for myself and one for my daughter, who's outside."

The saleswoman's brows raised. "For both of yous?" She'd no doubt seen Holly carrying a cell phone and dressed in jeans. Well, both Holly and Esther were dressed Englisch.

Esther's fingertips explored a bolt of cotton fabric, a vibrant cranberry she envisioned as part of a quilt. She turned to the twenty-something Amish saleswoman, her eyes round.

"I'm joining the Amish church," Esther said, "and it's about time I dressed properly. Now, my daughter—she's another subject. But we both need a dress and an apron."

The woman stared back in silent surprise.

"Mamm, does your treadle sewing machine still work?" Esther asked.

"As well as ever." Mamm shuffled over to them. "I almost gave it to Greta to take with her to Montana. Now I'm glad I didn't."

"If we can afford to, we should send her one as a Christmas gift." Esther had preferred her brother Isaac's wife over her other four sisters-in-law.

"That's a gut idea, Essie."

Esther admired the saleswoman's dress. "I like the color you're wearing."

"We call this plum." The woman moved toward an assortment of solid-colored fabric and selected a bolt.

Esther noticed it was 100 percent polyester—easy to wash and line-dry, and no ironing required. "Would you please sell me the correct amount of yardage? I'm a little rusty."

"Yah, glad to." The saleswoman carried it to the counter where another saleswoman stood cutting fabric for the Englisch woman, a brunette with short hair.

Holly wandered inside, stuffing her phone in her hip pocket.

"Come take a look at these fabrics," Esther said. "I'm going to sew a dress and apron for both of us, if you're serious about wearing them."

"If Mommy Anna holds up her end of the bargain." Her eyes met Mamm's, and she nodded.

In the past, Holly had borrowed one of Nathaniel's daughter's dresses and aprons; Esther was grateful Holly didn't suggest she use them again. Just thinking about Nathaniel made Esther's throat close up as if she'd bitten into a lemon wedge.

"What color do you want?" Esther asked her, trying to keep an uplifted expression on her face. She noticed Holly eyeing the expansive selection of black fabric displayed against a partition wall. "Look over here," Esther said, drawing her daughter's attention to the many colors suitable for an Amish dress. "You said you like blue and it suits you."

"How about this cobalt blue?" the saleswoman said, her hand on a bolt of fabric sandwiched between a whale-gray and a pale blue. The saleswoman unraveled it for Holly to see.

"I love it." Holly stroked its smooth texture. "This isn't for an Amish wedding gown, is it?"

"It could be worn at a wedding," the saleswoman said.

"No, it's for a work dress," Esther said. "What you can wear when you help me milk Pearly."

"But the fabric's so soft and pretty, I'd hate to get it dirty."

"Then I'll sew two dresses, if you like. Another one to wear while this is being laundered. It's about time I taught you how to do the washing without electricity."

"Okay, how about the cobalt and that one across the aisle with the sunflowers?" Holly demonstrated more enthusiasm than Esther had expected.

Esther scanned the rows and rows of ornate and unique fabrics. No store in Seattle could compare to Zook's. It took all her willpower not to stroll up and down the aisles. "Sorry, Holly, we'll need to stick to solid colors. Nothing with a pattern or that's extremely bright."

"All right, then, what about this chestnut-brown?" Holly gathered up a bolt of material. Esther wondered if Holly would adhere to her agreement. No matter, Esther would go along with Holly's scheme. Esther had always enjoyed sewing.

"Yah, that's pretty, almost the color of your hair."

"But Mom, are you sure you want to go to all this inconvenience? I'm only going to wear it for a week."

"I can sew quickly."

"I remember." As a girl, Holly had hated wearing Esther's handmade dresses; Esther hadn't blamed her for wishing to be like all the other girls.

"I might sew another for myself in this asparagus green." Esther pointed out the fabric to Mamm. "Do you think it would be prideful to have my dress highlight my eyes?"

Mamm gazed into Esther's face. "Nee, as long as in your heart you're not showing off."

"I would be, if honest with myself. Maybe I'll get the eggplant-purple instead." Growing up, Esther's parents had insisted she and her brothers obey stringent rules; God expected humility and obedience. Showing off was strictly *verboten*, but it seemed Mamm had mellowed.

Fifteen minutes later, Mamm yawned and stood near the cash register, a sign Esther needed to cut the trip short. They had yet to select their quilting supplies, but she quickly paid for their purchases. They left by the front door and rounded the building to the parking lot. Cheryl, their driver, helped them schlep their bags of fabric to the van.

"Now, shall we go for a bite to eat?" Esther asked.

"Nee, I'm too tuckered out," Mamm said. "I could keel right over."

With Cheryl's assistance, Mamm climbed into the van and sat next to Holly, who was getting in from the other side.

Esther slid in on Holly's right.

"I forgot thread," Mamm said as Cheryl shut Mamm's door to bar an attempted exit.

"We'll come back another day," Esther said. "We'll need quilting fabric, not to mention more yardage for capes."

"And slippers for Nathaniel," Mamm said, reaching for the door handle. "I told him we'd buy him a pair."

Ach, the last item Esther dared purchase. She was relieved Cheryl said, "I don't think Nancy's carries slippers."

Cheryl started the engine. "All buckled up?" She nosed the van out of the parking lot and onto the main road.

Esther wondered how long Mamm's recuperation from surgery would take. Esther guessed the operation would occur at Lancaster General Hospital, but she dare not speculate aloud.

"I've accumulated many a scrap of fabric over the years," Mamm said, capturing Esther's attention. "But I don't recall where I stored them. In cardboard boxes I s'pose."

"While Mom sews, you and I can have a treasure hunt in the house until we find them," Holly said to Mamm. "It'll be fun."

"*Des gut.* They've got to be around somewhere."

"If we can't find them, we'll come back here," Esther said.

"Is this too far to travel using a buggy?" Holly asked, craning her head to watch a high-stepping horse and carriage.

"Not at all," Mamm said. "Armin could bring us."

"Or I could," Esther said. "Do you think your mare, Topsy, will obey me, Mamm?"

"Yah, she's as cooperative as they come, like she can second-guess you. And she needs to get out more so she doesn't put on weight."

"I'm glad I never owned a car," Esther said, "so I won't miss it."

"Do you think I could drive a horse and buggy by myself?" Holly asked.

"Sure, if you start with a nice slowpoke mare like Topsy," Esther said.

"But how will I get her bridled and harnessed to the buggy? All those leather straps look so complicated."

"I think I remember, but Armin would do a better job teaching you."

"Yah," Mamm said. "You let Armin give you some tips. He knows horses like nobody else."

Holly crossed her legs at the ankles. "Then why did Galahad run away?"

"Could have happened to anyone," Mamm said.

Fatigue encompassed Esther; she let her spine ease into the cushioned seatback. In spite of her determination to stay focused on their conversation, Esther's thoughts careened back to Nathaniel. And his former wife. Esther didn't know the woman's name; it was never mentioned. She knew the Amish in general didn't dwell on the deceased. Still, to not even know her name? Now that Esther considered her and Nathaniel's courtship, she realized she'd only met Nathaniel's two daughters a couple of times, even though his Tina and her husband, with their three children, owned a farm two miles east, and Hannah and her husband dwelled down in Strasburg. Esther had chalked that idiosyncrasy up to the fact that each daughter had a spouse and a household to keep in order. Nathaniel had taken Esther by to meet each daughter, who'd both been standoffish and not invited her in. But Esther reminded herself she was Englisch, and she recalled how Holly had acted the one occasion she'd met a man Esther had casually dated—maybe twice. Holly had not wanted a replacement for her father, and Esther wondered if even now she wished Nathaniel would disappear from the scene.

More troubling thoughts clattered in Esther's head like pellets of hail. She figured Nathaniel had visited his daughters over the past few weeks and not mentioned it to Esther. His daughters must be waiting with bated breath, wondering if their mother were alive. Holly would be frantic in their position.

Esther must have dozed off, because suddenly she heard Holly speaking into her cell phone. "Mom's right here, would you talk to her?"

Holly handed her the phone. "Nathaniel?" Esther's voice came out a squawk.

"Sorry, no, it's Larry."

She reined in her volume. "Hello, Larry, I apologize. I thought—" They were headed north, driving by Nathaniel's farm, almost home. If she were not confined in the van she could speak more openly. How should Esther phrase her next question?

Larry saved her the embarrassment. "Nothing new to report," he said.

"May I speak to Nathaniel?" Esther asked.

"No can do," Larry said. She heard birds chirping in the background; he must be standing outside. "Nathaniel said he doesn't want to talk to anyone. He's pretty broken up. He's sitting in my car with his head in his hands. Say, could you put Holly back on?"

Of course Nathaniel would be on tenterhooks, but why would he not speak to her? "Yes, she's right here." Esther's hand shook as she passed the phone back to Holly.

"Tell me all." Holly leaned over to Esther and held the phone between their ears so both could hear Larry's voice. "Possibly a paranoid-schizophrenic, needing to be institutionalized," he said. "No ID, no friends. Nobody seems to know how long she's lived there. Over five years."

"Larry, you don't have to spend one more night there." Holly sat taller. "I'm sure Nathaniel will understand." Another pause, during which Esther's ears filled with white noise—just as well she couldn't hear Larry anymore. "Well, okay," Holly said, "I'll talk to you in the morning. And Larry? Thanks a million."

"I don't even know her name," Esther muttered to Holly as Cheryl drove around the side of the house. "Nathaniel's wife—I don't know her name."

"Larry said Nathaniel called her Deborah," Holly whispered in Esther's ear.

Esther remembered a girl named Deborah from her childhood, but couldn't recall her features, only that she was a few years younger, on the tall side, and shy.

Cheryl came to a halt in the barnyard and helped Mamm emerge from the van as Esther and Holly got out with their bags.

"Let me take those." Cheryl scaled the stairs and left the bags by the door, then trotted back down.

"How much do we owe you?" Esther brought out her wallet.

"Not a thing. Zach Fleming paid us ahead of time over the phone using a credit card."

"But surely you'd accept a tip."

"No, ma'am, he included one."

CHAPTER FORTY-ONE

"How did Zach know you were driving us?" I asked Cheryl as we stood outside her van in the barnyard.

"My hubby didn't tell me," she said. "Want me to call him and find out?"

"No, not necessary." I slipped an arm through the crook of Mommy Anna's elbow. "I'll ask Zach when and if I see him." Maybe he'd called every driving service until he struck gold.

"We're very grateful," Mommy Anna said.

"Yes," my mother echoed.

I was thankful too, but did I want a husband who gave generously from his wallet and not of his time? To me, time was of more value than money.

"Call Mel and me again when you need us," Cheryl said, and hopped into the van. She backed out onto the lane, turned around, and drove away.

Once up the stairs and in the kitchen, Mommy Anna thudded onto her favorite padded chair at the table. She polished the vinyl cloth with her hand. "I'm starvin'."

"Me, too, I'm famished." Mom brought out leftover meatloaf, cheeses, lettuce, chow-chow, and pickles from the refrigerator. I set the table for three, and sliced bread.

"I'm so hungry I almost forgot to thank the dear Lord again," Mommy Anna said, when we were all seated. "I can't recall such a busy morning."

We bowed our heads. I imagined our prayers—zinging around like flying saucers, vaulting through outer space, somehow reaching the source of all creation, to thank God for our blessings and that we were congregated together in harmony. Followed by diverse requests, ranging from Nathaniel, Mommy Anna's illness, Rascal's welfare, the mysterious doll, my future …

My Sunday school teacher in Seattle used to say, "Let go and let God." I prayed the Lord would lead me down his chosen road, not the other way around.

Our silent prayer culminated with "Amen."

"As soon as we're done eating, I'll clean the kitchen and then start sewing," Mom said. She constructed a meatloaf sandwich with plenty of mayonnaise and ketchup, and set it on Mommy Anna's plate.

We nibbled at our lunch and skipped dessert.

Mom and I cleared the table and stored the uneaten food in the refrigerator.

"Holly, why don't you take Mamm into the Daadi Haus for a nap while I start the dishes," Mom said.

"Okay." I helped my grandmother to her feet, using the full strength of my arms. In the Daadi Haus, she collapsed on her bed, her head landing on her pillow.

"*Denki*," she said. "We'll have our treasure hunt later."

"Sure." I removed her shoes and spread a quilt over my precious grandmother. "Have a nice snooze." Would she remember our agreement? In any case, I was going to forge ahead and do my part.

When I returned to the kitchen, Mom had wiped and dried the table and spread several yards of our newly purchased cobalt blue fabric across its surface.

"I'm starting your dress first." She held out a measuring tape and gauged my arm length, waist, and hips—I was used to the routine from my childhood. She jotted down her findings.

"Do you have a pattern?" I asked.

"Yes, passed on for generations. I'll make what we have fit. I may not get the apron done before Mamm wakes up, but you can wear. one of hers. And we'll find you a Kapp."

"My, you sure are in a hurry."

"I'd best keep my mind occupied so I don't stew over what's beyond my control." She brought out worn pattern pieces made of stiff brown paper and arranged them on the fabric. "When's Mamm's next doctor's appointment?"

"Thursday morning. I figured she has more energy before noon."

"Good thinking."

"The receptionist seemed ecstatic Mommy Anna's coming back."

The corners of Mom's mouth crescented up like a half moon. "Then I'd say we'd better get your week started, yah?"

"Yes, and I'm looking forward to it. Wait until Armin sees me."

"Armin's your number one choice?"

"No. Well—I don't know anymore."

I heard an automobile engine, and tires alongside the house. I bopped over to the window and saw Zach's pickup coming to a halt.

Mom placed the pincushion next to the fabric. "If that's Zach, please ask him in so I can thank him."

"All right." I had mixed feelings as I watched him get out of his pickup, like oil and vinegar gurgling in my stomach. But Mom was right about needing to thank him.

Opening the back door, I couldn't ignore Zach's confident posture, his handsome face. "Come on in," I called and beckoned with my hand.

He mounted the stairs two at a time. "How is Anna?"

"According to Dr. Brewster, she has hyperparathyroidism, if I said that correctly. And she needs surgery."

He wore a sober expression, how he might look when talking to pet and livestock owners. "Dr. Brewster is highly respected." He nodded, as if he understood the condition. "But you can ask for a second opinion if you feel unsure."

"No, the chance of getting my grandma to another doctor is about zero to nothing. And Mommy Anna agreed to the necessary surgery."

"That's fantastic. You've made great progress." He stepped closer, but I backed away.

"Well, not without a price." I led him through the utility room and into the kitchen.

My mother had finished pinning the pattern to the fabric and held a pair of shears. "Zach, thank you so much for paying for the driver and passenger van today." She set the scissors aside.

"It's the least I could do after promising Holly I'd take you. Any word from Nathaniel?"

"No." She took hold of the scissors and snipped into the fabric.

"Nothing confirmed yet," I said. "Mom's concentrating on her new sewing project—an Amish dress for me."

Zach scanned the material. "Nice color. Did you say it's for you, Holly?"

"Yup."

"Uh, does this mean you're planning to join the Amish church?"

"I'm fulfilling a wish for my grandmother, as part of a bargain. After a week, I don't know."

His lips parted a skosh; he looked flummoxed, as Mommy Anna would say.

"You have a problem with it?" I asked.

"No, but you've certainly caught my curiosity."

"*Dabbish* fingers," my mother said, and sucked her thumb. She must have poked herself with a needle or scissors. Not like her to be clumsy or careless.

Zach eyes riveted onto mine. "You want to come see Missy's puppies now?" He glanced at his wristwatch. "I have a couple hours of free time."

I did want to see them, but not Beth or whoever else might swing by.

"Why do you want me to see them so much?" I asked.

"Because I get pick of the litter. Several people are waiting in line, but I may choose first. And I want your opinion."

"Don't you know ten times more about dogs than I do?" I deliberated on his remarks about Rascal, and felt a wave of uncertainty regarding Zach's judgment. But maybe Zach had assessed Rascal correctly. Armin had mentioned he'd been a stray.

"I think I'd better stay home and keep my mother company."

"Nee, you go ahead," Mom said. "I'm happiest when my hands are busy. 'Idle hands are the devil's workshop,' Mamm told me many a time when I was growing up." She inspected her thumb. "But you could leave your cell phone, if you wouldn't mind. Or is that a mistake? Here I am sewing an Amish dress and wanting to speak on a phone."

"In this case, I think even the bishop would give you the green light."

"I doubt that," Mom said, but took my phone from me.

I turned to Zach. "Are you positive your mother will let me in her house?"

"Yes, we've already spoken. She says she's sorry she hurt your feelings, and so am I. Sometimes I don't understand her, maybe part of the reason she and my father split up for a few years. Boy, is my dad hopping mad since she told him she'd invited Victoria over."

"Will Victoria be there?" I recoiled at what I used to consider a beautiful name—one of my favorites. A possibility for my future daughter should I have one.

"Absolutely not," he said. "Say, do you want me to take your laptop to Mom's or to the office to get it charged? I should have thought of doing that weeks ago."

"It's weird, but I haven't missed using it, or watching the news, or picking up emails. There's so much going on with my family. Like I'm living in a soap opera, so who needs TV?"

I went outside with him and inhaled the resilient barnyard air. My heart brimmed with gratitude and hopefulness. Mommy Anna had a diagnosis! She'd agreed to surgery, a procedure Dr. Brewster said would reduce if not erase her symptoms. Yet I was hesitant about leaving her and my mother, whose future was anything but certain. And I was about to blunder into Beth's lioness den with a man I still didn't trust.

Zach seemed at ease, his arms swinging at his sides as we approached the pickup. I slowed my pace.

"Are you worried about my mother?" Zach opened the passenger door, but I made no move to get in. "She promised to be on her best behavior," he said.

"She's not our only problem."

"I'm telling you the truth about Justin—if that's what's on your mind." Zach steepled his hands. "I've done the math. Justin was born a year after Victoria got hitched. I certainly wasn't having relations with her. Maybe the little boy is someone else's child, but I'd swear using a lie detector, he's not my son."

"Then why is Beth sure he is?"

"My mother is apparently gullible. And she knows I'd like a family."

"Wait a minute," I said. "How can you be so glib about a woman you supposedly loved and a little boy who doesn't have a dad? You did love Victoria at one time didn't you?"

"Yes, I did." He pinched the bridge of his nose. "At least I thought I did."

"And you would have married her?"

"Yes." He blinked away a veneer of moisture pooling across his eyes.

"But now, you don't give a can of beans for her or her innocent child? What if you miscalculated and Justin really is your son?"

"Someday I'd like a child, more than anything. And a faithful, loving wife." He wiped the corner of his eye. "But I'm not his father."

His hands glided to my waist and he drew me toward him. "I'd better hug you now," he said, "before you start wearing straight pins."

He bent his head, his lips nearing mine. I felt him inhaling my breath, drawing me closer like a force of gravity I couldn't resist.

CHAPTER FORTY-TWO

Esther pieced together, basted, and sewed Holly's blue dress at a breezy clip. All she needed to do was hem the skirt, a simple assignment. As she threaded a needle, she recalled the many articles of clothing she'd crafted for herself and her brothers when she was a young teen on this very Singer treadle machine, her feet working the pedal. Who needed an electric sewing machine? Who needed electric anything?

"Holly?" Mamm entered the sitting room, passing through the front hall from the Daadi Haus. "Is Holly ready to go on our treasure hunt?"

"To look for quilting scraps?"

"Yah." Mamm stretched her arms. "They've got to be hiding somewhere."

Esther was astounded Mamm had remembered and hoped her memory wouldn't relapse in twenty minutes.

"Holly went out for about an hour to see Beth's dog's new pups." Esther held up her almost finished dress. "Like it?"

"You've done a fine job, Essie."

"Thanks. I need to hem it, and I haven't sewed the apron yet. Could Holly borrow one from you until I do?"

"Mine will be too big for a slender *Maedel* like Holly." Mamm patted her tummy, which seemed flatter. "I'll go up in the attic and see what I can find."

"No, I can't let you. The stepladder's too steep." Esther dreaded having to enter the dark and stuffy cavern, but said, "I'll do it, if you really think I'll find clothing."

"You remember where the attic is?"

"Yes. At the top of the stairs and down a few yards." A rectangle in the ceiling, a short length of twine to pull, and a stepladder would slide down. "Maybe we should ask Armin," Esther said. Nathaniel could surely reach the string and lower the ladder, but no use wishing for him to appear.

"I don't want to wait that long," Mamm said. "Let's be ready for Holly when she gets back. We might need to launder the apron."

"I'm not exactly a teenager myself," Esther said. "If I slip and fall, I might not get up again."

"Pshaw. Why would you fall? You've been in the attic a hundred times."

"That's when I was a girl. I'm in my fifties."

"Sounds young to me." Mamm grabbed hold of the banister and plodded up the stairs. "You coming?"

"Yes, wait up." Esther followed closely on her heels in case Mamm tumbled backward. As they proceeded Esther ruminated over Mamm's hanging on to her clothing from her youth and her heart swelled with gladness. "Did ya really know I'd return?" Esther asked.

"Yah, I knew the Lord would answer my prayers when he was good and ready." Mamm reached the second story, moved forward a few feet, and tilted her head back to survey the ceiling. "We'll need a chair, unless you can reach the pull." Mamm pointed at the three-by-four-feet rectangle of wood in the ceiling, a short cord dangling from it.

Esther had never been tall enough to snag the string, meaning she'd need a chair. "Ach, how did I get myself into this?" But her mind was occupied and less tormented over Nathaniel or receiving the doll, which she'd pretty much decided was a fluke.

She fetched the wooden straight-backed chair from her room— the bedroom she'd slept in as a child. She eyed the chest her father had made for her decades ago, still abundant with gifts for her future wedding. She might give the contents to Holly should Nathaniel find his wife or change his mind about marrying Esther—for any reason.

She climbed onto the chair and felt it wobble. Pulling on the string and opening the attic door, time seemed to repeat itself, like rewinding thread on a sewing machine's bobbin, layer upon layer. When would Esther understand why she was so all-fired determined to leave this home as a teenager and never return? Pride had played a role, and bigheadedness. She'd been *grossfiehlich*.

Her pastor back in Seattle promised her the blood of Jesus had paid for her sins, and Bishop Troyer agreed: her transgressions had been atoned. She didn't need to ask for forgiveness over and over like a never-ending loop-de-loop.

The wooden staircase—indeed more like a stepladder— descended to the floor at a less than forty-five-degree angle. Esther moved the chair aside and placed her foot on the first skinny step.

"Wait, take this." Mamm handed her a flashlight.

Esther had to laugh at herself. Did she think a light bulb awaited her? "Thanks, Mamm." Esther had never been afraid of heights, but a troubling sensation of impending disaster assailed her.

"Anything wrong?" Mamm asked.

"Nee." Esther didn't want Mamm worrying; it might send her backsliding when her mood was so nicely elevated. "You stay there or sit on that chair." Esther peered into the attic's dimness. The flashlight illuminated the sloped ceiling, and stacked cardboard boxes and trunks, casting eerie shadows into the bleak corners.

The dense air was woven with the aromas of dried cedar, mothballs, deteriorating fabric, and what could be an abandoned wasps' nest.

Using her forearms, she hoisted herself up and was able to stand erect. Dat, a tall man, had to hunch, as she recalled. She leaned over to speak to Mamm through the hole. "Shall I search in the boxes or trunks?"

"Try the trunks first." A moment later Mamm's head appeared.

"What are you doing?" Esther said. "Please go back down."

"Nee, I've come this far." She clambered into the attic with what seemed to be great satisfaction.

Esther assured herself that eventually Holly would return to help Mamm down the ladder. But really, they needed a man's strong arms.

Mamm extracted a small flashlight from her apron pocket and shone the beam around the attic, with its sloped ceiling. "I never thought I'd be up here again."

"Well, ya shouldn't be."

"If I slip and break my neck it'll save the cost of surgery with Dr. Brewster."

"No, the hospital bills will be even higher. Don't you dare fall, Mamm. I'll never forgive myself if you do."

She cackled. "For that reason alone I'll be careful." No sooner had the words floated out of her mouth than Mamm walked into a trunk and faltered, dropping her flashlight. Her hands reached out to steady herself on the wooden chest, almost waist-high. She picked up the flashlight and aimed it at the trunk. "Try looking in this one."

Esther lifted the heavy lid; it fell back against the sloped ceiling. A cloud of dusty air floated out. She slid her hands into the trunk and felt layers of aged fabric, some soft as a day-old lamb. She extracted several items, all clothing from her youth. Mamm had told the truth; she'd hoped for another daughter. Esther's father's untimely demise had killed that dream.

"Dat's death was in part my fault," Esther said, grateful her face was shaded in the darkness. "He wouldn't have been on the road that night if I hadn't left for California. I'd do anything to reverse time and undo my actions."

"It was God's will. My Levi's time had come. "'Tis *unsinnich*— senseless—to rehash the past." Mamm moved to Esther's side and pulled out a couple black aprons. "I admit I kept these for sentimental reasons too. I missed you so. I couldn't bear to part with your things."

"Oh, Mamm—"

"Hush, don't spoil our treasure hunt. These aprons might fit Holly." She held them out for Esther's viewing, then draped them over her forearm. "Let's keep looking. The scraps of fabric have got to be somewhere." Inching along, her toe hit a low object and she faltered again—into Esther's arms, praise the Lord.

"Who would leave something there, where a person would stumble over it?" Esther picked up a metal container and noticed its small latch.

Mamm said, "Ach, I probably did, silly me."

"What is it?" Esther asked.

"An old tin bread box."

"I think I remember it from when I was a child." Esther took the oblong metal container from her and was surprised by its weight, as if a loaf of bread were entombed within. "I'll bring it downstairs. We could use another bread box, but I hate to think what's inside." With Mamm's flashlight illuminating it, Esther undid the latch and was staggered to see dozens of unstamped envelopes.

"That's where I put them," Mamm said. "But how did they get up here?"

"The letters from Jeremiah Fisher?" Outrage inundated Esther, as if she'd sliced into a shoofly pie to find it made of mud. "Why didn't you send them to me?"

"Because Beatrice refused to put your last name on them. She said you weren't a Fisher. Essie, I confess I opened a couple and read them. I knew it was wrong of me, but I thought if my Esther reads these she'll never come home."

"You had no right." Yet Esther was reminded of her own lame excuse for not showing Mamm's many letters to Holly.

Esther rifled through them. Sure enough, only the name *Esther* was scrawled on the front of each envelope. "Never mind, Mamm, I understand you were trying to protect Holly and me."

"Thank you, daughter. I knew you'd come home and I'd give you the letters." She scratched her head. "Then I forgot about them. You want to read them now?"

"Not today."

CHAPTER
FORTY-THREE

I cuddled the border collie puppy and breathed in its honey-sweet aroma. I'd never held a newborn pup, its eyes still closed and its coat like velvet. It yawned and bobbed its head. "Looking for your mama?" I asked.

Missy stared up at me with wary brown eyes, but she stayed in the whelping box attending to the remaining five pups. Half the litter was male and half female; they were waking up hungry.

"It's okay," Zach said to Missy, and stroked her forehead. "Holly won't hurt your baby girl." He sat on a nearby chair, and I on the floor by the wooden whelping box Zach had built that resided in the TV room, off the kitchen.

"I'd better put you back," I said, and gently returned her to Missy, who nuzzled and licked her off as the puppy wedged itself among its siblings and latched on to her next meal.

I thought about each puppy transitioning, growing incrementally, until it reached the size of its mother, whose girth had shrunk substantially since I'd seen her last. It occurred to me there was wisdom to be learned from her about patience and loyalty.

I felt warmth kindling in my chest, a stirring in my abdomen. I ached for a child of my own. At my age, I might be infertile, for all I knew. Zach told me he wanted children, but could I provide them? He'd also mentioned possibly adopting when he'd proposed weeks ago.

I examined Zach's symmetrical features and wondered if he'd make a good dad. He was attentive to his mother—to a fault, in my opinion—and seemed to get along with his father. I'd assumed Zach would be an excellent parent, but in truth, I hardly ever saw him. Zach had always acted with kindness and understanding, but I'd also witnessed his antagonism toward Armin and Rascal. I wondered if he'd ever direct hostility at me. And really, if he wanted to marry me so much, why hadn't he spoken the three words I yearned to hear? That he loved me. Nor had we sat down with a calendar to set up a date. He must know it took more than twenty-four hours to plan a wedding.

"Found your favorite, Holly?" Beth said, strolling into the room from her kitchen, only yards away. She settled on the leather couch against the wall, situated across from a flat screen TV. A framed print of her husband holding up a whopper of a trout adorned the far wall.

"They're all precious," I said, not meeting her gaze. Beth had greeted me cordially at the door a few minutes ago, but I felt on guard, suspicious of the woman who'd originally welcomed Mom and me with open arms, before Victoria's arrival.

"I don't know what I would have done if Zach hadn't been here this morning," she said.

"Mother." Zach lowered his brows. "Please." From the tone of his voice I surmised they'd crossed words.

"Anyone want coffee?" Beth asked in a jovial voice.

Zach looked to me and I shook my head.

"No thanks," he said.

"How about a cup of Sleepy Time tea, Holly?"

I remembered my pleasant hours sitting at Beth's kitchen table chatting as if I were an honored guest. I contemplated asking her why she'd made a sudden turnaround when she heard Zach and I were getting engaged. No, my life was already in enough disarray.

"No, thank you," I said.

"Maybe when you come back next time." Beth watched the slumbering puppies.

"I'd better get home," I said, although I could have spent all afternoon with Missy and her brood.

"You're welcome to stay as long as you like," Beth said. "Zach has work, but I'll take you home later if you need a ride."

"Thanks, but I should go." I hadn't mentioned my grandmother's appointment or her impending surgery to Beth. Zach hadn't brought up the subject either. He seemed to be taking his cues from me.

"How's everything at Anna's?" Beth asked me. I noticed she hadn't mentioned my mother; I wondered if the two had really made up.

"Fine." I wouldn't reveal I'd agreed to dress Old Order Amish for a week and was going to attend church with my family this Sunday—even Zach didn't know. With Nathaniel, I hoped. And possibly Armin. I assumed he went to church on preaching Sundays—every other week.

"While you two are here is the perfect time for me to run to the grocery store," Beth said. "Go ahead and leave when you need to. So far, Missy is the epitome of good mothers."

Minutes later, I heard Beth jangle her keys and leave by the kitchen door. I was tempted to ask Zach if his father had in truth been absent this morning when Missy whelped her litter.

Zach pointed at the pup I'd been holding. "Is that little lass your favorite? You two seemed to be bonding." The litter of six was almost identical in color, but that particular female had struck me as special, perhaps because her black and white markings were exactly like her mother's.

"You can name her. Someday, whichever one you pick will be ours." His blue eyes scanned my face.

"To keep me company while you're working all the time?" I arched a brow.

He sat forward in the chair, rested his chin in his hands. "You're right. When patients call me I come running, probably more than I need to. I've turned into a workaholic like my father, something I swore I'd never do. Maybe I should think about hiring another veterinarian to man the clinic while I'm out treating livestock."

I admired his dedication. He was the kind of veterinarian I'd hire, but he seemed to lack balance.

I watched Missy licking her pups. "When will their eyes open?"

"Usually between a week and ten days, and their hearing kicks in too."

"They seem so helpless."

"They are, but once they're up on their feet, watch out. They'll be tearing around helter-skelter and gnawing on the furniture. I'll build them a fenced area by the garage. My mother will have a full-time job on her hands."

"Your mother, or you?"

"I already have a full-time job. I can't come over to babysit every day."

My thoughts ricocheted back to Rascal. As soon as I got home I'd walk over to see if he'd returned. I prayed that he was lounging around Nathaniel's farm, or was in a safe haven. I might ask Zach to drop me off there, which could ruffle his feathers. Too bad, Armin was my friend, and I hoped some day, as Nathaniel's brother, he would be a relative. Was Armin serious about courting me or did he just enjoy competing with Zach? If history repeated itself, Armin might take off again. I wondered if he'd really attend Lynnea's wedding, a brash move, I'd think. But the Amish were so forgiving, Lynnea's future husband would probably welcome Armin. I admired the spirit of forgiveness and their allegiance to God's Word, family, and community.

I thought about my mother at home sewing me an Amish dress and felt a sprinkling of excitement. I was drawn to the Amish in so many ways. I could make my dad proud.

From what I'd gleaned, the Amish church dated back to the sixteenth-century Reformation in Europe, when the Anabaptist movement split into the Amish, Mennonites, and Brethren. Amish were the most conservative, emphasizing separation from the non-Amish world. Bottom line: it was the hardest to join. Other than Mommy Anna and Armin, no one had encouraged me to become a member. I wondered what Bishop Troyer would think if I told him I was considering it.

I felt like a willow branch in the wind. Mom would say I should seek God's guidance at every juncture in the road. Today, I should be praying for my mother. No one's future was more tenuous than hers. Except maybe Rascal's.

"You're awfully quiet," Zach said to me.

"I'm thinking."

"About what to name the puppy?"

"I'm worried about Nathaniel and about Rascal." My life was like a puzzle, each piece needing to be jiggled into place. "Is there something you're not telling me about him?"

"You mean Rascal?" Tension grew around the corners of his eyes. "If you like, I could call the humane society and see if he's been picked up."

"That would be great. Thanks."

While he spoke on the phone, I watched Missy care for her pups—without going to motherhood school. Like the Amish, I thought. They learned everything they needed to know about farming and family at home.

I wondered if I'd be content following the strict rules of the Ordnung. Did contentment even matter when I rounded my bases and touched home plate at the end of my life? Mommy Anna and the bishop would tell me that obeying the Lord and spending eternity in heaven was all-important. How would I find God's best-choice plan for my life unless I gave my Amish week a 100 percent effort?

CHAPTER FORTY-FOUR

Esther heard Holly calling her from the first floor.

"We're up in the attic," Esther shouted. She listened to Holly's footsteps ascending the staircase, then watched her daughter's head come into view as Holly climbed the ladder.

"Both of you are in the attic?" Holly poked her head through the rectangular opening. "Mommy Anna, what are you doing up there?"

"Did ya forget about our treasure hunt?" Flashlight in hand, Mamm minced her way toward Holly.

"I remember," Holly said. "Please be careful."

"Yah, Mamm." Esther grasped hold of Mamm's elbow.

"How did Mommy Anna ever get up there?" Holly asked.

"A lot of gumption," Esther said. "I'm glad you're home. Would ya catch these?" Esther tossed the two aprons to Holly, who nabbed them.

"Cool," Holly said. "These aprons look almost new."

"Now, could ya help your grandmother down the stepladder?" Esther asked.

"I've been in the attic many a time." Mamm flicked off her flashlight and dropped it in her apron pocket. "Quit your fussing."

Esther bet her mother hadn't been up in this cramped, dusky space for many years, but no use arguing with a woman suffering from memory problems. Esther shone her flashlight on the floor to illuminate Mamm's path. "Can you see okay?"

Mamm's squinty eyes and lips stretched to a thin line revealed dismay. "Feet first?" she asked Esther.

"Yah. Holly's right there to assist you." Esther helped Mamm grope her way through the opening, then Mamm dangled her toes until they landed on a step.

"Take it slowly," Esther said.

"I know what I'm doing." Mamm sounded tetchy.

Holly descended in tandem to Mamm—right behind her—arms out, until Mamm's feet finally touched the hallway's wooden floor.

"Did you find the stash of quilting fabric?" Holly asked.

"Nee, but we found those aprons and an old tin bread box," Mamm said.

"I'll bring it down later." Esther felt obligated to let Holly know Jeremiah had written, but wished to peruse the letters first. If the pages held inflammatory statements, she should warn her daughter. Jeremiah seemed to harbor no further resentment toward Esther, except when it came to the doll. His wife, Beatrice, was another story.

Esther slid the tin bread box near the opening, but out of sight. Glad to have her hands free, she followed them, and left the ladder in place. "Holly, I'll bring down the bread box after you try on your new dress."

"Wow, you've already sewed it?" Holly said.

"It just needs hemming."

"Mom, you're amazing."

"*Denki*. I enjoyed myself. In fact, I got more satisfaction finishing one plain dress than working all day at the Amish Shoppe." As she sewed, Esther had decided she was done laboring behind a cash register forever. "Last week, I was tinkering with the idea of visiting Dori in Seattle to see how she's doing with the Amish Shoppe, but I have no desire to fly. I hated that bumpy ride, not to mention the nerve-wracking security lines. And taking the bus or train would take too long."

"Don't ya ever go back." With icy fingers, Mamm clutched Esther's hand. "Let your friend come visit you here," Mamm said. "What would the bishop think?"

Esther's other hand covered Mamm's. "No matter what happens, I won't leave you again," Esther said. A lump inflated in her throat as her thoughts wended back to Nathaniel. She felt like a woman wandering in a foggy valley, no tangible road mark or horizon in sight.

"Those aprons should fit you, Holly." Mamm took one and held it up for viewing.

"I could wash it right away," Esther said.

"It looks new," Holly said. "I can wear it as is for now."

"First you need to try on the dress for your mother." Mamm clapped her hands. "I can hardly wait ta see you."

Esther strode to the staircase. "Hold on to the banister, Mamm," Esther instructed. The three descended, with Holly supporting Mamm's waist.

"Are you losing weight, Mommy Anna?" Holly asked.

"Not intentionally. Not with all your mother's gut cooking."

"Yah, I think you're thinner." Esther noticed Mamm's double chin had shrunk. Weight loss was one of the signs of hyperparathyroidism, according to Dr. Brewster.

In the sitting room, Holly headed to the chair next to the sewing machine and scooped up the dress. "I love this blue color, like a cornflower."

Esther felt a round of jitters hoping Holly would like it—and also wondering if her daughter should be dressing Amish at all. In retrospect, she should have sewed her own dress first.

Holly dashed out of the room, and returned wearing the dress. "It's a perfect fit, Mom. Thanks!"

"Let me measure the length again while you've got it on," Esther said. "Won't take but twenty minutes to iron and hem it, and I'll be done."

"Don't make it too short." Mamm wagged a finger.

"No worries," Holly said. "My mother won't make it a miniskirt. At least she never would when I was a teen." She gave Esther a quick hug. "I apologize, Mom. I was a regular little brat when you sewed clothes for me."

"No matter, Holly. You were young and imagining everyone in the world was watching you. Seems we women spend far too much time worrying about what others think of us." Esther realized she'd been guilty of this transgression. Comparing herself to Lizzie, of all silly things.

"Holly looks so *lieblich* every unmarried Amishman in the county will want to court her," Mamm said.

"Thanks, Mommy Anna," Holly said, "but before we proceed, I want to make sure you're still intending on following through with the surgery."

"Uh, yah, I s'pose …"

"I'm not going one step further unless you promise me."

"Yah, I will. But I wonder if I should ask the bishop or the deacon. I wish my Isaac were here."

Esther was glad her strict brother Isaac, a minister, chosen by lot for a lifetime, was not around to put the kibosh on Mamm's surgery. His attitude toward their mother—that she was old so why attempt to extend her life?—exasperated Esther.

While they spoke, Esther pinned the hem at midcalf, and then, after Holly slipped the dress off, Esther ironed and hand-stitched the hem.

While she worked, Mamm showed Holly how to fastidiously part her hair down the middle and tame her wavy tresses with bobby pins, pulling it into a small bun. "Now, don't ya cut your hair," Mamm said.

"You mean in the next five minutes?"

Mamm clucked. "I mean for as long as you're wearing a Kapp. Wait here and I'll fetch one." She shuffled into the Daadi Haus, returned with a clean, pressed Kapp, and crowned Holly's head.

"I shudder to think what I look like." Holly patted her head, then gently tugged on the strings.

Esther glanced up from her sewing to see the majority of Holly's gorgeous hair was hidden. Esther was under the impression Holly considered her thick wavy hair her best attribute. What would she think when she caught sight of herself in a mirror?

Mamm straightened Holly's Kapp. "Ya couldn't look better."

"Should I tie the strings?" Holly twirled them.

"Most of the young women don't, but if the bishop pays us a visit it wouldn't hurt." Mamm reached up to straighten her own Kapp. "Ach, mine have come undone." Her fingers fumbled to knot the strings, then she gave up.

Minutes later Esther said, "Here you go." She handed the dress to Holly with a flourish.

Holly stepped into another room and waltzed back wearing it. "I want to use one of the aprons when I go over to Nathaniel's to see if Rascal's returned." She brought an apron to her nose and gave it a sniff. "Not too musty. I'll shake it out first, then pin it on. I hope I don't stab myself."

"I need to practice too." Esther motioned to the couch. "Mamm, this would be a perfect time to put your feet up."

Mamm sidled up to it and melted onto the cushions. "Guess I am a wee bit tired." She closed her eyes, held her breath for a moment, then relaxed into slumber.

"Mom," Holly said, "you have an anxious expression on your face. Don't I have this dress and apron on right?"

"Yes, you look just fine." Still, Esther wondered if she was influencing Holly too much.

"I'm dressing this way for a week only," Holly said, as if anticipating Esther's thoughts. "Although I might check out the Amish church. If you're joining it, it's got to be okay."

"My circumstances are far different from yours. I never learned to drive an automobile or owned a cell phone, although caving in to the temptation to use it is something I'll have to confess. And I'm grateful Larry owns a car. If I have these many internal struggles, what would it be like for you?" Esther wrung her hands. "Holly, now you look *drauerich*—sad in your face. Are ya regretting your agreement to dress Amish? You can change your mind."

"No, it's not that."

"Is it Zach? How did your time with him go?"

"The puppies are darling and Beth was civil. But on the way home, Zach was sullen when I suggested we swing by to ask Armin if Rascal had returned, so I said never mind, I'll walk over there myself." She pulled the prayer cap strings down and crossed them under her chin. "Any phone calls while I was gone?"

"Not yet."

Please bring Nathaniel home, Esther pleaded with the Almighty in her mind. If it's your will. I won't hold it against you if it isn't, but I'd be ever so grateful.

CHAPTER FORTY-FIVE

Hiking over to Nathaniel's, I felt *naerfich*—nervous—about seeing Armin dressed as I was.

Hey, I thought a word in Pennsylvania Dutch! How nifty was that? Proof I could learn the language of my forefathers whether I joined the church or not. Mommy Anna would be overjoyed.

I saw Armin next to the barn tying up Nathaniel's Holstein bull—the giant animal mostly black, save his white feet. It let out a snort as I neared them.

Armin turned to me. "Don't come any closer." His eyebrows lifted, Armin stared at my dress and apron, then his gaze fastened onto my prayer cap, its strings fluttering in the breeze.

I wouldn't take offense. Of course Armin would be surprised by the new me. "That bull looks like he belongs in a state fair," I said.

"He weighs over a ton. Don't ya ever get near him." Armin checked to make sure the bull was securely fastened. "He has his friendly days when you'll almost trust him, but the next minute he might gore you through."

I took a baby step closer.

"Stop, I ain't kidding!" Armin's hand jutted out, as if directing traffic. "I don't know why my brother keeps such a beast when he gets better offspring from artificial insemination. Nathaniel should have had him polled—his horns removed." They did look like lethal skewers.

I thought instead of talking about bovine propagation, Armin would rush over to me when he was finished securing the bull, but he stayed put. Was he deadly serious about protecting me or trying to maintain distance between us?

"*Wie geht's?*" he finally said. He'd switched back to his usual work boots, and a smear of mud marred the front of his trousers.

"I came over to see if Rascal had returned."

"Not yet. Maybe he found some swanky Englisch mansion where they serve prime rib." Armin's cavalier attitude struck me as false. He seemed too blasé, an act for my benefit so I wouldn't fear the worst.

"I hope so." I couldn't shake a premonition Rascal was lost or injured. "Any more reports of sheep or goats being attacked?"

"Not that I know of."

I did a pirouette to show off my dress and apron; the fabric swished around my legs, reassuring me. "Well, how do I look?"

"Fine."

"Come on, Armin." I batted my eyelashes. "What do you think?"

"You look gut."

"But evidently not irresistible."

"Ya look as *schee*—pretty—as the day we met."

A new reality stuck into me like an ill-placed pin at my waist. "Are you worried I'll join the Amish church as you suggested?"

"Why would I be?"

"Because I'd be available for you to court when and if you get baptized. Meaning you wouldn't be attracted to me anymore."

"I never said that." He straightened his hat, pulled down on the brim. "I like ya as much as ever. You caught me off guard, that's all."

I finally understood Nathaniel's vexation with his flip-floppy little brother. "Do you only want what you can't have, Armin?"

He let out a puff of air. "I was fixing ta stay right here on this farm, but now, what with Nathaniel either marrying Esther or his wife coming home, I don't know. I've gotten mighty used to doing things my own way." He moved toward me until we were a couple feet apart. I had to raise my chin to look into his face. He certainly was easy on the eyes, and I enjoyed Armin's witticisms—his *joie de vivre*. But I didn't want a lifetime of second-guessing this unpredictable fellow, who was too full of himself.

"Only someone brought up Amish would understand what I'm going through." He shifted his weight back and forth. "The finality of getting baptized. I've kept putting it off. If I do there's no turning back."

"Same with marriage, right?"

"Yah, especially if you're baptized Amish. Look what my brother's going through." Armin's hands skated up and down his suspenders. "You haven't heard from Nathaniel, have you?"

I marveled at his capacity to dodge the subject. "No, and I left my phone with my mother. Which is where I should be—helping her." I felt sorry for Armin, losing his dog—his best buddy. But at this moment I found his attitude toward me aggravating at best.

The bull pawed the ground, then lowered his massive head and bellowed.

"I've got chores ta do before milking." Armin angled his torso toward the barn.

I felt rejected. "Well, then, good-bye." I spun on my heels and marched across the barnyard and around the house. Striding along the path at the side of the road toward home, I recognized Zach's pickup headed my direction. It pulled off and stopped.

Zach lowered his passenger side window. "Is that you, Holly Fisher?"

"The one and only." I curtsied.

"I almost didn't recognize you. Want a ride?"

Conflicting thoughts reverberated in my mind. "You'd let me in your pickup dressed like this?"

"I'd be honored. Hop in."

I opened the door and climbed aboard. "Thanks, I should have worn a jacket." He cranked the heater up and I felt warmth bathing my legs.

"As an incentive, I'm dressing this way for at least a week, or until Mommy Anna has her surgery. And I might attend her church service Sunday."

"You could come with me to mine again." He accelerated the engine, conveying us away from my grandmother's farm.

Leaning against the seatback, I felt a pin sticking into my midriff. I relocated it. Okay, I didn't have the art of fastening the straight pins down pat, but would by the end of the week.

"You wouldn't be embarrassed taking me to church dressed like this?" I pulled down the mirror on the back of the sun visor and felt a moment's grief for the loss of my hair.

"Never."

"What if people ogle?"

"They won't. You've been to our church. All are welcome."

We passed several farms and fields, then motored through a forested area. I cracked the window and breathed in the rich essence of pine needles, and fallen maple and oak leaves mulching into the soil. "Where are we going?" I asked.

"Anywhere you'd like."

"Where do you live?"

He chuckled. "Is that your way of asking to see my humble abode? I didn't know if you'd think it proper for me to invite you."

"In this day and age?"

"You're the woman I want to impress, but it seems most everything I do goes wrong." His grip tightened on the wheel. "Would you like to see my house?"

"Is it far away? I need to get home pretty soon."

"Just down in Gordonville—five minutes."

As he drove, he waved at several other motorists and an Amishman driving a horse and buggy. He pulled into the driveway of a modest buttermilk-yellow one-story home with black shutters on its two front windows. A carport extended from what must be the entrance to the kitchen, but when we got out he led me around to the front door, painted cherry-red—a nice touch I hadn't expected.

He removed his jacket and draped it over my shoulders. I viewed the small and nicely clipped lawn. Evergreen shrubs obscured homes on either side, and a Japanese maple tree, still clinging to its garnet-red leaves, stood next to the carport.

"You live here by yourself?" I asked.

"Yes, I do. Never had a housemate." I assumed he'd disclosed that tidbit to quell my reservations about Victoria. "My folks invite me over a lot, and I usually accept," he said. "Who likes to sit home alone?"

"But soon you'll have a wiggly puppy to keep you company."

"Yes, and I hope a new bride. You, Holly." He escorted me to the door.

I turned to him and said, "You'd want to marry into my oddball family? If Mom and Nathaniel get together, Armin and you will be related."

One corner of his mouth hinted at a grin. "You'd want to marry into mine? My mother would be your mother-in-law."

"Don't think I haven't thought of that." Not a tactful remark, but I figured bare-bones truth was essential.

He maneuvered the key into the brass lock and swung open the door.

"Please, come in to what I hope will be your future home."

Ahead lay a beige-carpeted living room with a brick fireplace, built-in bookshelves standing on either side, a velour couch, and a matching loveseat. A coffee table displayed several magazines, having to do with veterinary medicine, and yesterday's newspaper, unopened. Above the fireplace hung a framed photograph of an Amish farm. A nice room with potential—in need of a woman's touch.

"It's beautiful," I said, "but I don't like sitting at home alone, either."

"Yes, I work too much. That's why I need to block out three weeks on my calendar, time to get married and take a honeymoon."

"How will you manage?"

"I called an old friend, a retired veterinarian, who said he'll fill in for me. He claims he's been bored stiff since he sold his practice five years ago." Zach's hand rose to the nape of my neck; his fingers traced the bottom edge of my prayer cap. I thought he'd suggest I remove it, but instead he straightened the strings. "If you could travel anywhere on our honeymoon, where would it be?"

In my mind, tropical paradises enticed me, but I stayed practical. "I can't go anywhere until Mommy Anna has her surgery."

"Understandable. Plus, we'd want her to attend the ceremony."

"Wait a minute, this conversation is galloping along too quickly."

"I thought you said I was moving too slowly." Zach plopped down on the couch.

"Well, you were." I pointed to my left hand. "No date and ring." I sank down next to him; the cushions were spongy and comfortable.

He moved closer, gingerly—I assumed to avoid the pins. "But you decided you didn't want a glitzy engagement ring," he said.

"True, but there's no reason not to choose wedding bands, if you're serious."

His arm reached around behind me and he kissed me tenderly. But I would not allow myself to tumble into the abyss until I knew for sure he loved me.

I leaned away from him, gazed into his luminous eyes, and tried to interpret what lay behind them. We sat there for a moment, until he blinked and withdrew his arm.

"I'd better get you home." He let out a wistful sigh. "Your mother will be worried."

"Okay." I took a last look-see around the pleasant living room I might never see again.

"Or how about you and I go out to dinner instead?" He got to his feet. "Just the two of us. If your mother still has your cell phone you can call her from here."

Not wanting to part yet, I agreed.

CHAPTER FORTY-SIX

Esther brought out several yards of plum-colored fabric, stretched it across the clean kitchen table, and lay out the pattern pieces for her new dress. She should be giddy with expectation, but she felt helpless—like a snared rabbit waiting for a fox to pounce on her.

Unable to concentrate on her sewing, she decided to tromp upstairs for the bread box and read Jeremiah's letters. No, she needed to unravel the mystery of the doll and silk first, even if it turned out to be the more painful task.

Holly's cell phone in hand, Esther located Chap McLaughlin's number on the phone's contact list and pushed the button. After a couple rings, she heard a twangy male voice. "Yo, this is Chap."

At first Esther's tongue refused to obey her. Finally she said, "Hello, this is Esther Fisher, the woman you sent a doll and silk to."

"Great, I'm glad you called. I was going to answer your letter—" He cleared his throat. "Sounds like you're not convinced I located the right Samuel Fisher."

"I have my doubts. There are many Samuel Fishers."

"You're telling me."

"Could you please describe what this Samuel Fisher looked like?" Replaced by Nathaniel, Samuel's image at age eighteen had become hazy in Esther's mind, as if looking through the wrong end of a telescope. But she'd never forget him.

"I have a photograph of a bunch of us," Chap said. "Want me to send you a copy?"

"No. Thanks for your kind offer, but we're not supposed to have photos."

"Huh? Well, let me think. Sam had brown shaggy hair, long sideburns, and a mustache."

"My Samuel never would have worn a mustache or sideburns."

"He could have grown them over there, ma'am. Lots of guys did—Well, they did all kinds of things they wouldn't have done at home."

Not wanting to hear the repugnant depictions of war, Esther said, "Can you tell me more about him?"

"He was one of the nicest guys you'd ever want to meet."

"Did he like to sing?" She recalled Samuel's tenor voice crooning for spare change on San Francisco corners before he was inducted into the army. Out the window she saw the sun lowering itself, a salmon-colored orb. But its radiant beauty brought her no joy.

"I can't say I recall hearing him sing," Chap said, "but he was a regular jokester, always keeping us in stitches and trying to rally a poker game. You know, five-card stud, Texas hold 'em."

"That can't be my Samuel. He'd never bet on a card game." He would never gamble, unless, like a butterfly reverting to a caterpillar, he'd mutated into a totally different person while in Vietnam.

"Sam made a fortune off us suckers. But it gave us something to laugh about, so we were grateful for him when he wasn't out on a mission."

"You mean in the jungle?" She'd seen photos of the dense terrain, inaccessible to vehicles and pocketed with hiding places for the enemy, on the news while Samuel was serving his term.

"Yes, we lost many in our unit. Sometimes guys called him Lucky Louie, the way Sam dodged land mines and bullets, and kept coming back in one piece."

"When Samuel wrote, he told me he worked as a medical aide." Dangerous in itself; the enemy was always lurking.

"Sam's team usually went out by helicopter to care for the wounded," Chap said.

"I see—" Maybe Samuel had wanted to spare her the gory descriptions.

"He told us he was married and that his wife lived in Seattle."

"I moved there after he went into the army."

"Don't that beat all?" Chap said. "I might have hit the jackpot."

"I still don't believe my Samuel would buy such a doll." She doubted Chap would understand that it was an inappropriate gift. On the other hand, she and Samuel were living like Englischers back then.

"Lots of the guys sent them home," he said. "I did."

"Still, there are many men called Samuel Fisher."

"Don't I know it. I've gone down multiple rabbit trails. Did you recognize his handwriting on his note?"

"There was no note." Her mouth felt stuffed with cotton balls.

"Yes, I left the letter at the bottom of the box, where I found it."

"Ya don't mean it. I can't believe my ears." She warned herself not to get her hopes up.

"It's under the tissue paper," he assured her.

"I'll say good-bye, then, and go look." She sprinted to the sitting room to locate the box. It lay jammed between the arm of the sofa and the wall, tipped on its side, where Mamm must have dropped it. Esther knelt on a cushion and reached to retrieve it, then tore the remaining crumpled tissue out. A handwritten letter fluttered to the floor. She recognized her Samuel's penmanship on the lined paper from five feet away.

A cloak of dread paralyzed her. Her ears began to ring. Her breathing increased, but she could barely inhale, as if her ribs were tightening, bending in like giant fingers, cutting off her air. Moisture accumulated under her armpits and around her waist.

A heart attack?

She didn't care. She would read the letter! Feeling light-headed, she leaned over and picked it up with trembling hands.

She mouthed the words:

Dear Esther,

I meant to send you these gifts and to come clean months ago, but kept putting it off. Now it looks like I'm being shipped back to the States so maybe I'll send them from there.

In your last letter you hinted you want to visit your family after the baby is born. There's no easy way to tell you I won't be going with you. I was never cut out to live the plain life and don't want anything to do with my parents' guilt trips. Or to be a father. I'd make a crummy dad. I'm not the man you thought I was. I let myself get drafted. You heard me, I knew what I was doing: escaping!

I'll probably stay in San Fran. I've kept in touch with a friend there who has an extra bed.

I'm sorry, Sam

She read and reread the letter. A farewell note! All these years she'd held herself responsible. She was appalled and then disgusted. Her legs giving out on her, Esther's eyesight diminished, blinding her for a moment, blackening the room. She crumpled down onto the couch,

What would Holly think when she saw her father's letter? Well, she never would; Esther would make sure of that. It would break her daughter's heart. She blinked her eyes open and saw her surroundings with clarity. Without a qualm, Esther shredded the letter into strips. She pulled herself up and mounded them in the fireplace, then lit a match, filling the air with sulfur. The flames hungrily curled and consumed the paper in less than a minute, leaving nothing but ashes and a puff of smoke.

———

That evening, after Esther had milked Pearly, she ate a light supper with Mamm. Holly had called earlier to say she was dining at a restaurant with Zach. Esther must be *verhoodled*; she'd thought her daughter had headed to Armin's. And Armin hadn't stopped by for supper, either.

After washing the dishes, sprucing up the kitchen, and helping Mamm into bed, Esther knew she wouldn't sleep, not with her mind gyrating with questions about Samuel's letter. Ach, he must have been on drugs, suffering from post-traumatic stress disorder, or perhaps he had simply fallen out of love with her. She decided it was for the best that her daughter never found out. She'd allow Holly, Jeremiah, and Beatrice to hold Samuel up on a pedestal—second to

God, of course. She'd give the doll and silk to Holly, and ask her to keep them out of sight, for everyone's sake.

She stood at the table cutting out fabric pieces for her own dress. A combination of fatigue and worry encompassed her, causing her hand to shake as she directed the scissors through the plum-colored fabric. A sloppy job, she noticed.

Another surge of incredulity pummeled Esther as if she were wading out to sea while the tide was rising, each incoming wave thrashing against her legs, swelling in multitude, until she'd be washed away.

"Help, Lord," she said softly. Only Jesus was perfect, she reminded herself. "Please, help me forgive Samuel." She'd never be alone as long as she called out to God. His Spirit was in this very room, could hear her inner moaning, and would intercede on her behalf.

She felt her lungs expand and contract in a relaxed manner, her anger subsiding. She didn't want to dwell on Samuel anymore.

If only Nathaniel were here.

She carried the cut fabric pieces into the sitting room, sat at the sewing machine, and found a bobbin with thread almost the same color. She inserted it into the machine, and then threaded a newly purchased spool to match her fabric. Not like Esther to be so lackadaisical, but she didn't care if the threads were a slightly different hue.

Esther sat before the machine, placed two fabric shapes—side-seams—together, and lowered the pressure foot. Pumping the treadle, she noticed her line wasn't as straight as it should be, as it had been only hours ago when she'd assembled Holly's dress—before she had read the letter.

She heard someone knocking on the back door.

She checked the battery-run clock on the wall and saw it was 11:59. Who would visit at midnight? No one she wanted to entertain. She decided to ignore the person. She was in no mood for chitchat. Holly would let herself in the unlocked door, and so would Armin if there was a problem.

Another rap-rap. Again she ignored it.

Esther recalled a biblical story about a neighbor knocking on a man's door begging for loaves of bread at midnight. Luke 11:7, she thought. The man of the house said, "Don't bother me. My door is already locked and my children and I are in bed." But because of the neighbor's boldness and persistence, the man in the house was eventually prompted to get up and give his neighbor what he needed, as God provided for him.

Esther dragged herself to her feet, trudged through the kitchen, and opened the door.

"Nathaniel!"

"Sorry to disturb you so late," he said, removing his hat.

"*Es macht nix aus*—it doesn't matter. You're back!"

She searched his gaunt face and saw haggard eyes and anemic-looking lips. Of course he'd be weary from the trip, but she wondered if he'd brought with him bad tidings. Ghastly information!

"*Kumm rei*—come in," she said.

"I should get back home and let you go to bed. We can talk in the morning."

"Nee." She grabbed Nathaniel's jacket sleeve. "You've got to tell me what happened. I won't be able to sleep a wink until I know."

"Got room for me in there?" Larry said, making his way through the utility room. He wore jeans and a yellow T-shirt with the words

"Earth is now, Heaven is forever!" written in a bold red font on the front.

"Sure, welcome, Larry." Esther stood aside as Larry passed her carrying his jacket and overnight bag. He looked beat too, his eyes bloodshot.

"Thank you for all you've done," she said to him. "Why didn't you call?"

"We wanted to surprise you," Larry said.

As Esther put Nathaniel's hat on a peg, she heard an automobile pull up and a car door shut. Moments later, she recognized her daughter's vivacious voice.

"Having a party in my absence?" Holly sashayed into the kitchen. "Hi, Nathaniel."

Larry swung around and saw her Amish attire. "Wooo—isn't that outfit a bit over the top?"

Holly's hands moved to her hips. "Larry, weren't you just traveling with an Amishman and staying at an Amish house?"

"Well, actually I slept at a B&B with Internet connection and electricity. But I had my meals at Nathaniel's cousin's." He gave her a thorough looking over. "Are you planning to dress that way from now on?"

"Awhile, anyway." Her Kapp strings swung freely, as if still in motion. "It's a long story."

"Where were you just now?" His brows raised, then lowered.

"Out to dinner with Zach."

"Dressed like that?"

"Yup." Holly glanced to Esther and Nathaniel. "Come on, Larry, let's give these two some privacy."

When Esther and Nathaniel were alone again, Esther said, "You must be hungry. I'll fix you a snack."

"Nee, I couldn't eat."

"Then something to drink? Hot cider or tea? Or I have decaf coffee, thanks to Holly."

"Yah, I am thirsty, now that you mention it." He sat at the table, across from Esther's usual chair. While the coffee brewed, she cut a wedge of pumpkin pie, positioned it and a fork on a plate, and set it before him. He dug into it like a starving man.

"'Tis the best pie I've ever had."

Pleased, she lowered herself onto her chair. "Why did ya come home so late in the day?"

"The local sheriff heard tales of my situation and came to see if he could help, bringing with him a swarm of newspaper reporters, snapping pictures left and right. I tried to shield myself, but I wouldn't be surprised if one caught my image and my face and the story ends up on the front page."

"Sounds *greislich*." Esther wanted to dive into the conversation both feet first, but she didn't shower him with queries about his trip to Ohio. When he was ready to unfold the story, she would listen.

He swallowed another mouthful as she poured him coffee.

"Maybe I'll have a snack too." She brought out another cup and a platter of peanut butter chocolate chip cookies.

"Those reporters ne'er scared that woman to death, poor thing." He selected a cookie, took a bite. "Turns out she's *ab im Kopp*—her mind's higgledy-piggledy. And she ain't my former wife—no doubt about it."

"Are you sure?" Esther sat across from him.

"Yah, we spoke to several neighbors in the area and found out her name is Coleen O'—something. She's from Tennessee. Not even Amish. I don't know what my cousin was thinking. But then, he was young when I married Deborah."

There, he'd finally voiced his former wife's name. But Esther wouldn't ask about Deborah either.

Esther wondered what would come next. "I'm so sorry for all you've gone through," she said.

He sipped his coffee again. "This is a mighty gut cup of coffee."

"Don't tell Mamm it's from Starbucks."

"Ach, that's why it tastes so gut. Larry's got me hooked too." He grinned, revealing the laugh lines she adored. "Do ya suppose we should confess to the bishop?" he joked.

"As a matter of fact, I invited Bishop Troyer to stop over tomorrow when he has time. No matter what happens between you and me, I'm bound and determined to become baptized."

"That's fine-gut news, Esther."

She waited for him to say more. It seemed she'd waited most of her life, as if buried under an avalanche of snow. She'd waited for Samuel, but he'd never returned. She'd waited for Nathaniel, but this time had been rewarded for her patience.

She nibbled into a cookie and savored its sweetness. The Lord Almighty was in control at midnight, and all day, every day. He ruled over the universe, no matter how Esther had tried to manipulate it.

"I want to be here when Bishop Troyer arrives so we can speak to him together," Nathaniel said. "Because I'm as bound and determined to marry you as ever."

"Truly, ya are?" Her hand covered her heart. "I was so afraid that even if you didn't find your Deborah, you'd choose somebody better."

"There is none better—for me. So count on planting as much celery as quickly as you can in the spring. Or we'll buy it at the supermarket, if we must."

Celery, Esther knew, was eaten in copious amounts at Amish weddings. The image of the leafy green stalks emboldened her. She leapt to her feet, rounded the table, then plunked down on the chair next to him. As she approached, his arms spread out to enfold her.

Ach, the best embrace in the world. Then he kissed her lips with fervor. After they reluctantly parted, he drew his head back. "*Ich liebe ich,* my dearest Esther."

"I love you, too, Nathaniel."

"Do ya still remember how to sing *Das Loblied* from the *Ausbund*?" he said.

"Yah. '*O Gott Vater, wir loben dich.*'—Oh God the Father, we praise you." The second hymn sung *a capella* every preaching Sunday for about fifteen to twenty minutes while the ministers prepared the service was ingrained in her mind since infancy.

Nathaniel gazed into her eyes. "How about the hymn from the *Ausbund* we sing at weddings?" he said.

"Yah, I remember it, too."

"Shall we ask Armin to be a *Forsinger*?"

"If you think he'll show up."

"Not agree to be a song leader for his own brother's wedding? He'll be there." He reached for her hand, brought her fingertips to his lips.

Esther was so ecstatic she felt like singing the hymns right now!

CHAPTER FORTY-SEVEN

With the door to the kitchen shut, I lounged on the sitting room couch and Larry slouched in the easy chair. His bold yellow T-shirt was incompatible with my demure Amish dress, apron, and prayer cap—or maybe not. Both spoke a message loud and clear: God was at the helm. Yet my ship was adrift and my future obscure. When Zach had dropped me off after dinner, he gave me a peck on the cheek and hadn't even made plans to see me again.

"We can never repay you," I said to Larry, determined to harpoon myself out of my ocean of insecurities.

"I'm the one who should be thanking you all," Larry said. "I wouldn't take back my trip to Ohio for anything. I learned more from watching Nathaniel confront his greatest fears with patient godliness than I did spending four years in college and listening to the best of sermons."

His statement got me wondering: What had I learned over the last few weeks about humility, forgiveness, and honesty?

"Larry, wait here, I'll be right back." I scrambled up the stairs and returned with the Tiffany's box.

He stood and put out his hand.

"I didn't open it," I said, and placed the box in his palm.

"Can't say I'm surprised." To my amazement Larry sounded more relieved than bummed. "I figured it was a dumb idea."

"The ring is waiting for the right woman," I said. "Your future soul mate. The lady who wins your heart will have a fine husband."

"And how about you, Holly? Are you tying the knot?"

"I'm still not sure."

"When you make up your mind, do I get an invite?"

"Absolutely, you're like a family member now. You've proven yourself to be more than a nice guy and a good businessman. You have my admiration."

"Thanks." He gave me a one-armed hug. "Do you think God urged me here on a commission, to drive Nathaniel?" he asked, his arm still on my shoulder in a brotherly fashion. "I thought I'd come to Pennsylvania to sweep you off your feet—"

"Holly!" Zach barged in from the kitchen. He stopped short, stared at me and Larry, then his gaze honed in on the blue box.

"Hey, man, I'm back." Larry tossed the box in the air and caught it with his other hand. "How's it going?" He extended his arm to shake Zach's hand, but Zach ignored his gesture and strode over to me.

"Well, I guess I'll put my gear away." Larry stuffed the Tiffany's box in a pocket and carried his overnight bag toward his bedroom. "Call me if you need me, Holly."

"She won't," Zach said, then turned to me. "At least I hope she won't."

When Zach and I were alone, he took my hand and said, "I've been sitting out back in my truck wondering what my problem is. I have something to tell you."

Seeing his taut, grim expression—like he was a pole-vaulter about to attempt to scale an impossibly high bar—I braced myself, wanting to stave off the inevitable. He'd changed his mind. He thought I looked dumb dressed Amish and had seen how plain I really was. This moment, before he spilled out his feelings and thoughts, might be the last time I could hold out hope for the two of us. I closed my eyes and tried to prepare myself.

He drew me to him and said, "I love you, Holly Fisher."

My eyes popped open. "You do?"

"Yes. You and only you. I should have told you before. I was afraid I'd botched things up so badly you'd vamoose. Well, I was acting like a coward, is what I was doing. Please tell me I'm the man who's swept you off your feet."

He bent forward, and his free hand gently guided my mouth to his. He brushed his lips against mine until my lips softened. Then he bestowed a passionate kiss, my lips melting into his, my body going limp. I closed my eyes again and allowed myself to be swept into the luxury of his powerful embrace.

As we parted, Zach said, "I'll love you for the rest of my life—that's never going to change. Please tell me you'll be my wife."

As his words replayed themselves in my ears, I felt my fragile heart overflowing with gratitude and devotion—my brokenness mending.

"I love you, too, Zach—so much I can't imagine life without you."

He held me close again, lifting me off the ground for a moment, then setting me down and cupping my cheeks with his hands.

"And Zach?" I said. "My answer is yes."

EPILOGUE

Anna Gingerich never thought she'd cry at an Englisch wedding, particularly her granddaughter's. As Anna listened to Holly and Zach repeat their vows, she recalled her own blissful wedding in her parents' home, so many years ago.

"To love and to cherish …" Holly wore a flowing white long-sleeved satin gown and a demure veil. "In sickness and in health." Her face gleamed with elation.

Yah, Anna was conflicted. What Amish grandmother wouldn't be? She prayed God Almighty would forgive Holly for not choosing to join the Amish church. Not like Anna's once rebellious Esther—soon to be baptized Amish and wed to Nathaniel, who sat beside her. In preparation for their wedding, Esther had hired Lizzie, seated a few rows back, to come over once a week to help. Anna had grown right fond of that spritely *Maedel*, and it wondered Anna that no man was courting her. Maybe Armin, if that footloose young man didn't take off again. She hadn't seen him today.

"As long as you both shall live."

Anna wasn't even offended when the pastor pronounced Holly and Zach man and wife, and the two exchanged a brief kiss right in front of everyone in the house of worship, the building alive with jubilation and brimming with well-wishers.

As Holly and Zach turned to the congregation, Jeremiah, seated on the aisle, and Esther, on Anna's other side, helped Anna to her feet.

Beth Fleming and her husband, Roger, stood across the aisle. Beth was dabbing the corner of her eye, but Anna could tell by Beth's smiling face she was delighted. Earlier, Anna had seen Esther's and Beth's arms linked, like sisters. Watching Holly and Zach stride toward them, Anna was grateful for Zach, whose veterinary skills were rejuvenating Cookie. Why, it was as if the aged mare were receiving a second chance at life, as Anna had ever since her surgery. Nathaniel had insisted he pay for Anna's medical expenditures, his early wedding present to Esther. Anna might even feel strong enough to visit her sons and their families in Montana, but she knew a long frigid winter lay before her, a season to quilt and reflect on the Lord.

When Holly and Zach neared Anna, they stopped. Holly reached out her arms, hugged Anna, and kissed her cheek. Then the newlyweds proceeded, a bounce in each step.

ACKNOWLEDGMENTS

I'm grateful for every reader. I can't thank those who sent encouraging letters, emails via my website, or Facebook posts enough! I wish I had room to mention each one by name! Two who gave me special assistance are Karla Hanns and Mary Hake.

Many thanks to Professor Donald Kraybill and Professor Emeritus C. Richard Beam, who were extremely gracious. Thank you, Emma Stoltzfus, Herb Scrivener and the staff at Zook's Fabric, Sam and Susie Lapp, and the Lancaster Mennonite Historical Society, among others in Lancaster County and across the nation for answering my barrage of questions! Thank you, Larry Bodmer, and several Old Order Amish farmers who advised me about aspects of farm life and milking cows. Thanks, Lisa Ravenholt, for answering my horsy questions. Thank you fellow author Renee Riva for your insights, and bird expert and author Connie Sidles. Thank you, Buddy Gilbert and Wesley Fisk, for sharing your experience and knowledge of the Vietnam War.

A humongous thank you to my fabulous editor, Don Pape, and David C Cook's stellar team, including Karen Stoller, Ingrid Beck, Amy Konyndyk, Renada Arens, the tireless sales force, and many others. Thank you, Jamie Chavez. Special thanks to Sandra Bishop—once again my agent of the year!

I am indebted to my critique group: Judy Bodmer, Roberta Kehle, Kathleen Khohler, Thornton Ford, Paul Malm, and Marty Nystrom.

I love hearing from readers via my website, www.katelloyd.net, and on Facebook at www.facebook.com/katelloydbooks, or follow me on Twitter @KateLloydAuthor.

... a little more ...

When a delightful concert comes to an end,

the orchestra might offer an encore.

When a fine meal comes to an end,

it's always nice to savor a bit of dessert.

When a great story comes to an end,

we think you may want to linger.

And so, we offer ...

AfterWords—just a little something more after you

have finished a David C Cook novel.

We invite you to stay awhile in the story.

Thanks for reading!

Turn the page for ...

- **Discussion Questions**
- **About the Author**

DISCUSSION
QUESTIONS

1. Which character do you identify with the most and why?

2. If you were Holly, which man would you pick for a mate and why?

3. How would growing up without a father affect Holly's opinions about relationships with men? What would you have done in Holly's position, if the person you loved were accused of fathering a child?

4. Esther and Holly see themselves as opposites. What characteristics do they have in common and what obstacles do they share?

5. How does harboring unforgiveness affect relationships? What is the best way to rid oneself of the burden of holding on to resentment and bitterness? How is maintaining a grudge hurting you more than the other person, who may not even know you harbor it?

6. Esther continues to blame herself for past mistakes and struggles with bitterness and accepting God's forgiveness. Do you think she and Beth have truly forgiven each other? Has Esther's mother, Anna, forgiven Esther?

7. Would you consider living on an Old Order Amish farm? Do you think Holly could be content without modern conveniences? What are the benefits of being a member of a defined, close-knit community, and what conflicts do you see as inevitable?

8. Do you think people can change the course of others' lives, as Anna and Esther have attempted? Have you had someone try to interfere with a decision you've made? If so, how did you feel?

9. Why are our greatest times of adversity also our best opportunities for growth and reliance on God?

About the Author

Kate Lloyd is a novelist, a mother of two sons, and a passionate observer of human relationships. A native of Baltimore, Kate spends time with family and friends in Lancaster County, Pennsylvania, the inspiration for *Leaving Lancaster* and *Pennsylvania Patchwork*. She is a member of the Lancaster County Mennonite Historical Society. Kate and her husband live in the Pacific Northwest, the setting for Kate's first novel, *A Portrait of Marguerite*. Kate studied painting and sculpture in college. She has worked a variety of jobs, including car salesman and restaurateur.

Kate loves hearing from readers and can be reached through her website, www.katelloyd.net, on FB at www.facebook.com/katelloydbooks or followed on Twitter @ KateLloydAuthor. Or write her at:

Kate Lloyd
PO Box 204, 4616 25th Ave. NE
Seattle, WA 98105

A WARM & WINNING DEBUT
for novelist Kate Lloyd

When single mom Marguerite Carr's son leaves for college, she feels as though her life has lost its purpose. When a friend drags Marguerite to a drawing class—her first since college—she rediscovers her long-lost passion for painting, finds unexpected love, and most of all learns that God's tender forgiveness covers all—even our worst sins and our deepest, darkest secrets.